THE DUFORT DYNASTY

BOOK SIX

JULIETTE N. BANKS

COPYRIGHT

Author: Juliette N. Banks
Editor: Crystal Durnan
Cover design by: Elizabeth Cartwright, EC Editorial

ABOUT THE AUTHOR

Juliette is an independent author who has taken the romance genre by storm, writing hot heroes readers fall in love with.

Juliette also has a vast background in consumer marketing and previously published with Random House. She lives in New Zealand with Tilly, her Maine Coon kitty.

www.juliettebanks.com

DEDICATION

I dedicate this book to the people of Maui.

While writing *Ruthless Temptation* my characters flew to the island of Maui. I wrote this on the same day the tragic fires destroyed too many lives, homes, the town, and historical landmarks in Lahaina.

Hawaii is my soul home and has brought me much happiness over the years as it has millions of people around the world.

I hope we can all contribute in some way to helping the Hawaiian people heal, rebuild, and thrive once more.

Aloha (love), Maui.

ALSO BY JULIETTE N. BANKS

Get all my books at www.juliettebanks.com

THE MORETTI BLOOD BROTHERS
Steamy paranormal romance
The Vampire Prince – **FREE ebook**
The Vampire Protector
The Vampire Spy
The Vampire's Christmas
The Vampire Assassin
The Vampire Awoken
The Vampire Lover
The Vampire Wolf
The Vampire Warrior
The Vampire's Oath
The Vampire's Fate
The Vampire's Obsession

THE DARK KINGS OF NYC
Steamy dark mafia romance
The Darkest King - **FREE ebook**
The Ruthless King
The Savage King
The Avenged King

THE DUFORT DYNASTY
Steamy billionaire romance
Sinful Duty - **FREE ebook**
Forbidden Touch

Total Possession
Desire Unbound
Dark Surrender
Ruthless Surrender
Naughty Festivities
Wicked Praise
Beautiful Ruin

THE MORETTI BLOOD WOLVES
Steamy paranormal shifter romance
The Claimed Wolf - **FREE ebook**
The Alpha Wolf

REALM OF THE IMMORTALS
Steamy paranormal fantasy romance
The Archangel's Battle **- FREE ebook**
The Archangel's Heart
The Archangel's Star

CHAPTER ONE

Aidan pushed his Armani sunglasses over his eyes as he stepped out of the private jet into the sunshine. The tropical scents of Hawaii made him smile as the heat melted away the January East Coast winter he'd just flown in from.

He began to descend the stairs toward the waiting vehicles.

Aidan had been in NYC when his cousin, Daniel, had offered him a seat on the Dufort jet. Given they were all headed in the same direction for Logan and Emma's wedding, it made sense to accept the offer.

Global warming and all that.

He sent his own plane home to Philadelphia and joined them.

Aidan had been looking forward to escaping the cold, but there was also something, or rather *someone*, else he was looking forward to during the week he was spending on the Hawaii islands for this brother's wedding.

A little sacrificial lamb if you like.

Or she soon would be.

Lily.

One of Emma's bridesmaids.

"Hello, Hawaii, you beauty," Harper declared from behind him in her kiwi accent. "I've missed you."

"It's been six weeks," Daniel said, and they could all hear the eye roll in his voice.

"Six and a half," Harper replied, winking at Aidan as she joined him on the tarmac.

"That's about six hundred in Hawaii years for Harper," added Kristen, her best friend, gripping the handrail and stepping down. Her husband, Jackson, followed.

"Well aware," Daniel said and tossed his bag into the backseat of the SUV.

As they watched their luggage being unloaded from the plane and put into the vehicles, Fletcher and Olivia debarked the jet with their newborn, Baxter.

"Oh, my God it's so gorgeous here," Olivia said, holding her hand over the baby's face.

"This is just the airport. Wait until you see… everything!" Harper declared.

"Jesus, someone should just give you the ambassador's job." Daniel shook his head and leaned his elbow on the open door of the SUV. "Aidan, you coming with us, or Fletch?"

"Ah." He took one look at Baxter, who was stirring, and made his mind up. Not that he had anything against babies, but Aidan was a bachelor, and playing house was something he was actively staying well away from.

For as long as he could.

Which wouldn't be long if his father, Andrew Dufort, had anything to do with it. Which he didn't, and yet the old guy had suddenly got on his case about getting married.

It was only a thirty-minute drive into Waikiki, so not a big deal, but when Harper and Kristen began hula dancing, Aidan decided the party was in their car.

"I'll hitch a ride with our Hawaiian tour director," Aidan said, grinning at Harper.

"Let's go," Daniel said.

"See you there," Fletcher said, guiding his wife into the other car.

It was great to have his cousins back in his life.

They—meaning he, Logan, and their sister Amelia—had reacquainted with the three Dufort brothers at their grandmother's funeral after more than two decades.

Their fathers had fallen out.

His younger cousins, Blake and Jacob, never knew them, but Logan was the eldest and so he and Daniel had been impacted the most.

Now, the two were building a new bond, both their women, Emma and Harper, good friends and fellow authors.

In fact, Harper was Emma's other bridesmaid.

Aidan and Daniel were the best men.

"I thought Hunter was flying over with us," Jackson asked, his palm spread across Kristen's thigh. Her own hand fell naturally on top of it with her shiny new rings.

The two had got married quietly a month ago.

Jackson's mom had cancer and while Aidan understood she was receiving the best treatment, they had decided not to wait.

There had been a lot of weddings in their family recently and if his father had his way, there would be another one.

Over my dead body.

But he was excited to see Logan get married—again— his first had not ended well. Emma, however, was no Zoe, and Aidan was certain the two would live a long, happy life together.

Not that he was an expert on romantic love. He'd never been in love.

Lust?

What aroused him were submissive women who spread for him. Forget lust. Aidan felt a euphoric rush when he was with the right lover.

Being in control. Bringing them pleasure. Hearing them plead.

The week ahead would be busy with Logan and Emma's wedding and festivities here in Hawaii, and he had plans for the little bridesmaid he had met at their engagement party in Philadelphia three months earlier.

It was true; he was a confident—some would say cocky—man, but Aidan would put money on Lily thinking about reconnecting with him today.

A lot.

He smiled to himself, his cock swelling a little.

God, he couldn't wait.

He was going to find some time to get her alone and do all the delicious things he wanted with her.

Just thinking about how many times Lily had tried to relieve the pressure he'd created in those short moments he'd touched her…fuck it made him hard as hell.

Those fingers of hers would have been between her thighs many times.

Thinking of him.

Now it was his turn to devour her.

"He's flying in tomorrow," Harper explained. "Addison was working, then dropping Sammy and Sienna off at her ex's for the week."

Sienna was Addison's daughter, and Sammy belonged to Olivia and Fletcher. The two little girls were best friends.

Aidan tilted his head. "She couldn't take today off?"

Harper shrugged. "It's a lot of holidays to take."

Daniel gave him a *don't-go-there* look, but it was too late. The words were out of his mouth.

"Hunter's a billionaire. Why is she working?"

Jackson shook his head and glanced away, hiding his smile.

"Tried to warn you," Daniel said as the two women began to go at him.

"She's an independent woman. I still work," Harper said as Kristen simultaneously cried. "I've started my own business now. I'm living in the United States and married."

Aidan held up his hands.

"Sorry. God. My bad."

"And they aren't married," Harper said, shooting Daniel a look.

"Let me explain one last time, my darling wife. I am not in charge of my brother's marital status. Hunter will propose, I repeat. Hunter *will propose* when he is good and ready."

"You girls need to stop hounding him. The more you do, the less likely he is to do it." Jackson shrugged.

"But he loves her." Harper sighed.

"Don't marry a romance author," Daniel said over his wife's head and got an elbow in his side for it.

"I'm in no hurry, no matter what career she has." Aidan laughed.

Then Kristen and Harper began reeling off names of women they could match him with.

He ignored them because it was unlikely they would be his type. He was a true dominant, and the submissives he met—and fucked—at the sex club he visited frequently were all businesswomen looking for relief from being in charge.

Aidan was looking for a rare unicorn.

Which is why, when he met Lily at Logan's engagement party, his cock had sat right up and screamed *hello, gorgeous.*

The blushing beauty could barely look at him. When she had, those cheeks went dark pink and giggles poured from her, making him want to grip her throat and find out if her pussy was the same color.

It didn't matter that Emma and his brother had warned him away from her, Aidan had already decided he'd be fucking her this week.

End of story.

The way they left things, he knew that pussy would be wet and ready for what he had planned for it. Then he would taste his little peach again.

This time, all of her.

CHAPTER TWO

First class was way fancier than Lily had expected. But she *had* expected Emma and Logan to book her the pricey seat after refusing the offer of being flown to Hawaii from Chicago on a private yet.

It was very tempting, but didn't sit right with her.

She was just a girl from the south side, after all, who just happened to be best friends with a bestselling author.

Who just happened to be marrying a Dufort.

So here she was in first class, and it was incredible. Not that she'd been on many flights before, but she was pretty sure being served champagne and lobster wasn't normal.

Also, her pod was enormous and reclined into a bed where she'd actually slept. There was even a shower where she got to try out the little bag of goodies, which turned out better than the *"Gift With Purchase"* at her local department store.

It was so much fun Lily was already looking forward to flying home. She was pretty sure no one said that when they were going to Hawaii.

Of course, given it was January, she was very much looking forward to the sunshine and palm trees.

And most of all, being Emma's bridesmaid.

They had been friends since they were little girls and remained friends. Even when Emma had moved from Englewood, on the South Side of Chicago, into a fancy apartment in the city. Even when she'd become a successful author and Lily was still working at Martha's Fashions.

Her role had been called fashion assistant, but Lily knew she'd been nothing more than a glorified cashier. It was her first job out of high school, and she'd stayed for way too long.

In fact, she'd only left a year ago and was now working as a PA in a legal office. It wasn't her destination—Lily had aspirations—as life had delivered a few bumps in the road for her.

Her parents hadn't had enough money for her to go to college and she had only just missed out on a scholarship.

She'd taken the job at Martha's as a temporary gig to save money for college.

Lily wanted to be a teacher.

Correction: she was going to become a teacher.

Eventually.

But those bumps were not things she could look away from. Her parents were only just making ends meet and Lily had helped out.

The first year the fridge had needed replacing. Then their stove. Then a year and a half later, a storm hit the area and tiles on the roof had come loose. When water began leaking inside the house, she had no choice but to call the company to come and repair it.

That had taken a huge chunk from her savings.

After that, and watching her teaching dreams drift further away, Lily decided to move out of her parent's home to be more independent. She knew it would slow down her savings, but by this time, she was in her mid-twenties and needed space.

Things had become easier last year when she started working for Harris & White and Associates. The new job came with a very nice increase in pay and her boss, Matt Harris, seemed to really appreciate her.

She was only a few streets away from her parents, so saw them regularly. Lily would be forever grateful for staying close to home and spending more time with them than other people her age.

Because her dad was diagnosed with cancer a year ago. Colon cancer.

As a family, they'd been devastated.

His medical costs had been a lot, but Lily had the rest of her life to become a teacher and only limited time left with her dad.

Flying across the country to Hawaii felt like a big deal, even though his condition was stable. It wasn't just her dad. Lily had never left the continental US.

Unlike Emma, who had traveled as an author to different parts of the country and overseas. And dined in fancy restaurants and met celebrities with her billionaire husband. Lily lived a mundane life in little old Englewood on the South Side of Chicago.

Lily was proud of her best friend, but she felt like a fish out of water in Emma's world. In fact, traveling to Philadelphia for her engagement party was the first time she'd left Chicago.

She was a little embarrassed.

These people were far more worldly than her, and Lily was only there because of Emma. Because of a childhood friendship that hung on by a thread.

Yet no one had made her feel like she didn't belong. Everyone was very friendly.

Then there was Aidan.

Her cheeks heated as the memories of that night returned, just as her plane landed on Oahu.

He was everything she was not. Wealthy, worldly, successful, sexy, and clearly very confident with his sexuality.

Lily had only slept with two boys.

Men.

Actually, no, they were boys.

Number one had been Todd Bueller when she was a senior in high school. What a fumbling mess that was. So much so, she wished she could forget it altogether.

Especially the moment with the condom.

Lily had been told it was her job to put it on a man, so she'd taken it from him, ripped it open… and it had fallen out. Simultaneously Todd had grabbed at it, and the thing had slipped out of both their grasps onto the floor of the car.

Yeah, this all happened in the back seat of his dented Toyota.

It got worse.

When it fell to the floor, both of them went diving for it, in their anxiety, and their heads banged together. While Todd rubbed his head, Lily retrieved it and forced the rubber onto his now semi-hard member. Cue the awkward smiles and groping while Todd got interested again.

Her boobs still ached from all the squeezing.

Ugh.

Then there was Joe Goodman. He'd worked in the store down from Martha's and every day the tall dark-skinned man would walk past the shop and stare. One day he winked through the window at her, and she'd blushed, wishing he would introduce himself.

Her wish was answered. That night after work, he was waiting for her outside on the street.

"Can I walk you to the bus?" Joe had asked.

"I don't even know your name," Lily had replied, figuring she shouldn't be too easy.

"Name's Joe." He had held out his hand, and she'd shaken it.

"How do you know I catch the bus?"

"Because you're the prettiest girl I've ever seen, and I've seen you catch it every day for six weeks."

It was the first time a boy had made her feel beautiful. They'd dated for two years, and while Joe was a lot more confident and skilled than Todd, and Lily had mastered the condom, there were not a lot of sparks between them.

Joe ended up being offered a job in the city and they'd both known it was time to say goodbye. They made empty promises to each other to stay in contact, and neither of them had.

Since then, Lily had gone on a few dates, which ended in the odd kiss, but she'd never wanted it to go any further.

Not because she didn't like sex—she did.

She was just hoping for a bit more spark, like she saw in the movies or read about in books.

Then along came Aidan.

Never had she reacted to a man the way she had him. In fact, Lily wasn't exactly sure what had happened that night.

But she did know she was aching to see him and find out if he would deliver on his promise. And terrified he would.

He was way too much for her.

Too rich.

Too powerful.

Too erotic.

Too sexual.

He'd probably forgotten all about her. It would be better if he kept his husky voice and magical fingers to himself.

FORTY MINUTES LATER, Lily pushed her trolley through the doors of the airport and heard a squeal. Her face broke into a smile as Emma came running toward her.

"You're here!" Emma cried, wrapping her arms around her.

"Oh my God, it's so hot," Lily cried, fanning her face with her hand. "How do you have a tan already?"

"I'm getting married. It's fake." Emma said, taking control of the trolley. "Plus, we've been here a few days already. I've been trying to keep out of the sun, so I don't get any tan lines."

"If that's your greatest worry in life, sweetheart, then you're doing well," a male's voice said.

Lily glanced ahead of them to where Logan was leaning against a concrete pillar with one hand in the pocket of his long shorts.

"Hey, Lily." He grinned and walked over to plant a kiss on her cheek.

"You both look so tropical," Lily said, glancing down at her Target capri jeans and T-shirt, which she was eager to rip off.

It was a lot hotter than she'd expected.

A car pulled up beside them a second later and a man climbed out and began loading her luggage into the trunk.

Ah, that's right. Billionaires.

They climbed into the white SUV.

"I can't believe I'm in Hawaii. And you're getting married," Lily said excitedly as the car pulled away from the curb.

Logan reached out and took Emma's hand. The two of them smiled at each other and Lily was sure it was one of those moments where the world disappeared and no one else existed.

She'd never had that.

Well, except for that moment when Aidan's fingers had—

No. *Don't think about that.*

"So we have a huge week ahead," Emma said. "Tonight, we have the cocktail party on the rooftop at Altitude Bar just before sunset. So, when we get you checked in, you can just unpack and relax."

Lily was looking forward to seeing the Dufort Hotel. It was one of the most luxurious in the world-famous tropical location and owned by Logan's cousins.

"Everything is on account, so order room service or whatever you need while we are here," Logan said, leaning forward to catch her eye. "We don't want you worrying about anything like that, okay?"

Lily nodded.

There was no point in pretending this trip wasn't outside her budget. She was a PA from Englewood. Logan was a billionaire. And now, so was her best friend.

Actually, she didn't know if that was true. Their finances were none of her business. But regardless, she was worlds apart from meeting them in the financial stakes.

Lily had a feeling that over time, she and Emma would drift apart as their lives became more different. For now, she was happy to be her bridesmaid and celebrate her friend finding the love of her life.

"Thanks. I won't take advantage, though," Lily said.

Logan barked out a laugh, his Rolex-clad arm still lying on Emma's leg. "Take full advantage, Lily. Do your worst."

Lily deadpanned him. "Sir, you clearly have no idea just how many twenty-dollar candy bars I am capable of eating in a day."

Emma snorted. "Lil, you're in one of the fancy suites. That shit is free. But by all means, order a fancy dessert platter every night."

Lily gasped. "You… I don't need a suite."

"You're our bridesmaid," Logan said. "Plus, I know the owner, so we're getting a good rate."

"And it's only for a few nights. We're heading to Maui, remember?"

The wedding itself was taking place in Maui at a beautiful home on a private beach.

By home, she meant mansion.

"Just keep away from my brother." Logan shot her a pointed look. "I know he was flirting with you at our engagement party. Let me know if he crosses any lines."

Heat warmed her cheeks, so Lily turned to look at the Honolulu landscape as they drove along the highway toward Waikiki.

Too late.

Lines had been crossed.

"It was harmless flirting," Lily replied. "I'm sure he'll be distracted by all the beautiful tropical princesses."

"Oh, you could meet a cute Hawaiian and have a holiday romance. Imagine if he ends up being the man you marry? Now that would be a good story to tell your kids," Emma said.

"Okay, now you sound like Harper." Logan shook his head.

Emma shrugged. "I sound like a romance author. Which I am."

"It's true. It never stops." Lily grinned at Logan as he lifted his arm and put it around his bride.

"I suppose I can put up with you for the rest of my life." He fake sighed.

"It's too late. There's no backing out now," Emma said against his lips.

Ugh, they were too damn cute.

Lily turned back to the window and gave them their privacy. While Aidan and Logan weren't twins, they certainly looked alike enough, with all that dark hair, bright intelligent eyes, and large frames, to set off a strange sensation in her body.

Anticipation.

Soon the car pulled into the sweeping entrance of the Dufort Hotel and butterflies swarmed her tummy.

Suddenly Lily knew.

Aidan was waiting for her. He'd said he would and now she had arrived, Lily knew he'd hunt her down and make true on his promise.

He was going to eat her alive, lick by lick.

CHAPTER THREE

Aidan stepped out of the elevator and lowered his sunglasses over his eyes. As he made his way across the rooftop bar, he slid his phone into the pocket of his long, tan Armani shorts.

It was a private event tonight for his boisterous family, who he could see surrounding the bar, dressed in their designer tropical attire. They were all holding huge cocktails and chatting animatedly.

As he approached, Emma and Harper laughed at something, and Daniel lifted his hand an inch to order another drink.

As CEO, Aidan wouldn't be surprised if he only had to blink to have his employees running to please him. Fletcher and Hunter might also hold executive titles and equal shareholding, but the title Chief Executive Office was a powerful one.

They were all powerful and wealthy in their own ways.

Logan owned Dufort Liquor, which had just gone global. Watching him with Emma now, seeing the genuine happiness on his face, was almost a relief.

It might not have been a therapist's approved solution, but Aidan had saved Logan from losing everything. He had spiraled after finding his first wife in bed with someone—their bed—and the board of his company was ready to remove him.

Aidan had pulled the Macallan bottle out of his hands and taken him to the sex club HEAT, he frequented in Philly. His brother had then used it as an outlet for fucking.

Again, he wasn't gunning for shrink of the year, but sometimes you had to take one step onto the ladder before you could climb back up.

Not that there was anything wrong with sex clubs. He was a regular. If you went for the lifestyle and respected both yourself and those attending, then great.

Logan hadn't done that.

He'd been fucking away his anger.

Then along came Emma, and after some nail-biting moments, the two had fallen in love and were wasting no time building a life together and saying *I do.*

Aidan was happy for them.

He spotted his sister.

"Hey, sunshine." He kissed Amelia on the top of her head.

Short ass.

She had sad-*ish* eyes, which meant she was probably grieving some guy. Another one. He wasn't sure who, as this one must have happened fairly recently. A Christmas romance, no doubt.

Aidan was surprised it had slipped past them. He and Logan kept a close eye on her, as all big brothers did.

Okay, they might be a little more protective than most. The last thing they needed was for her to fall in love with some hot guy who was after the Dufort dynasty.

Or even her own pot of gold.

As an artist, Amelia had sold some of her sculptures for mid-six figures. She wasn't the struggling artist he teased her about.

But she was the worst romantic and could be terribly naive.

"Hello, annoying brother." Amelia tiptoed up and kissed his cheek. "Fancy seeing you here."

He glanced down at her dress.

Jesus. The damn thing only just covered her ass.

"Hope you got a discount on that thing. Did they forget the bottom half?" Aidan frowned as Amelia rolled her eyes and tugged the fitting sundress down.

"I said the same thing," Logan said, turning from where he was standing a few feet away, speaking to Jackson.

"If you two are going to be like this all week, I will find a new hotel." Amelia crossed her arms and glared at them.

"It's been going on all your life, so why would we stop now?" Aidan was momentarily distracted as an enormous fruit-laden cocktail was handed to him by a server. He lifted it and perused the contents. "What the hell is this? There better be whisky in here."

"Uh," the server started, looking uncomfortable.

"Just drink it," Logan groaned and glanced over his shoulder.

Got it.

The bride had organized them, so he was not to upset Emma.

Aidan slid the straw between his lips, closing his eyes so he wasn't stabbed by the umbrella/pineapple/strawberry/cherry/melon on the stick.

Jesus, there's a goddamn orchard on this thing.

He shuddered as the creamy, sweet liquid slid down his throat. When he opened his eyes, something far sweeter had appeared in his line of sight.

Well, hello there.

Fuck, she'd somehow gotten hotter than the last time he'd seen her. Was hot the right word?

No. Lily wasn't a hot chick. She was pretty.

Delicate.

Breakable.

Perfect.

"Logan, Aidan is eyeballing your bridesmaid," Amelia the cockblock said, following the direction he was looking.

He snarled at his sister.

"Do not touch the bridesmaid, Aidan," Logan said firmly.

"Just to be clear, I can't touch her, but if she ties me up and wants to have her way with me, that's okay?"

Logan didn't smile.

He turned to Amelia, who held up her hands and said, *I'm gone,* then made her way over to the girls.

Traitor.

"I'm serious, Aidan."

"So am I." Aidan smirked.

"Look, she's Emma's best friend. I may not know all your kinks, but I think we both know they won't be the kind of thing Lily is looking for," Logan ground out.

Aidan took another sip of the fruit bowl in a glass and grimaced. He placed it on the bar and casually slid his hands into his short's pockets.

"Lily is a submissive. I'm exactly what she's looking for," he said quietly yet firmly, meeting Logan's stare head on. "If she says no, I will walk away. But until then, I'm pursuing her."

Like a predator.

Logan cursed and said something about Emma going to kill him, but Aidan had already glanced away and had found his target.

Lily looked as if she were a deer in the headlights, unable to look away. His lips twitched and heat rushed through his body, straight to his cock. Then he watched as she nervously swallowed.

When her lips slightly parted, he felt a rumble start deep inside his chest. Aidan's smile faded, and the energy flowing between them intensified.

Narrowing his eyes seductively, he ran them over her body and back up again. He would own every inch of her, fulfilling the promise he'd made to her three months ago.

He saw the moment she lost control.

Her mouth shuddered and the cocktail glass she was holding slipped through her fingers, smashing to the ground.

Everyone leaped back and Dufort employees quickly arrived and began sweeping the glass away.

"Oh my God, are you okay?" a few of the girls cried, grabbing Lily's arm.

She never looked away from him.

Logan turned, still holding his bouquet-sized cocktail, and glared at him. "You will break her."

Yes, but she will enjoy it.

"I'll put her back together again before she returns home," Aidan said, slapping his brother on the shoulder. "Now, if you will excuse me."

Seeing Lily again had only increased his desire for her. He was going to enjoy watching her crumble to pieces in his hands.

Sweet Lily, your pussy tastes like peaches.

He knew that already.

But just to be sure, he was going to taste her again. This time with his tongue. While she was stretched out on his bed, tied to… well, he didn't know what. Stupid hotel rooms made that type of thing difficult.

Maybe he would just bind her wrists.

Or push her down onto her elbows, spreading her wide, so he could help himself to her sweet, wet flesh.

Aidan walked over to the chaotic scene, moving in behind Lily. He leaned into her hair. "Little peach, did I scare you?"

She whipped around. "Aidan,"

Crunch.

He glanced down and saw blood trickling from her little toe. That wasn't okay. Without thinking, he reached down and scooped her up.

"Hello, sweet thing," he said as she gasped.

Aidan winked at her, and as Lily gripped his shoulders and biceps, he began to move her away from the broken glass.

"Logan," Emma called, but he was already taking off with their bridesmaid.

"You need to put me down," Lily cried, her nails digging into his skin.

You'll be doing that with my cock inside you later.

"Do I?" he calmly asked.

"Yes,"

"Relax. You're bleeding." Aidan dropped Lily onto one of the sun loungers beside the pool.

A staff member appeared. "Can I get you anything?"

"Napkins and a few bandages please," he said and crouched down by her feet.

"Aidan, please," Lily said, tugging down her skirt, which was pointless as it fell nearly to her knee. Amelia could borrow half of it. "It's just a scratch."

"He's not hurting her," Logan growled from behind him. Here we go.

"Are you okay, Lil?" Emma asked.

Aidan didn't look around. He remained crouched at the foot of the sun lounger with his eyes on Lily, who was chewing her bottom lip and waiting for his permission to answer.

Fuck me. Aidan's cock turned to stone.

He had to force himself from pointing at her and saying to his brother *Exhibit A. One sexy submissive.*

He almost purred as he gave her a little nod.

"Yes." Lily then glanced back at Emma.

Aidan couldn't help it. He swiveled around and caught Logan's watchful eye. They both knew a pure submissive when they saw one and she was submitting to him as they spoke.

Logan cursed and laid a hand on Emma's shoulder, nodding to Aidan, as if to acknowledge it wasn't up to them.

Regardless, Aidan planned to keep things discrete. In this family, if you showed any interest in someone, they were trying to marry you off in the next breath.

Including his father.

However, Andrew Dufort wouldn't be doing that with Lily. He'd already made himself clear on that matter.

"We'll get you another drink," Logan said as the first aid kit arrived. He tugged Emma away.

Daniel and Harper came over.

"All okay here?" Daniel asked, and Aidan nodded, wondering how he had himself a whisky.

Aside from being the owner.

Harper joined them and glanced down at Lily's bleeding toe. "Ouch."

"Seriously, it's just a minor cut," Lily said, sounding exasperated. Her gaze shot to him again, and he realized she was overwhelmed by the fuss.

"You don't want it to get infected while on a tropical island. Good work spotting it, Aidan," Harper said, patting his arm as he stood up and handed the first aid kit back to the employee.

"Thank you, Harper," Aidan replied. "The bandage should stay on overnight and we'll check it in the morning."

He reached down and helped Lily to her feet.

That was when his younger cousins decided to show up.

"What's up, Aides!" Blake greeted him with a back slap.

"Cuz," Jacob said, grinning.

His Aunt Samantha, Andrew's sister, had added to the family a few years after Amelia was born, so they were the youngest of the Dufort pack.

Well, except for Baxter now.

"You remember Daniel and Harper, right?" Aidan asked.

"We met in Philly," Harper said, reaching out her hand. "At the engagement party."

"Good to see you again, boys," Daniel said.

They all shook hands while Aidan found himself placing a hand on the small of Lily's back to keep her steady as she kept the weight off her foot.

"And this is Emma's bridesmaid, Lily," Aidan said.

"I met them in Philly, too."

Aidan had been very distracted at the engagement party, so of course, they had all met. Right now, he didn't like the way Blake and Jacob were smiling at Lily.

"When is your mom flying in?" Daniel asked.

"Monday, for the ceremony," Blake said. "Your parents arrive tomorrow, right?"

Aidan nodded.

"What about Uncle Jonathan? Was he invited?" Jacob asked.

"Yeah, no, he won't be attending." Daniel smirked.

There was still bad blood between both their fathers. Aidan knew he had been invited, but despite the air being sort of cleared, it was still awkward having them both in the same room.

Long story short, they had both loved the same woman and while Jonathan had married Margaret and had a family, it was Jena, the love of his life, who was the one who got away.

Aidan had to wonder if it had all been worth losing his brother over. Especially as he divorced Margaret years later, and now was reunited with Jena.

Oh, yeah, and Jena was also Jackson's mom, making him Daniel, Hunter, and Fletcher's half-brother.

"Plus, Jenna is undergoing a special cancer treatment and can't travel right now."

Oh, shit, he didn't know that.

"I'm sorry," Aidan said, and his sentiments were echoed by his cousins.

"That's very sad," Lily said, and he noted the heavy tone in her voice.

"You know Jenna is Jackson's mom, right?" Harper added. "So he and Kristen will be heading right back to NYC after the wedding."

"Yes," Blake said. "Mom doesn't like to gossip, so we got the information out of the big guy here."

Aidan lifted a shoulder.

It was true, he'd updated them on the family gossip. They deserved to know.

"Dude, your mother is a huge gossip. She's just super subtle about it." Aidan laughed.

"Maybe she didn't want to gossip about a dying woman, dude." Jacob frowned at him, and he held up a hand in defense.

Harper leaned into Lily. "Sorry for the family politics. There is a lot in this one."

"Behave, wife," Daniel said and cupped the back of her neck, forcing her to turn. Daniel dropped his mouth to hers.

Beside him, Lily shivered and lifted her eyes to Aiden's.

I'll scratch that itch for you soon, peaches.

They all headed back over to the bar, and Aidan had begun to follow when, beside him, Lily cleared her throat. He glanced down.

"Thanks. For—" Lily pointed at her foot. As she made to walk away, Aidan angled his body, stopping her progress.

Big eyes lifted to his.

"It was the least I could do, given I caused it," Aidan said as she pressed her lips together, looking nervous. Aidan tilted his head. "You're scared of me."

She shook her head.

Liar.

"You're scared of the way I make your body feel. The way I *made* you feel that night." When she began to speak, Aidan took a step closer and lowered his voice. "I meant what I said back in Philly. I intend to have all of you. When I come for you, you'll know."

Then he took a step back and let her return to the bar.

CHAPTER FOUR

Shit.

Shit, shit, shit.

Lily's foot was aching. The glass had cut quite deep—not that she needed stitches, but enough she wobbled a bit walking back to the bar.

That and her pride was wounded.

She felt like such a tool in front of Aidan.

He was just as gorgeous as she remembered. Probably more. He might look like his brother and cousins—all of them insanely good-looking—but there was something magnetic about him. He was a little taller than all the others. Not as broad as Daniel but still very muscular, with what she could only describe as juicy, round biceps.

Aidan's thighs were thick and powerful and, yes, Lily had checked out his ass when he'd first arrived. But it was those green eyes that sparkled full of mischief that undid her.

When they'd locked onto hers, it was as if they were reminding her he'd had his hand inside her panties not long ago.

Sure, it had been three months, but during that time Lily had fantasized about him way too many times.

Hence losing control of her senses and her cocktail smashing to the floor.

What an idiot.

Then Aidan had snuck up behind her, and she'd stepped on a piece of glass. The next minute, he had her in his arms and was carrying her away, whispering in her ear.

Lord.

She was not okay.

Aidan was playing with her, and they both knew it. Fine, she liked his attention because he was a very hot guy, but someone might hear the things he said.

Little peach.

Gah!

Firstly, vaginas do not smell or taste like fruit. Anyone who tries to claim that is either sticking fruit in their va-jay-jay and will end up with a UTI, or slapping some highly perfumed chemical crap on it, and, same deal.

Secondly, he needed to stop talking dirty to her.

He made her feel all…wobbly.

And warm.

Aidan seemed to thrive on shaking her foundations. His smirks and dirty glances. Lily wasn't as confident and outspoken as some of the women here but then again this wasn't her world.

She was surrounded by successful people and billionaires. It wasn't an even playing field and his poking make her feel a little uncomfortable.

Vulnerable.

But, Lily couldn't ignore that when Aidan was close, and when he'd held her in his arms, not only did a flush of arousal shoot through her, she felt almost safe.

Grounded.

Lily joined Emma, Olivia, and Fletcher as she reached the bar, and they pulled out a barstool for her. She climbed onto it and turned to face out across the pool, avoiding Aidan's glances.

When I come for you, you'll know.

Holy hell. There was no way she could let what happened in Philly take place again.

No way.

Lily blamed the champagne. It was Cristal, after all.

Logan's house had been incredible. It wasn't a house—it was a mansion with numerous bedrooms and the most incredibly entertaining area outside.

When she was introduced to Aidan, she had found him funny and charming.

And drop-dead gorgeous.

That night he was in a suit and looked every inch the wealthy entrepreneur she knew he was. Tailored jacket, a large silver watch that was worth more than her parent's house, and polished shoes.

Lily knew his attention was a bit of fun, because men like him didn't end up with girls like her.

So when Aidan had offered to show her Logan's art collection, she'd just grinned and accepted it, looping her hand through his arm.

They started in the living room where everyone was milling around, and slowly made their way up the stairs and along the hallway, stopping to discuss each piece. One of them was a Picasso.

Which apparently Lily had thought was a good time to tell Aidan she loved to sketch, as if it was the same.

She'd blushed as he'd said, "*Oh yeah? Is our Lily an artist?*"

Ugh. She'd felt dumb.

"No. It's just a hobby. Some people read. I sketch to relax," she'd replied.

Not that she had a lot of time.

While Lily enjoyed her job, her boss was very demanding of her time. He was very nice, and they had a good relationship—too good, Emma said.

Matt was good-looking.

He'd divorced last year and sometimes his behavior was a little inappropriate. Nothing that she had to worry about, so Lily just brushed it off.

She needed the job.

From time to time, his hands went to places that made her pause. On her arm, on her knee, brushing a hand over her hair.

It wasn't okay, but he never took it further and the overtime she got paid was helping to boost her savings and pay for stuff her dad needed.

Lily figured Matt was handsome enough, and because he had his own law firm, he'd find a girlfriend eventually.

And lose interest in her.

So Aidan's advances, while she had no idea why he was interested in a girl from the South Side of Chicago, were much of the same. Lily decided to just sip her champagne, relax, and enjoy it.

As much as one could relax with a powerful and masculine man like him towering over them.

Then things had escalated.

He was a terrible flirt, and she had no game. She had just giggled and fluttered her eyelashes like a Jane Austen heroine.

At one painting, Aidan placed a hand on the small of her back and leaned in. "You see, the skill of the stroke here, Lily?"

She had shivered.

Then his hand had slid down her arm at another print. "How do they make you feel?"

By then, her heart rate had been off the charts. When they got to the top of the stairs, Aidan's hand was on her hip. Unlike Matt, Lily didn't want him to move away.

She continued to follow him and to this day, she had no idea what art she'd seen from that point onwards.

Except the last one.

Logan's office.

There was a large painting hanging on the wall opposite an impressive bookcase. It was a landscape with rolling waves and an energy that took her breath away. Lily had stood staring as she'd felt the heat of Aidan's body at her back.

He'd moved closer. Then closer.

Soon she was no longer able to focus on the painting before her. Aidan's breath had slid over her neck as his hands fell to her hips, rendering her frozen.

"Do you like this one?" he asked huskily, and they both knew he didn't mean the painting.

The champagne made her say *yes* as his lips gently brushed over her collarbone, distracting her as he tugged up the hem of her dress.

"Tell me what you like," Aidan rasped.

She knew he'd meant the painting as part of the game they were playing.

"The power," she'd replied.

"Good girl."

Oh fuck.

Her panties had been wet already, but with those two words, Lily knew she was now drenched.

She didn't want him to know.

When she tried to move, his grip on her hip tightened, sending a fire soaring through her. Which was just the beginning because then his fingers felt the hem of her panties and she began to tremble.

"Move your legs apart for me," Aidan ordered.

Despite her mouth parting, Lily was surprised to find that she obeyed.

Just like that.

No question.

Her body was on autopilot, following instructions.

Aidan didn't wait for an invitation; he simply lifted the edge of her panties aside and pressed his fingers into her flesh.

She'd arched, letting out a moan as her head fell back onto his chest.

"Christ, you are fucking soaked," Aidan had growled into her hair. "I could slide my cock into you so goddamn fast right now."

No.

Yes.

Then his other hand had almost lifted her off the floor, spreading her wider as his fingers plunged inside her pussy.

Fucking her fast and vigorously.

"Quiet," he ordered as she began to moan.

Then they stilled when they heard footsteps out in the hall.

Aidan released her.

That's when he did it.

Lily spun around and as he slid his fingers into his mouth. With fire in his eyes like a devil, he grinned. "Lily Peterson, you taste like peaches."

Her eyes had been wide.

No one had ever gone down on her before, so the thought of a man licking *that stuff* was…arousing.

"Lucky for you, peaches are my favorite fruit, so I plan to have my mouth on that pussy one day soon. Unfortunately for you, I intend to eat you alive."

Right at that moment, Emma had walked in, interrupting them. "Come on, it's time for some photos."

Lily was still not sure whether her best friend had saved her, or interrupted what was probably going to be the best orgasm of her life.

She'd never know.

But no masturbating had relieved the itch.

Not in three long months.

THE COCKTAILS HAD created a nice warm fuzzy feeling inside her tummy. Lily swung her legs back and forth, watching the sky turn bright orange as the sun set, from her barstool.

It looked like every postcard she'd ever seen of Waikiki and couldn't believe it was real.

She couldn't believe she was here.

In Hawaii.

Olivia and Fletcher were beside her, tending to the baby, her enormous diamond ring sparkling brightly, and Lily wondered what it would feel like to have the price of a house—hell, probably two houses on your finger.

It was another world.

Emma's ring was big, but not as big. Harper's—well, that was a whole hotel she had on her ring finger.

No wonder they had personal security dotted around the place. Lily had noticed them immediately and Emma had whispered to just take no notice. That they would blend into the background.

"Fletch, you're such a natural baby daddy," Emma said, leaning into Logan.

"Trust me, I'm simply motivated by sleep." Fletcher replied.

Olivia smiled up at him, her eyes full of love. When he winked back, Lily felt an odd sense of envy spark within her.

Not because Fletcher was handsome and wealthy—he was—but because Emma was marrying into such an awesome family. She'd never had a relationship solid enough to even consider what her in-laws might be like.

The Dufort's all looked like carbon copies of each other. Or more to the point, like Aidan. Even his sister, Amelia, who was gorgeous, looked like her brothers. Which no girl wanted to hear, so she kept her thoughts to herself.

Her brothers were relentless in teasing her, and while Lily couldn't help giggling, she could imagine it was stifling and annoying.

As a single child, she couldn't imagine it.

"Could someone please bring my sister a towel? She forgot her skirt," Aidan said, attempting to tug Amelia's skirt down.

To be fair, it was extremely short, but she had long gorgeous legs and a great tan, so why not show them off?

"Stop it, Aides." Amelia slapped his arm. "That joke is getting old. It was old the first time and while you keep going on about you're also getting old."

Aidan snorted, while Emma and Lily giggled as the poor Dufort employee reached for a towel, looking confused.

"Don't encourage him. He'll be your brother-in-law in a few days and don't think these two won't start on you," Amelia chided.

"Let them try," Emma challenged, poking her tongue out at Logan. Who snapped at her with his teeth.

Lily tuned out of the conversation, chewing her lip and playing with the butterfly charm on her necklace, as Amelia's words sunk in.

Aidan would soon be Emma's brother-in-law.

Which meant if she let anything more happen between her and Aidan, it would always hang awkwardly between them.

Forever.

When Emma had children. At anniversaries where she and Aidan would both attend. Single or one of them shacked up.

Awkward.

So she wasn't going to go down the path that would inevitably lead to *hey remember that time in Hawaii we...*

No.

Not to mention she was well aware he was way too much for her to handle.

I'm going to eat you alive.

Yes, he probably would.

Plus, she was here for Emma and had bridesmaid's duties. And late at night, she would be ringing home to Chicago to check on her dad.

Lily sucked down the last of the Pina Colada and placed it on the bar behind her. Turning back, she avoided Aidan's stare. She could feel him watching her, but Lily had made her mind up.

Nothing was going to happen.

Nearby, Harper, Kristen, and Jackson were dancing. Amelia downed her drink and skipped over to join them.

Blake and Jacob followed.

Daniel took the baby from Fletcher and held him up in front of him. Then he tucked him into his arm.

"Take it all in, little man. You and your cousins will be running this place one day."

"Daniel Dufort. Are you getting clucky?" Olivia smirked, pulling her baby back onto her shoulder.

"Don't be insane." Daniel handed Baxter back to Fletch.

"You are most welcome to start teaching him how to be the next CEO of Dufort Hotel Group, but not before bedtime," Fletcher said, taking the baby. "And on that note, we're off to pretend to sleep."

Olivia rolled her eyes and gave Lily a wink.

"Fletcher Dufort, stop pretending you are sleep deprived. You sleep in our spare room most nights. The *soundproofed* spare room."

Lily laughed.

Her eyes accidentally drifted to the wrong Dufort man, and her tummy twisted.

Thankfully, he wasn't looking.

But she took a moment to take in his thick dark hair, stunning green eyes, and dusting of hair on his jaw.

He was so sexy.

"I have a billion-dollar organization to run," Fletcher retorted.

"You had it soundproofed?" Aidan frowned.

"Trust me." Fletcher cast his eyes around the men. "Get ahead of the game and get it done now."

"I think I'm good for at least another ten years."

Aidan laughed.

Noted. He didn't want kids.

Which was not relevant to her.

Olivia shook her head. "Let's go. See you all at breakfast."

"Golf," Logan said. "Tee off at ten a.m."

"We're heading to Lanikai Beach for SUP yoga, if you want to join us?" Emma said to Olivia. "No pressure."

The stand-up paddleboarding wasn't Lily's idea. She wanted to go shopping after hearing how great it was in Hawaii.

Emma said they needed to do a group activity, and that shopping with billionaires was not something she wanted Lily to suffer through after having her own nightmare experience in the Hamptons.

"Oh, yeah. Gotcha," Lily had replied during their phone call about it, remembering her friend's visit to Long Island. "I'll wait until after the wedding."

She had an extra day on Oahu, so would sneak off to the outlets then.

Lily glanced down at her sundress. It certainly wasn't designer. In fact, she was pretty sure it was from Target.

Or maybe she'd splashed out on a Gap dress.

Hard to remember when it was over five years old.

Which begged the question: why was Aidan even interested in her? When she glanced over at him again, he was sipping his whisky and watching her.

Emma leaned against the bar, distracting her. "How's your foot?"

"It's fine. Aidan was just being dramatic."

"He does that," Emma laughed. "Think you can SUP tomorrow?"

Lily frowned.

"Harper said I need to be careful it doesn't get infected. But I should be fine," she replied, kicking out her leg, and they both stared at the bandage. "I think she has a point."

"Yeah." Emma touched her chin and hummed.

The next minute, her foot was back in Aidan's hands. "If it does, we'll get you some antibiotics. The saltwater will be good for it."

Lily felt her face flush once more.

His touch had her squeezing her thighs together and when their eyes connected, the blaze she saw in those green globes told her he was well aware of what he was doing.

And he was just as affected.

Nope. Brother-in-law. Can't go there.

She tugged her foot back and nervously played with her butterfly pendant.

"Aidan has a point," Emma said as Logan and Daniel joined them.

"I should head back to my room, soak it in the bath, and have an early night. Jetlag and all that," Lily said.

He did, but she could feel her defenses slipping now that the alcohol was kicking in.

Aidan stepped away as everyone returned from their dancing.

It was now dark. Around them, the hotels were lit up and she could hear the sounds of tourists and traffic from below them in Waikiki.

The atmosphere was happy and tropical.

And full of anticipation.

"We're heading to one of the hot local night spots," Jackson announced. "Who's in?"

"Me," Blake said, high-fiving Jackson.

"Me?" Jacob said, leaning on the bar and asking for water.

"Me three," Kristen called out.

Emma turned to Lily in question.

"You're not going home, are you?" Amelia asked. "It's early. Emma. Aidan. Tell Lily she has to come dancing with us."

"I'll carry you if you can't walk," Aidan offered, and Logan shoved him.

"I can walk." Lily slid off the stool and ended up bouncing on her foot, landing right up against Aidan's chest.

He didn't move.

His hands gripping her arms.

"I can walk," she said. "It's not broken, it's just a cut, which is stinging a little."

"You heard her. She can walk." Logan shoved him again, and Aidan smirked and took a step back.

"So, are we doing this?" Harper said as Daniel nodded to one of the personal security guys.

"Two cars," Daniel said as one of them walked over.

"Three," Aidan corrected.

Daniel recounted the bodies and nodded. "Three,"

"I can walk," Lily said. "Or Uber there and meet you all."

Emma laughed and looped her arm around her neck. "Just follow my lead. Billionaires do things differently."

Right.

No Ubers.

No walking.

"We should ditch the guys and make this your bachelorette party," Harper said.

"No!" Kristen and Daniel said firmly at the same time as they all stepped into the elevator.

"Party poopers." Harper crossed her arms. "I don't plan for us to get arrested this time."

Lily's mouth fell open.

"She's joking," Emma said, bumping her shoulders.

"She's not," Kristen mumbled.

"Okay, I need to hear this story," Aidan said. "Spill."

"So," Harper began.

CHAPTER FIVE

Aidan reached into the vehicle to help Lily when they arrived at Aloha Bar. There was a queue—which they wouldn't be waiting in—and the music was pumping even from out here.

She looked like a deer in the headlights, and it was doing strange things to his nether regions. After all, submissives were his thing.

"I truly can walk," Lily said softly, smoothing down her dress after climbing out. "You don't need to make a fuss."

"Perhaps I'm being a gentleman," Aidan purred.

"Is that what you're doing?" she asked, and her touch of sass took him by surprise.

Aidan smirked. "No,"

Daniel's personal security positioned themselves, and the rope was lifted so their group could enter. Groans behind them sounded out.

Just another day in the life of a Dufort.

Aidan followed his cousins up to the bar to get drinks while the girls found tables and hit the dance floor.

The place was busy and now they were in the air conditioning and couldn't see the palm trees outside. Aidan felt they could be in any bar in LA or NYC. Red lights flashed, music thrummed with a heavy base, and bodies heaved.

For the next few hours Aidan watched Lily dancing—despite her damn foot—and tossing back shots. He kept his distance, mostly because he was ready to tilt her neck and lick his way down to her aching nipples.

Meanwhile, Blake and Jacob had made friends with two gorgeous, tanned news anchors. They'd made themselves comfortable at their table and were flirting like mad.

They were a sure thing.

Together.

A tough call. Threesomes were hard to say no to, especially if they were both eager to please and would submit. He'd already figured one of them, Kalea, had a praise kink.

The way she'd preened when he'd Blake had said *good girl* and run his hand over her ass. Her friend, Nalani, was less secure and eager for Aidan's attention. Or Jacob's. She didn't seem to be fussed about which one.

They could talk her into both.

But Aidan had zero interest in fucking with his cousins. So he would leave the Hawaiian women to them.

His eyes were on Lily, but she didn't know that. Her smile had stiffened when she saw the company he was keeping. That had pleased him immensely.

His little peach was jealous.

"I need to move to Hawaii," Blake said. "I had no idea the women were so gorgeous."

Liar.

"Everyone says that until they learn the cost of living here," Kalea responded, lifting her glass to her lips.

"Don't think I'll starve." Blake smirked.

Aidan watched Kalea take in Blake's forty-thousand-dollar timepiece and then glance around the table.

Welcome to the party, sweetheart.

"What did you say your surname was?" she asked Jacob, who was on the other side of her.

"I didn't," Jacob replied, tossing back his vodka shot.

Aidan wiped away his smile.

Out of everyone he knew, Jacob worked the least to get a woman. They just sort of crumbled at his feet. Aidan made a note to invite both of them to the club one night. It was possible his cousins had a kink or two they could lean into without fear of being exposed in the media.

Which these two women fronted.

Daniel and Harper returned from the dance floor, and that's when the penny dropped. Daniel Dufort was a well-known face in the media across America.

"Oh my God. Dufort." Kalea glanced at Aidan, and he nodded to let her out of her misery.

Daniel stiffened.

"They're just having drinks. You girls won't do anything silly, will you?" Blake asked.

Or, rather, informed them.

"Scout's honor," Nalani said, lifting her fingers and shooting Aidan a look.

"Good girl." He smiled seductively.

She leaned into him, and suddenly Aidan wanted out of this game.

It was Lily he wanted to feel against his body, not anyone else.

He turned back to the dance floor and found her wiggling her sexy fucking ass with a strange man.

Hell no.

"Excuse me," he said and nodded to Blake and Jacob, his eyes darting at the women, all *help yourself, boys*. Then he made his way over to the dance floor.

Aidan hadn't realized Lily was the only one in their group still dancing. How long had this guy been pursuing her? He was way too close, and she was letting him.

Not okay.

Clearly he needed to make his intentions louder, so Lily knew that she was his.

Only while she was in Hawaii.

Then she could fuck who she wanted.

Over the next few days, she was his.

Aidan stepped up behind her, catching the guy's eye. "Can I cut in?"

His voice was dark and authoritative, letting him know it wasn't actually a question. The man frowned and Lily turned and wobbled on her foot.

Aidan grabbed her hips. "Woah, sweetheart, let's get you off your feet."

"Hey, wait a minute. We're dancing. Do you know this guy?"

"She knows me," Aidan said firmly. "Let's go."

"I—"

"Hey, man. Let the lady decide."

No thanks, pussy.

"Lily," Aidan growled, his eyes locked on hers.

When her eyes lowered and he felt her body relax under his touch, he felt her submission and his cock thickened.

Desire poured from him as Lily swallowed.

I am ready to fuck you right now.

"Yes, I know him. Sorry," she said, glancing back at the Hawaiian man.

He shot Aidan an annoyed look, then wandered off.

"That was a little rude," Lily said.

"Little peach, let me be clear," Aidan whispered, moving them deeper into the moving crowd so they had privacy. "Your body is mine while we're in Hawaii. And I don't share."

He couldn't see her cheeks, but Aidan knew they had gone red with excitement and arousal.

"Aidan, stop. You're soon going to be Emma's brother-in-law."

"So?"

"So… it's not right. I am her best friend."

Aidan frowned. "Did someone not tell me about a law? You're older than seventeen, right?"

Lily frowned back at him. "Of course I am."

He was being obtuse. She was nearing thirty-one, which he knew because so was Emma was around the same age.

"And you're not my sister." He tugged her hips up against him and Lily's hands landed on his pecs.

He fucking loved her hands on him.

"Don't be silly."

"You're also not my sister-in-law," Aidan continued, and lowered his mouth to her neck, breathing in her natural scent.

"Aidan, please."

"Tell me your panties are nice and moist for me,"

"Stop,"

"I promised I was going to finish what I started in Philly. Until I hear you crying out to God while my mouth is on that sweet pussy, you are mine. Understand?"

Lily's forehead dropped to his chest.

Aidan smiled.

He lifted her face to his, a finger under her chin.

"When I knock on your door, you will open it. Do you understand?" he instructed.

Blink, blink.

"Do you understand, Lily?"

She nodded.

"Tell me you understand," Aidan rasped.

"I understand. But—"

"I understand, what?" He could feel her body tense and begin to shake under his touch.

"Wh—"

"Sir," Aidan said, lowering his hand to her hip again and moving them to the beat of the music. "When we're alone, and when I am giving you instructions, you will call me sir."

"Don't be absurd," Lily replied, shocked.

Aidan grinned and nudged her chin to close her gaping mouth. "Better not do that or I'll drag you out the back, push you to your knees and fill you with my swollen cock."

Lily took a step back and shook her head. "I can't do this."

He glanced down at her sniff nipples and when their eyes connected, he said. "I think we both know you will."

CHAPTER SIX

Lily closed the door of her suite behind her and tossed her purse on the coffee table. Then she flopped down on the sofa and threw her head back.

Her nipples were aching.

Her panties soaked.

The last hour at the bar had been painful. Walking away from Aidan on the dance floor was all she could do.

She wanted him to kiss her. She wanted to drop to her knees and undo his pants. She wanted relief from this pain and torture, but calling him sir?

No.

No way.

That was going too far.

It was *all* going too far.

So fine, she was using the brother-in-law angle as an excuse. They both knew that, but he was overwhelmingly gorgeous, and it scared her.

There was no way she would be the lover he wanted. Not to mention she didn't do casual sex.

Or play bedroom games where she called a lover, sir. Did he have a *Fifty Shades* kink or something?

And telling her what she would do, instead of asking… well, it was shaking her to her core.

Worse, she wanted it.

She wanted him to force her legs apart and give her instructions.

Yet, it felt so wrong.

Even now her body disagreed. Her nipples pressed harshly against the cotton of her dress, and she was dying to slide her hand between her legs.

"Damn it. Why don't I own a vibrator?" Lily said out loud.

Before she relieved the ache, she had a job to do. She glanced at the time on her phone and did a quick time zone conversion.

It was six thirty in the morning in Chicago. Her mom would be awake. She found her number and pressed send.

Her mom answered. "Lily, darling, how is Hawaii?"

"Hot. Beautiful. Sunny," she replied, "Well, it's nearly two in the morning, but it *was* sunny."

She let out a giggle, wishing she could tell her about Aidan. Her mom was her best friend. So was Emma, but in recent years, as their lives drifted further apart and she shared the responsibility of caring for her father, her mom and her had become a tight team.

But this wasn't something she wanted to tell anyone.

What would she say?

I'm highly aroused by a man who wants to own my body for a few days. He's making me have the dirtiest thoughts. But he's out of my league and I think he's playing me.

Still, Lily was tempted to let him.

Just for a few days.

Then she would return home to the South Side and pretend it never happened.

"Sounds like you're having fun. Wish Emma and Logan all the best from us."

"I will. How's Dad?"

"The same," her mom answered. The same answer she gave most days, and the one Lily was hoping to hear.

It wasn't going to get any better than that. Not at this point.

Her chest relaxed. "Good."

"Enjoy yourself while you are there, Lily. Don't worry about your dad," Angela Peterson said. "There's nothing we can do except let him go when it's his time."

Lily sighed. She knew that, but the waiting was hard. It was a cruel juggle of wanting to freeze time and sardonically wanting the torture to be over.

Grieving someone while they were alive was exhausting. And yet, she felt heavy with guilt even thinking about herself.

Lily had been close to her father, Gary, all her life. She was unashamedly a daddy's girl. He'd always been a cuddly father and taken her everywhere.

When she was small, he'd carry her on his shoulders. When she started school, he helped her with homework and taught her to ride a bike. Lily and her mom always went to watch him play football, and as she got older, she would go with him and help sometimes when he coached local teams.

Soon he wouldn't be with them, and a gaping hole would be left behind.

In some ways, he was already half gone. Gary had lost so much weight and was half the man he was. He had no energy and his smile looked way too ethereal for her liking.

"I know. I will, Mom," Lily said.

"I better go. I have to get to work after making your father's breakfast."

"Call you tomorrow." Lily ended the call and walked into the bathroom.

Her mom was right. She needed to relax and just have fun. She *was* having fun.

Heck, she was staying in a beautiful suite in the Dufort Waikiki, hanging out with some of the wealthiest people in America. She'd just danced the night away at the infamous Aloha Bar and a gorgeous man was attracted to her.

But.

Lily wasn't going to forget what her priorities were. She was going to keep her feet on the ground and not get to wishing she was this wealthy, or hope to fall in love like all the wives and girlfriends in the family had.

She didn't fit into this world.

Her goals were clear.

Help her mom with her dad until he left them. Work hard at her job—ignoring Matt's wandering hands—and save until she could go to college and get her Bachelor of Education.

Then she would finally fulfill her dream of becoming a teacher.

There would be no Chanel dresses or huge diamond rings in her future. No private jets or first class.

Lily would meet a local man and fall in love and make her dad proud by living an honest life.

But while she was here, on this dream vacation, Lily was going to have fun.

Lily shook her head at the huge spa bath, a shower with seven hundred shower heads—okay, fine, five—and two basins. On what appeared to be gold-plated hooks were two luxurious bathrobes and two pairs of fluffy white slippers on the floor below them.

She walked over and ran her hand over the silky robes and giggled. "I need more bodies."

Knock knock.

Oh shit.

"God, I was only kidding."

She stood there frozen, wondering what to do, because she knew exactly who it was. Lily wasn't sure she was ready for this.

Maybe she could pretend she was asleep.

"Lily, open the door," Aidan called out.

Crap. She padded across the hotel suite on her bare feet and reached the door.

"Now turn the handle," he said quietly as if he could see through the door and knew she was standing there.

Lily drew in a deep breath and let it out.

Then opened the door.

Aidan walked straight in, grabbed her by the hips, let the door close behind them as his hand glided through her hair and bent her backward.

"Now, where were we, peaches?" he growled.

Lily gasped as his mouth smashed down on hers.

WELL, WHAT DO you know, Lily tastes like peaches up top as well. Aidan released her lips, after thoroughly kissing her gorgeous mouth, and waited for her to get her bearings.

He might have been doing the same thing because, damn, he was ready to fuck this woman.

"I've waited way too long to do that," he said as she pulled in a ragged breath.

"You can't just walk in here and kiss me," Lily said and pulled out of his arms.

Yes, he could.

He had.

And he was just getting started.

"Just did," Aidan said, squeezing her bottom as he walked past her and sat down on the sofa. Then he patted the cushion beside him. "Come, little peach."

She hesitated, then padded over.

"Stop calling me that," Lily said, and he grinned, grabbing her legs and pulling them across his lap after she sat.

"Why?" he asked, taking in the bandage on her foot. "How does this feel?"

"Sore, but the alcohol has helped," Lily replied softly. "And you need to stop calling me that because it's inappropriate."

Liar.

That wasn't at all why she didn't like him calling her that.

"It reminds you of the time I sucked your juices from my fingers. Doesn't it?" he asked, then grinned as her face bloomed with embarrassment.

Bingo.

"Yes. So please stop," Lily murmured, shaking her head and then attempting to remove her legs from his lap.

"Little peach, there is nothing to be ashamed about. You taste incredible. Don't you want to feel that same feeling again?"

Lily stilled under his touch and those deer eyes found his.

"You've been thinking about it, haven't you, Lily?" Aidan said, his hand drifting north. "Have you touched yourself to ease the ache up here?"

"Stop," she whispered, glancing away.

He stopped.

When her eyes shot back, he didn't smile. He locked, held them firmly, and began to move his hand again. "Say it with meaning and I'll stop."

A little moan escaped her lips.

"No means no in here. No exceptions, but if you lie to me, I will keep going," Aidan said. "Do you understand?"

Lily nodded.

"Do you want me to keep touching you, Lily?" His palm was on her upper thigh now, his thumb inching between the gap. He moved over her panty line, watching her chest rise and fall as her breath became shallow and needy.

"Answer me, peaches."

"Yes. I shouldn't, but I do," Lily answered, and the electric charge between them intensified.

Aidan leaned closer. "Yes, what?"

It was time to push her completely out of her comfort zone and into the pleasure zone.

She tried to move.

Aidan clenched her thigh, keeping Lily on his lap, then he nudged them open a little wider.

"I can't," she gasped, but there was little heat and truth in her words.

"Yes, you can. And you will. To please me," Aidan said, and this time his thumb brushed her clit.

She jumped.

"Say it or I will stop and leave."

Lily gasped.

"Good girl. Say it. Yes…" Aidan prompted.

Her eyes lowered. "Sir. Yes, sir."

"Tell me what you want me to do?"

Lily let out a little groan.

Aidan allowed himself a private smile, then pushed it away and lifted her chin with his free hand.

"Words, Lily."

Hesitating again, those pretty eyes of hers grazed his face, then she swallowed and said, "Yes, sir. I want you to touch me."

Aidan's smile stretched wide. "Good, girl."

To reward her, he pressed his thumb against her clit and rubbed in a circle. Aidan watched her mouth fall open and felt his cock swell as she let out a delicious sound.

"Spread your legs wider for me," he instructed.

As she did, submitting further, Aidan got a sense he could get addicted to this petite creature.

She was tiny compared to him. Slim limbs, long blonde hair in curls, and rich brown eyes. Lily was pretty, but not enough to stand out in a crowd.

Yet those doe eyes had made him erect the moment he'd seen her.

The need to dominate and own this being almost overwhelmed him now.

Aidan leaned over and sucked her bottom lip. With his free hand, he lifted her dress to her waist and tugged her white lace panties aside.

"Look at yourself, Lily. Look how spread open you are for me," he said, sliding a finger between her pink lips. "Wet and hot."

"Ohh, hell,"

The sounds of her sex filled the room as he pressed two fingers inside and began to pump them.

"Aidan," she cried, grabbing a handful of his shirt.

"Watch as I fuck this pussy with my hand and control your pleasure."

"God, oh, God,"

"Shall I stop?" he asked.

"No, no," Lily replied, her eyes widening.

"Pull your breasts out so I can see them," Aidan ordered.

Lily tugged at her straps and nudged her dress down eagerly. Two little tits fell out, sitting propped up on the metal frame of her bra.

Fuck, they were gorgeous. Her nipples were pink and hard, the darker pink areola puckered with arousal.

"Good little girl," With his fingers still plunging inside her, Aidan leaned down and sucked one of them. Then, twirling his tongue around it as he lifted his eyes to hers, he released it and sat up. "Pinch them and roll them between your fingers."

"Yes, sir," she answered unprompted and fucking hell. He nearly whipped out his cock and shoved it inside her right there and then.

Instead, he began to rub her clit again.

"Oh my God, Aidan. Shit."

"Good girl, keep rolling them."

"I'm going to come," Lily cried.

"No, you're not," Aidan said firmly, and Lily's mouth parted, her eyes questioning. "Not until I give you permission."

When her lips pressed together, he slapped her clit. "What do you say?"

"Yes, sir," she groaned out. "But oh, God."

Pulling his fingers out, he nudged her legs open wider and slid his slippery wet digits down close to her ass.

Her hips lifted off him.

"A little virgin ass." Aidan smiled. "I might take that if you keep being a good girl.

"Sir, Aidan, please."

"Begging will get you everything, peaches." He leaned in and sucked her bottom lip, pressing his fingers back inside her pussy.

Then plunged his tongue inside her mouth and fucked her hard, his thumb back on her clit, circling in just the right spot he knew would send her to heaven and back.

Lily's writhing was rubbing against his cock, creating such need he was moments from reaching under her and slipping it out of his shorts.

"That's my girl. Now come for me." Aidan sat and watched her glistening pussy. "Come, while I watch this hot cunt shudder around my fingers."

Immediately Lily's body contracted, her pussy clenching greedily.

"Fuck, oh, holy cow," she cried as he played her like a fiddle. Stroke after stroke, he felt her ride the ways of her orgasm.

"Feel good, peaches? Fucking my fingers. Do you like it?"

"Yes," she gasped, her cheeks in full blossom.

Gently slowing, Aidan removed his fingers and lifted them to his mouth. Eyes locked with Lily's, he licked them one by one. All she did was blink and watch him like he was the orgasm God.

For her, this week, he would be.

"Now let me prove your nickname to you," he said, cupping the back of her head and bringing her to his mouth.

The moan was more than his cock could handle.

As their tongues entwined, Aidan moved Lily's body to the sofa and climbed over her, tugging his shorts down.

His cock snapped out and hung thick between them.

Part of him wanted to play with her more, but with the taste of her on his tongue, the memory of her tight pussy around her fingers, he had run out of patience.

Now he was going to fuck this little blonde submissive and own her as she took every single drop of his come.

CHAPTER SEVEN

Lily felt like she was in a daze as Aidan lay over her. Somehow, her dress had disappeared, and then she felt him rip off her bra and panties.

"I'm not on the pill," Lily shared when she realized he was going to penetrate her.

She felt stupid not thinking about this and hoped to God he didn't ask her to put one on. Call it PTSD, but she had always let the man do it since that fumbling first time.

Flashes of Aidan laughing at her for the next few days, if she couldn't get a condom on him, appeared before her.

Please, God, no.

Instead, Aidan retrieved a rubber from his shorts and held it up. "This is where you say stop if you don't want to continue, peaches."

Then he ripped it open with his teeth.

Did she want this?

Lily knew this would be a one-night thing. She'd seen him with the two Hawaiian women tonight. After conquering her, he'd lose interest and turn his attention to someone else.

She had no expectations of Aidan, and her life goals were well and truly cemented in her mind.

So she nodded.

The way he ordered her around was so sexually thrilling Lily doubted she'd ever meet anyone like him. Ever come as hard as she just had.

For one night? Yes.

"I want to," Lily said, and when she saw his eyes glower, she added, "sir."

"Such a fucking good hot girl," Aidan replied, and then sat back, gripping his cock, staring down at her for a moment.

His eyes roamed over her body.

"Sit up," he finally said, giving her space to move. "I want you to lick it,"

Oh.

Lily didn't have much experience giving blow jobs. Heat spread across her face as she leaned forward, taking possession of his cock.

By not much experience, she really meant zero.

If this was her first time, then she wasn't unhappy with Aidan, because as far as dicks went, he was very nice.

Long, thick and… tidy.

Groomed.

She thought back on every magazine and romance novel she'd read for quick instruction, but the moment Aidan's cock hit her tongue, her mind blanked.

And her body took over.

"Jesus, Lily," Aidan moaned, and she felt a slice of power run through her. She could make him feel the same pleasure she just had.

Quickly she moved to take him in her mouth, but just the tip. She sucked it, glanced up at him, and repeated the action while he continued cursing.

She felt herself become aroused again as his cock filled her mouth and her hand slid over his muscular abdomen.

His body was hard and powerful, sending an urgency through her.

She wanted all of him. She wanted to be dominated by him. To have his enormous, strong body lie over her as his cock thrust into her.

Aidan reeked of control, whereas she'd always been someone who could stand back and let others own the room. In some ways, Lily saw herself as having quiet confidence.

But with Aidan, he seemed to suck her soul into him and take ownership. Except right now. Staring up at him with his cock in her mouth, she felt strong. She felt like she was in control, even though they both knew he was.

A light fired inside her as she continued to pump him with her lips.

"Take me deep inside that hot mouth, peaches," Aidan said, placing his hand on the back of her head. "All the way down,"

His thick smooth flesh hit the back of her throat and she drew in a breath through her nose.

Holy hell, it felt like he was getting bigger.

"Pull back, and that's it. Take me again," Aidan ground out. "Jesus, it's like fucking heaven in there."

Lily wanted to purr. She was so aroused and wet. She began to move faster as her pussy throbbed. Without thinking, she reached down and slid her fingers between her legs.

Aidan suddenly pulled out of her mouth and grabbed her face.

"Remove your fingers." His tone was dark and authoritative. "I'm in charge here, in case that wasn't obvious."

"Sorry, I—" Lily started, her heart pounding.

"Now lick them," he ordered.

She frowned.

It was one thing to take herself from his mouth, but her own hand.

"Lick them or we stop."

No.

"I just—"

Aidan made to move, and her hand went flying into her mouth.

"One more hesitation when I order you, and you are going over my lap and getting spanked," Aidan threatened. "And sweetheart, I will like it."

Spanked?

"Like a child?"

"On your naughty cunt," he said, climbing off the sofa.

"Wait," Lily began, but Aidan was pulling her to her feet. He led her around the sofa and gripped her hips.

"Bend over and let me see this glistening pussy." He placed a hand on her back and pressed her down, so she was face-planting the cushions.

She'd never felt so vulnerable in her life.

Her ass was in the air and her legs spreading wider as Aidan nudged them apart. Then she felt his cock at her core.

A jumble of indecipherable words fell out of her mouth as she pressed back into him.

"You ready to be fucked, peaches?" Aidan said as she heard the rubber snap on. Then the cock of his head entered her, and her body flared alive.

"Yes, sir," she answered, and then the fullness of his member slid inside her and she arched. "Ohmygod."

"Fuck, you're tight. Tight, hot, and wet."

Inch by inch, Aidan pressed in further, his hands squeezing her ass as she pressed her face into the cushions, panting.

Aidan was the biggest man she'd ever had, and her walls were stretching to accommodate him. He seemed to be aware of it with the way he was moving out and then pressing back in.

With his last thrust, he was fully inside her and she arched up with a cry.

"Easy there, peaches. Just let your body adjust."

"Oh God," Lily cried as one of his hands slid over her backside and up her back.

It calmed her.

"Good girl, my cock is surrounded by your delicious pussy,"

Then he moved.

And it hurt.

"Oh shit. I don't think this is going to work," Lily gasped.

"I fit, just relax," Aidan said, pushing her back down and repeated, "Relax."

His hand circled around and flicked her clit, sending pleasure flying through her body. Lily sucked in a breath and all at once he moved and her body accepted Aidan's thickness.

Her ragged breaths filled the air as he groaned and thrust in and out of her.

Then Aidan lifted her, so her back was against his chest, slightly angled over the sofa. The angle change had her crying out.

One hand on her breast, the other on her hip, Aidan's husky voice in her ear. "Feel that, peaches? That's how much I've wanted to fuck this sweet pussy. For fucking months."

Thrust. Thrust.

And oh God, she was burning with desire for this man.

This could be the worst or best decision of her life, but right now Lily didn't care. Wrapped in this gorgeous and successful man's deliciously dominant arms, she wanted him to own her.

Completely.

All night long.

After a time, Aidan pulled out and carried her down to the bedroom. With more care than she expected, he lowered her onto the bed and climbed between her legs.

Then his mouth was on her. Lapping, sucking, and working her until she climaxed all over again.

Sweet beads covered them both as he moved up her body and stole her mouth. It was like their words had disappeared and only guttural moans were left.

Aidan's cock found its way back to her core and slid in effortlessly.

He gripped her neck, surprising her, as he began to pump harder. A mix of panic and arousal flooded her body as those green eyes glowered down at her with absolute power.

In this moment, Aidan Dufort owned her.

And Lily wanted to be owned by him.

She felt his cock swell and watched his eyes begin to roll back as she arched into him, taking him deeper, feeling his body press into her clit.

The sensation as arousing and erotic as the gorgeous man above her took everything.

Lily could only hope that when the time came to leave the island, she could one day forget him.

She knew there would never be another moment like this. They weren't destined for each other. He wasn't her forever. But she would take a piece of him with her.

And in a few days return to her life and responsibilities.

CHAPTER EIGHT

"Fuck, my head hurts," Blake complained as Aidan reached into the cup to retrieve his golf ball.

"My cock hurts," Jacob groaned.

"Amateurs." Aidan smirked as his two cousins followed him to the golf cart.

Just as they climbed on board, another cart headed their way. When he saw who the passenger was, Aidan suppressed a groan.

"It's Uncle Andrew." Blake pointed out the obvious as his father, driven by a Turtle Bay Resort staff member, approached them.

God, he was in a bad mood.

Like Blake, Aidan had a hangover.

Or was it just a lack of sleep?

He'd left Lily asleep, reluctantly, after she'd collapsed on his chest.

Aidan had wanted to go another round, but she'd already succumbed to five orgasms, and he could see she was struggling when he pressed his cock inside her pretty little mouth for the final time and her eyes began to flicker.

So, he'd laid them both down and rested for a moment. The next minute, he heard her breathing deepen.

Lily was out like a light.

But she'd exceeded his expectations.

Aidan had known she would submit to him beautifully and relish the pleasure it would give her.

She'd climaxed quickly each time. He was, after all, a skilled and well-practiced lover.

What he wasn't expecting was the way he'd reacted to her sexy moans and the way the timbre of her *"yes, sir,"* made him so fucking hard.

It was like he couldn't get enough of his sweet peach.

At one point, he saw a little challenge in her eyes when his cock was down her throat. She liked the way she pleased him and thought the power had shifted.

It hadn't.

But he liked that she was playing with him.

Except she needed to understand that any dominance she displayed would encourage him to break her.

To own all of her.

That was the source of his surprise. Once he left a woman, he was fulfilled, and sure he might want them again, and did. But he was satisfied.

He wasn't satisfied with what he'd done with Lily.

Sexually? Fuck yes.

Closing the door behind him when he left had felt wrong. He wanted to wake and sink his cock inside her.

He wanted to shower and have her kneel before him and pleasure him.

He wanted to watch her eat breakfast naked while his fingers slid inside her.

An overpowering need to completely own this woman was making it hard for him to concentrate.

He'd found himself glaring at her at breakfast and knew it had made her uncomfortable.

Then Logan had glared at him, and Aidan had nearly told him to fuck off.

What this meant was he would just have to fuck her every chance they got before they both flew home to their different states.

By then, she would be out of his system.

And his cock would be falling off.

"Aloha," Andrew greeted them as the cart stopped a few feet away.

"Dad," Aidan replied, leaning his forearm on the steering wheel. "You're late."

"Do you want to tee in?" Jacob asked. "We're just playing for fun."

Aidan nearly snorted.

His father didn't do anything for fun. It was competition from morning till night with this man. But then again, he'd taught them all to strive for excellence, and that trait was serving him, Logan, and Amelia well in their lives.

"No." Andrew shook his head. "I'm just saying hello. I'll hang around for a while, then go find the groom."

Aidan nodded, mumbling *lucky Logan*" as he pressed his foot on the accelerator.

As they bounced along the green, he took a sip of his *barely iced* coffee and wished, not for the first time in the last ten minutes, that the drinks cart would hurry up and come around again.

Or maybe he just needed a whisky.

He'd need it to deal with his father.

It wasn't that they had a terrible relationship. He'd been a fair father. Stern and strict, but not abusive.

Less so on Amelia, but Aidan figured he had his reasons.

It was Andrew's recent behavior that was driving Aidan a little nuts.

Like all the Dufort men, Aidan was very successful. Even Jacob and Blake were extremely wealthy at the age of twenty-two and twenty-three.

While he respected his cousins and siblings for their achievements, Aidan had done something very few people had. He'd invented a piece of technology that was so impactful it touched nearly every human on earth.

He'd invented a microchip delivery housing.

Boring, yes.

Yet this small but mighty creation was now connected to every microchip in just about every single piece of technology used today.

In other words, a shit ton. Just ask his accountant.

Aidan was wealthier than Daniel, Hunter, and Fletcher combined. He just kept that little bit of information to himself.

Although he had a feeling, many of them were well aware. *Forbes* tossed all their names about in random order, guessing most of the time.

Unlike Dufort Liquor—Logan's business—and Dufort Hotels, Aidan's income was not public knowledge.

And it was certainly far greater than his father's.

Not that this was a *my-bank-account-is-bigger-than-yours* game, but the fact that he was now riding his ass about protecting his wealth was ludicrous.

It had started several months ago.

"When you choose a wife, Aidan, make sure she's of good breeding."

He'd nearly choked on his drink.

"Jesus, Dad. Did I just get transported to Downton Abbey?"

That had got him a dark glare.

"I'm not joking around. Who you marry is extremely important. A family like ours—now with your success—makes us one of the wealthiest in the United States," Andrew had said.

At the time, it hadn't surpassed him that his father had included his cousins in that total figure.

Aidan knew all his numbers.

"Relax. That's what prenups are for." He'd taken a casual sip of his Macallan.

"Aidan. I will not have some floozy joining this family. You'll marry someone with a good standing in the community. Someone smart, educated, and committed to the Dufort name," Andrew had said firmly.

Aidan had lowered his brows, squinting at the man, then shaken his head. "Thanks for the relationship advice, Dad, but I'll marry someone I love. Someone I desire."

Andrew had leaned forward on his elbows. "Listen to me, Aidan. This family is broken enough. I will not have a cast of former daughters-in-law taking chunks of our fortune and dancing off into the sunset a few years after you and your brothers have had a taste of their pussy."

Gross.

Was this the sex talk he'd been waiting for all his life? Because, if so, it had gone down a completely different road than he'd been expecting.

"You'll choose someone who understands what it means to join this family. And our way of life."

Rich folk, in other words.

Aidan had let his father rant. When he got in a stubborn mood, there was no stopping him.

It was clearly a passing phase, but he'd been wrong.

The thing was that his father had no authority or influence over his life decisions, but that didn't mean it wasn't irritating as fuck.

Let's face it, Miss Sweet Home Alabama was not the type of girl Aidan was interested in.

Submissive? Yes.

But he liked them sweet in the kitchen and dirty in the sheets.

The women his father was referring to were after his bank account and surname. That wasn't to say he thought all rich women, or even trust fund babies, were unattractive. He'd fucked a good number of them.

But marry one of them?

Not unless they got on their knees and purred out *sir*.

He wondered if Logan had been given the tenth degree when he announced his engagement to Emma. Aidan wasn't privy to any private conversations between his brother and their parents.

He was close to Logan, but since falling for Emma, his brother had changed. Not in a bad way. Logan was simply protective of his soon-to-be wife, and Aidan respected that.

A few weeks after their engagement party, at a family dinner, Andrew had invited him into the library for a chat.

They had some investments together, so it hadn't occurred to him this might be about his love life. Especially with Emma now in the family. Aidan had truly thought the insane phase was over.

Wrong.

"Your mother wants you to take Diane Winslow on a date," Andrew announced, pouring two fingers of Macallan into a crystal glass.

Aidan had laughed. "I'm sorry, what?"

His father had handed him a glass with a pointed look. "You heard. This Thursday there's a fundraiser. Give her a call and tell her you will pick her up."

Aidan had taken a long draw on the expensive whisky and then placed it on the polished oak table between the two leather chairs they were sitting on.

He kicked out his legs and crossed his ankles.

"I'm not going to do that for two reasons. One, Diane will get the wrong message and that's not fair to her. Two, I'm going to be in Seattle for a meeting that evening."

And three he didn't need anyone arranging dates for him. Especially not with society women who wore plaid and had no career prospects other than being his wife.

"Aidan—"

He stood. "If you have any business to discuss, tell me, otherwise I am leaving."

Andrew had scowled at him and tossed back his whisky. "I saw you with that girl at Logan and Emma's engagement party."

"I wasn't with any girl," he'd snapped, becoming angry that his father was about to comment on Lily.

"I saw the look in your eyes. I was a young man once. I know what it means," his father said.

Aidan laughed. "I want to fuck her. So what? That's none of your business."

"Fuck her if you want, privately, but the girl is going to be in Hawaii at Logan's wedding. She no doubt has aspirations to the Dufort name. I want you to start dating appropriate women and choose someone to settle down with. But do not lead her on. And do not fucking marry her."

Aidan shook his head.

Jesus Christ. He'd had his hand inside her panties and his father thought they were going to plan a life together.

Was this nineteen fucking sixty-five?

"I'm not even thirty yet, Dad. Calm the fuck down."

"And a Dufort. A multi-billionaire who will end up a dirty wealthy playboy if you don't start planning ahead. Don't step into your thirties unmarried. Before you know it, you'll be forty and the options will be limited. Honestly, Aidan, it's not a good look."

He scrunched his nose. "You need to drop this, Dad. All of my money and assets are in a trust. None of it is at risk. Who I fuck—which I need no permission to do, by the way—is not anyone's business."

When Andrew went to speak, he held up a hand.

"If I bring a hooker home, then by all means, slap me around the chops, but I've never brought anyone home to meet my family," Aidan continued, crossing his arms. "Marriage is the furthest thing from my mind right now, and I'm not going to start looking for a bride because you are riding my ass."

His father had leaned forward. "You don't have the life experience yet to understand how these things can impact your life. Look at Logan. Zoe almost cost him his company. Twice."

Yeah, well, Logan had been pussy whipped by that bitch. He wasn't Logan.

Although right now, Aidan wasn't so sure after a night with Lily. Fortunately, he was the one doing the whipping.

Figuratively, as he hadn't brought any with him.

They climbed off the cart and lined up their shots.

Blake went first.

"Where's Mom?" Aidan asked.

"Christine stayed behind at the hotel with Olivia."

Aidan nodded.

At breakfast, Olivia had announced she wouldn't join the girls for SUP yoga at Lanikai Beach after a long night with the baby.

Fletcher had rubbed his eyes while Olivia reminded him that he'd slept four hours and she'd had only thirty minutes.

"I think she's ready for some grandbabies," Andrew added.

Blake let out a snort beside him.

"I'm sure Emma will be popping them out soon," Aidan said, undoing his Velcro golf gloves and doing them back up.

Unnecessarily.

"Are you dating anyone, Blake?" Andrew asked.

Aidan burst into laughter.

"Ah. Am I dating?" Blake asked, twisting his Nike cap awkwardly.

"It's a simple question," Andrew replied, crossing his arms.

"Dad, he's twenty-three," Aidan replied as Blake shot him a look that screamed *help.*

Jacob took his shot, and they were all momentarily distracted.

"And it's a hole in…not one. Goddamn it," Jacob cried.

When they turned back, his father was still staring at them.

"Right. Dating. Who am I dating?" Blake said, still fiddling with his cap.

"The entire women's baseball team, the last time I counted," Jacob said, nudging him with his club. Then he slid it into the bag and did the inverted commas thing with his fingers and said, "*dating.*"

Aidan rubbed his hand over his mouth, loving that the attention was off him for a minute.

"Jesus, are all the men in this family playboys?" Andrew shook his head.

Jacob grinned.

"Lighten up, Dad. The boys are young. Hell, I'm still young," Aidan said.

"Debatable," Blake coughed.

Cue the play fighting as he kicked out his leg and caught him around the thighs.

Blake's knees weakened, and he stumbled. "Hey!"

"Christ. I'm off to find your brother," Andrew said as Blake hooked his arm around Aidan's neck. "Hopefully, they're playing a better game of golf than you fools."

They all laughed.

"Oh, and Aidan, remember what I said back in Philadelphia."

About Lily and keeping away from her.

Oops too late.

Aidan deadpanned his father while he returned his stare. Then he walked over to his cart and zoomed off across the green.

"What's his deal?" Jacob asked.

"It's probably just wedding fever," Blake said. "Mom gets like this whenever someone gets married or has a baby. Starts interrogating us about our love lives."

"It better be a phase. He's been riding my ass for months," Aidan said. "I have zero interest in walking down any aisle. Someone even does my grocery shopping."

Jacob laughed. "Go take your shot, dork."

Blake slapped his hand under his brother's water bottle, causing it to spurt everywhere.

"Hey," Jacob cried, wiping his face.

This was more like it, Aidan thought, as a stupid grin spread across his face. Life was serious enough. There had to be play and fun, or what was the point?

His mind wandered, and he hoped Lily was enjoying her day out. He'd worked her body hard last night and, along with her hangover, he knew the SUP yoga would be a struggle.

Aidan had left her a note with his mobile number and instructions to sext him.

She wouldn't, but he liked knowing it would have rattled her.

If she thought he was going to leave her alone now, she was mistaken. That was just the first course.

CHAPTER NINE

"I'm pretty sure I'm going to put my back out doing this," Harper said, running her hand over her chin and staring at their instructor. "I'm an author. The only core strength I have are my steamy sex scenes."

Emma burst out laughing. "Me too, girlfriend. Me too."

"Why didn't Amelia join us?" Lily dropped her sundress onto her beach bag and felt like a glow stick standing in her bright pink bikini. She hadn't seen the sun in months, and it showed.

Beep, beep.

Lily frowned as she saw Matt's name show up on the phone. She'd expected he would leave her alone while on holiday, but clearly, she was wrong.

Lily quickly answered his question, knowing he could have gotten the answer about the file location from the receptionist, and dropped her phone into her bag. Then she followed the girls down to the water's edge.

"Amelia's meeting a friend who has flown in. She was a little vague. I think it's a guy. For God's sakes, don't mention it around her brothers," Emma said.

Lily let out a little laugh. "They are rather protective."

"It's a Dufort trait," Harper said.

"Everyone gets into everyone's business in this family." Kristen nudged Harper. "Including this one."

Harper shrugged. "It's because I care."

Emma burst out laughing, then she pointed at Lily. "Hey, you need lotion. No strap marks on Monday."

She was referring to the wedding.

"Oh, let me take off the straps," Lily said, reaching to tug them off.

Emma helped, and they handed them to the SUP assistant, who ran up the beach and threw them on their bags and towels.

None of them were worried about security, as Harper's personal security guy was with them. Lily couldn't imagine living like that, but then again, she didn't have to worry about anyone trying to kidnap her or rip an enormous diamond ring off her hand.

Why they didn't leave them at home? She had no idea. Unless their husbands wanted them to wear them.

Yeah, that was probably it.

She could see Aidan being like that with his wife one day. He was pretty bossy.

Even if it was sexy.

She tugged up her bikini even though it was snug and took another look at the board.

Emma bumped her hips. "Ready? I've been wanting to try this for ages."

Lily didn't feel quite the same. In fact, she would've happily stayed in bed for a few more hours.

And drink another four cups of coffee at least.

She was a little hungover, very jetlagged, and Aidan had fucked her to within an inch of her life. She didn't remember falling asleep or him leaving.

Lily woke to a note beside the bed with his number and a request for sexy images. Which he would be waiting forever for.

There was no way she was doing that.

He got a good enough look last night. And now she was expecting him to find someone else to play with.

Lily didn't know how she felt about it. Mostly tired. She was just focused on getting through the day and falling into bed after dinner.

"I'm half excited," she answered. "With my luck, I'll fall into the water, so I'd like to skip that part."

The SUP instructor stepped in front of them. He was a good-looking Hawaiian man around their age.

"Okay, ladies. Do you remember what I taught you? Legs hip-width apart, lean forward, and keep your eyes up."

Kristen and Harper climbed on the first one, and after a bunch of giggles and messing about, they finally stood up and got moving.

Lily was a little worried about her legs holding up. She had aches in places she didn't know she *could* ache after her night with Aidan.

She played with her butterfly necklace and chewed her bottom lip as she recalled the things he made her do.

Being on her knees.

Calling him sir.

His hand around her throat.

Aidan stroking his cock and spilling onto her outstretched tongue.

She loved every second of it and knew she'd remember it forever.

"Let's go," Emma said, doing a little dance in the sand.

The two of them waded into the water to the instructor. He handed them a paddle each and then indicated to Lily to go first.

"Keep your legs shoulder-width apart and you won't fall."

"If I fall, you better, come save me." Lily shot him a grin.

He pointed to Harper and Kristen, who were fooling around. "They're going about one mile per hour. It's safe."

Emma giggled and took hold of the board. "Get on; I've got it."

Lily lifted her leg and kneeled on the board, placing her paddle in front of her. Then brought her other leg up and stood.

Woohoo.

"Emma, you're up next," their instructor called and when Lily glanced around her, she saw Emma looking at her weirdly.

Her smile fell.

"What—" Before she had a chance to ask what was wrong, Emma moved behind her and climbed on.

A few minutes later, they were paddling along a little wobbly but doing their thing.

"Wow. Look at us," Emma said. "I'm getting married and SUPing."

"I think I'm going to pass out," Lily said. "I need either a Mai Tai or a burger. I don't care in what order."

"Someone drank too much," Emma teased. "And it was me."

Lily laughed. "You drank less than me, I'm sure of it."

Her friend went quiet.

Lily could tell something was wrong but had no idea what brought it on so suddenly. Was she getting cold feet?

No way.

"Hey, Lil? Is everything okay with you?" Emma finally asked her, and when she tried to turn, the board wobbled. "Words. Use your words. Don't look at me."

They both laughed.

When the board was steadied, Lily replied, "I'm fine. I mean, I'm dehydrated and need some salty carbohydrates urgently, but I'm in Hawaii with my best friend for her wedding. Why wouldn't I be fine?"

Emma was quiet.

"And did I mention the incredible suite and flying first class?"

"Okay. Cool."

No, she wasn't. Lily went back over their morning in her mind and tried to work out what could have given Emma the impression she was unhappy.

"I'm just hungover and jetlag. Honest," she repeated and turned her head.

Wobble.

"Shit."

"I'm just worried. Please don't hate me for bringing this up but I'm your best friend so it's my job."

Lily felt her body stiffen.

Had she seen Aidan leave her room?

Or heard them? Oh God, she had been loud.

"I saw the marks on the inside of your thighs and so... I dunno. Are you self-harming?"

What?

"You know you can talk to me. Or talk to someone. Just because I'm living in Philly now, I'm still here for you," Emma said, but Lily hardly heard the rest of it because she was still stuck on the *marks on the inside of your thighs.*

Bruises.

From sex.

Who the hell was she right now?

Her silence triggered Emma further.

"Fuck it. Just move to Philly. I'll talk to Logan. We'll find you a job. Move in with us."

"Em—"

"I know, I know. Your dad. But we have a jet. You can be there back in Chicago in just a few hours if something happens."

"I can't—"

"It's your boss, isn't it? Matt. Did he fucking touch you? If he did, we can file a report and make sure he never touches anyone again."

Oh, my God.

How did Lily tell her the marks between her legs were made by her future brother-in-law?

She didn't.

Worse, they were probably still forming and going to get even more obvious over the next few hours.

Did she have them on her neck? Her breasts? Her arms?

Oh, God. She was going to look like she'd been beaten up, and how on earth did she explain it had brought her pleasure?

Lily did bruise easily, but it had never occurred to her it would be an issue.

Shit.

She couldn't have sex bruises in Emma's wedding photos. She needed Arnica cream and fast.

But where?

She didn't know the shops in Hawaii.

Worse, she couldn't even lower her eyes to see how bad it was down there, or they'd fall off this damn board.

"Did he rape you?" Emma asked, bringing Lily's attention back to her friend.

Who?

Oh, Matt?

"Stop. No one raped me. I don't even know what you're talking about."

"Are you sure?" Emma's tone was tentative, and she felt terrible for lying, but not everything needed to be shared with her friends. Some things were private between two people.

Even if those two people were never doing those things ever again.

"I'm not self-harming and no one has sexually abused me," Lily said. "Also, I'm not moving to Philly. Dad needs me and he doesn't have much longer."

"So, where are the bruises from?"

"I fell over at the airport. Landed on my suitcase. You know how easily I bruise, so it was likely that."

Then she prayed that there were no bruises anywhere else on her body.

AN HOUR AND a half later, they all made their way back up the beach and grabbed their beach towels.

Kristen flopped onto the sand and fell back. "I'm dead."

Lily felt her legs shaking. She was so tired. But quickly wrapped the towel around herself to hide the bruising.

"I can't believe how much of a workout that was. It looks like the laziest sport on the planet, but my God," Harper said, dropping down beside Kristen.

"My legs are killing me." Emma laughed, drying off. "Not the smartest move before walking down the aisle. Hopefully, I won't stumble."

"Two words," Kristen said. "Hot tub. Spa bath. Whatever you call it here in the US of A."

"Hot tub," Lily and Emma both replied and laughed.

Kristen and Harper were both kiwis, and she'd already heard them use different names for things that sounded foreign or made no sense.

"Good idea," Emma said, and as the three girls chatted, Lily reached down into her beach bag and grabbed her phone. She found the name she wanted, then typed out a text.

I'm covered in bruises. Emma noticed and thinks I've been sexually abused. *frown emoji* Can you get some Arnica cream? I can't have them walking down the aisle.

How short is this bridesmaid's dress?

Lily actually frowned.

Don't be silly. You were rough in other places.

I wasn't rough. I was in control. Did I bruise your neck?

Lily chewed her lip. She wasn't sure.

Maybe. I'm on the beach.

Take a photo and send it to me.

I'm not sexting you.

Peaches, I'm not asking you to spread your legs and play with your clit. I'm asking for a photo of your neck.

Jesus.

Her core clenched at his dirty mouth. Or rather fingers. She'd had a good dose of both already.

Stop blushing. You liked it.

Ugh.

She angled the camera and took a photo. Emma saw her and, thinking she was taking selfies, jumped in.

Next, Harper and Kristen joined in and then Harper's security guy, David, was given her camera and was instructed to take a group shot.

"Ah, Lily. Someone is messaging you." He smirked.

She grabbed the phone.

Shit.

Her notifications were set to permanent banner, so it was sitting right at the top of her screen for David to see.

Oh, dear God.

If you're playing with that pussy, you're in trouble. Send me the photos.

Heat filled her face, and she glanced up at him. Fortunately, the girls had gone back to their beach bags and were pulling on their clothes.

David lifted his hand and did the international lips-sealed action.

She gave him an uncomfortable smile, then fired off a few photos to Aidan.

Can you get the Arnica please?

I can't see any bruises on your neck. I'll get the cream, but only if I can rub it on you.

No way. What they did was a one-night thing, and she needed sleep. A lot of sleep to make up for the measly hour or two she had got.

When she didn't respond, Aidan texted again.

The correct response is yes, sir.

Arousal plowed through her body, her pussy clenching at his instruction. When she just stood there biting her lip, the phone rang.

Aidan.

Oh, my God.

Emma glanced up at her.

Shit.

She took a few steps away.

"Hello," she answered casually, as if it was no one special.

"Peaches, when I give you an order, you need to do as you are told," his deep sexy voice said, and holy hell, it was like he had a hotline to her hormones.

"Aidan, I can't do this." Lily kicked at the sand.

"Don't tell me your pussy isn't wet right now. Wanting to be owned by me."

She let out a quiet moan.

"Maybe you should slide your fingers into your bikini and swirl it around your sensitive nub?"

"Stop," she breathed.

"Are your pretty nipples hard? Pressing against your bikini,"

Dammit, they were.

"Stop," she repeated, glancing behind her.

"Stop, *please, sir,*" Aidan said.

Ugh.

"Stop, please, sir," Lily grit out. "I mean it. It was one night. Please, just get the cream and I'll pay you back."

"Is that what you think? That I was going to fuck you once and not want seconds? Wrong, Lily. I am thirsty for you. My cock is throbbing to get back inside you."

Oh, Jesus.

"I'll get the Arnica—and do not offend me by offering me your money—then I'll rub it on while my tongue laps up the juice from your sweet pussy. Or no deal."

Lily clenched her thighs.

How was he able to do this to her? Have so much control over a phone call.

"See you soon, Lily." Aidan hung up with a click and she let out a sigh.

When she returned to the group, Emma asked, "Everything okay?"

"Yes, just Mom checking I'd arrived safely."

Another lie.

CHAPTER TEN

Knowing he'd marked Lily's pretty skin was making Aidan happier than he cared to admit. Right now, that sexy little blonde was on a Hawaiian beach across the island with bruises between her legs.

His bruises.

Bruises he'd made while fucking the life out of her.

It was nearly as rewarding as the fact she'd reached out to him to get the Arnica. Whether Lily realized it or not, she had come to him for her aftercare.

When they'd caught their breath in between orgasms, Aidan had grabbed a cloth from the bathroom and cleaned her a few times. If he hadn't slipped out before morning, he would've made sure she was well-hydrated and fed too.

This wasn't a proper D/s relationship, and aside from letting her know she could say no at any point, Aidan hadn't framed it as one.

Still, she'd come to him, and he liked it.

When he'd gotten off the phone, he'd ordered the product and had it sent to his penthouse. Then smiled at the opportunity to care for her. Aidan was ready for take two, but first he would ascertain how bad Lily's bruising was and how sore she was.

But one thing was certain: tonight he'd be back inside her again.

One night? No.

Lily, I am having you all week. Then I will set you free.

Despite his father's comments.

WHEN THEY RETURNED to the hotel later that afternoon, Hunter and Addison had arrived. Aidan headed to Daniel's penthouse to say hello.

"Hey, man," Aidan said, shaking his cousin's hand.

"Saw you had a fun night last night?" Hunter smirked.

What?

Hunter sniggered.

"Don't be cruel, Hunt. You, Blake, and Jacob were tagged on Instagram by some local girls," Addison said, leaning across the back of the sofa and twisting her head to smile at him.

Oh.

Jesus, he wasn't sure what he'd expected them to say, but it had something to do with Lily, and all he felt was relief that it wasn't.

So, the news anchor girls had gone social with their night with the Dufort boys. Damn them.

"Harmless fun," Aidan said, crossing his arms. "Has it gone viral?"

"Yes." Daniel shot him a look. "Fortunately, without my photo."

"I'm on maternity leave," Olivia said, pointing to the baby. Liv was the Dufort PR manager who dealt with all the media. "But I checked, and it was mainly Blake and Jacob."

"Present," Blake said as he walked in. "What have I done?"

"Did you take those two girls home last night?" Logan asked as Emma sat down in his lap.

Jacob walked up behind him and the smirk on his face said yes. Then the two of them turned to stare at one another and their smirks turned to grins.

"That's a yes," Aidan laughed.

His mom and dad arrived and wandered across the room, sitting down on one of the sofas.

"For, you know, a nightcap," Jacob said, eyeing his aunt and uncle.

"I have two boys, Jacob. Don't bother." His mother laughed.

"Hey, I never brought a girl home," Aidan said, and it was true. He'd taken them to hotels instead.

"Make sure you don't this weekend, either," Andrew said. "This is your brother's wedding. Let's respect that."

Aidan raised his brows. "Ex-fucking-scuse me."

"Aides," Logan growled.

"When have I ever created a sex scandal?" he snapped. "I'm not Tom Brady, sure, but every single Dufort in this room hits the columns at least once a month, with some journo second guessing our romantic lives."

"Not this weekend," Andrew said firmly.

Jesus Christ.

"I left with Logan and Emma. Ask them."

"He did," Emma said.

"I can confirm. The media ch—girls came home with us," Blake said.

Aidan did a one-eighty to triple-check if Lily was in the room.

No.

Thank fuck.

He didn't want her hearing this family bullshit. And it was bullshit.

"I don't know what's gotten into you recently, but you need to get off my ass," Aidan said.

"Former Manhattan Playboy here." Fletcher cleared his throat and raised his arm. "Most of what they say is rubbish and people know that."

"At least fifty percent." Daniel shrugged.

"Not helpful." Fletcher frowned.

Andrew grunted as Amelia walked into the room. "Hey, ho…oh. What did I miss?"

She read the room fast.

Aidan spun back to his father and put his hands on his hips. Then nudged his head back at his sister. "You going to ride her ass, too?"

"What did you do?" Amelia asked.

"Language, Aidan," his mom said.

"Okay, you know what, I'm going to play in another sandpit." Aidan stood. "Oh, and by the way, my newest invention just won an award. Found out this morning. Can I go stay at a friend's place overnight so I can celebrate?"

Harper snorted.

But if his father was going to treat him like a kid, then he'd rub it right in his face.

"Enough." Andrew glared back at him.

"Guys, please stop fighting," Logan said. "As you pointed out, Dad, this is my wedding week. We are in beautiful Hawaii, so let's just drop the drama."

"Leave your father, he's just—"

"I can speak for myself, Christine," Andrew snapped.

"Enough," Logan growled.

"Agreed." Aidan backed him.

None of them let his father get away with speaking to their mother poorly.

"Mom, how about you show me your wedding outfit?" Amelia said, as if on cue. The three of them had this process well practiced.

Logan shot him a look as Christine patted her husband's leg, gave him a small smile, then stood and walked over to Amelia. "Come on then, darling. I got the dress I sent the photo of."

"I'm coming," Harper said.

"Me, too," Kristen said.

"Same," Addison said.

"Better follow the girl gang." Olivia smirked and handed Fletcher the baby.

Baxter let out a little gurgle.

Emma stayed put with Logan, and Aidan loved her for it. But right now, he only had one girl on his mind, and he wanted to get away from his father.

Aidan suspected Lily had gone back to her room and was waiting for him.

"See you all tonight. I've got a few things to take care of," he said and headed to the door.

When it closed behind him, he shook his head. There was something going on with his father, and he had no idea what.

He wasn't going to sit back and let him throw out bullshit comments like that, whether they were in private or company. Andrew should know by now Aidan wouldn't put up with it.

Logan was a powerful businessman, but Aidan had always been the one to speak his mind. Which meant he and his father had clashed over the years on different topics.

But he'd never tried to dictate his life like this.

Aidan would get to the bottom of it, but right now, he had a date between Lily's legs.

And her pretty blushing smile.

When she opened the door to her penthouse, that was not what greeted him.

CHAPTER ELEVEN

Lily leaped up when she heard the knock. She pulled the door open and when she saw it was Aidan, she almost relaxed.

Almost.

"H—"

"Thank, God," she said, grabbing his T-shirt and pulling him inside the room. When she released it and was about to ask if he had the Arnica cream, something caught her eye. "Is that a Prada T-shirt?"

She knew the answer as the logo was clear as day on the hem.

Aidan was a tall man, so he stood towering over her, looking like he was about to kiss her, when he frowned and glanced down at his top.

"Yes. Why? What's wrong with it?"

Nothing was wrong with it.

The gray cotton knit top hugged his muscular frame like a glove. It should be illegal. Its short sleeves were slightly bunched, and Lily was sure more than one girl on the island would have enjoyed the sight today.

But it wasn't that.

She shouldn't have said anything. It just seemed like an insane amount of money to spend on a T-shirt. She could understand buying a special dress from a luxury designer or even a handbag if they could afford it, but a T-shirt?

That's like buying designer socks.

Stupid.

Maybe she was just too practical.

Or poor.

"Nothing. Doesn't matter," Lily said and began to walk off.

Aidan caught her arm and tugged her back.

Right up against his chest.

His Prada-clad chest.

"Explain." His voice was low.

"Have you got the Arnica?" Lily asked, hoping to distract him.

"You don't like my top?"

"I have marks on my inner thighs," she said, hoping to distract him.

"You play a mean game," he growled playfully. Her cheeks flushed as Aidan dropped his mouth to hers, their lips touching. "Show me."

When he let her go, she took a step back and lifted the white sheer sundress she was wearing over her pink bikini.

"Okay, sunshine, let's do this properly." Aidan scooped her up and Lily let out a squeal.

"I can walk."

"And I can carry you. You'll remember I had you wrapped around my body up against the wall last night."

Lily pressed her face into his chest and mumbled, "Yes, you are very strong."

She did remember. She remembered very clearly and had been thinking about it several times today.

His strength was incredible.

Lily figured he worked out a lot. He had to. But then again, all the Dufort men were large and strong men.

Aidan placed her on the edge of the bed and crouched down in front of her.

Then pushed her legs open.

She stifled a moan, focusing on what he was seeing. It was the first thing she'd done when she got back to her room.

On her thighs were little dark bruises the size of his fingers.

"Hmm. Let's see. Shall we play doctor-patient?" Aidan smirked.

"Let's not. Hand me the cream, please," Lily said, holding out her hand.

Aidan slapped it away. "They are not too bad. Let me see what I can do."

Lily bent over. "Not bad? There are fingerprints between my legs, Aidan."

He smiled.

Smiled!

"*My* fingerprints, peaches," Aidan said and pulled the Arnica out of his short pockets. She tried to grab it and he pulled back. "Uh, uh. My bruises. My job."

Lily let out a sigh and let him continue. She knew there would be no arguing with him. Aidan was a dominant personality and seemed to always get his way with her.

"Emma was the one who spotted them," she said as he squirted the herbal cream onto his palm and began to administer it across her thigh. Lily noticed the gentle care he was taking.

She also noticed how nice it felt and the warm feeling growing at her core.

Dammit.

"What did you say when she asked?" Aidan asked, his attention between her legs.

"That I fell over at the airport."

His eyes lifted. "Did you?"

"No."

"Lily Peterson, you liar," he teased.

"I had to. What was I going to say, Aidan? That you forced my thighs open and were licking my va-jay-jay all night?" she snapped.

Then she pressed her lips together as the warm feeling roared to a furious fire when he brushed his hand over her bikini.

Her eyes shot to his and the same heat reflected back at her.

"Choose your words carefully, baby. I am trying hard to control myself and care for you right now."

Her eyes moved to his shorts, and she saw the curve of his erection.

Lily drew in a jagged breath.

The next minute, his fingers were rubbing cream where she knew there were no bruises, his attention on her face.

"I think that's all," she whispered.

"I missed a bit." Aidan's fingers brushed over the material covering her core once more and she was done for.

A groan slipped out.

"Turn over. I need to check the back," Aidan rasped.

Leaving her little choice, he took her by the hips and spun her over. She rested her elbows on the mattress and felt extremely open and vulnerable.

"Let me see." Aidan ran his hand over her butt cheeks, his fingers following the seam of her bikini bottoms. "No good. I need to remove these."

"Aidan," she gasped as he pulled her bottoms down.

"Say no if you mean it. Right now," he ordered her.

Lily stayed silent.

Her body was now throbbing with arousal. Her nipples were hard against her bikini, aching as she shivered with need. The warm tropical air teased her exposed wet flesh and then Aidan blew on her.

"Oh fuck," she cried.

"I'll take that as a yes. Remember, no means no, baby. Say it and I'll stop." Aidan's hand ran up the inside of her thigh.

Touch me, dammit.

His mouth kissed her ass, her legs, and everywhere but the place she needed it the most.

Then, finally, he touched her.

His mouth following.

"Fuck!" she cried again.

Aidan pressed his fingers inside her, his other hand grabbing a handful of her ass, and a flood of pleasure burst through her body.

All she wanted at that point was his cock.

Now.

Lily pressed back into his hand.

"Eager, peaches. Be patient," Aidan instructed in a growl.

"No. I need… it. You," she moaned.

"You know the words."

"Sir. Please. I need it," Lily begged as her core throbbed.

"It? I think you can use a better word than that."

Aidan loved to push her outside her comfort zone. It was only that her body was now trembling with need, despite all the orgasms she'd had last night, that she forced the dirty words out.

"I need your cock. Inside me. Now. Please. Sir," she purred in what she hoped was a sexy voice.

It worked.

"Fuck me," Aidan cried, and the next minute she heard him move his shorts and felt his fat tip at her entrance. "You want me inside you, Lily? You ready for more of my cock?"

When she nodded, clenching the bed linen, he gripped her ass and pressed inside her.

"More." Lily pressed back into him, pleading, "I want more."

"You want to be fucked, peaches? You want me to fuck you with my thick cock hard?" Aidan pressed nearly to the hilt.

"Yes,"

Then he slammed into her. Pulling back and slamming again. Thrust after thrust.

"Like this, Lily. Fucking all of you,"

Holy shit.

"Yes, sir."

His hips pounded at her over and over.

"Fucking your sweet pussy and owning this body. You want me to mark every inch of you?"

Yes. She wanted him to own her. Savagely. And never stop.

His hand reached out and gripped the back of her head. "Submit to me, Lily. Give me everything while I come inside your cunt."

Jesus.

Aidan swelled inside her, his hips slamming harder as his grunts increased. She clenched her muscles around him as sweat dripped down her face and chest.

Every part of her body was aroused and exploding as the heat of his orgasm filled her.

Oh, shit.

Suddenly, he pulled out and flipped her over.

Aidan tugged her bikini top down, exposing her, and stroked his cock, spilling the rest of his come over her breasts.

His passion-filled eyes found hers as his strokes slowed. "I'll take care of this,"

He didn't need to explain. They both knew he'd come inside her without a condom.

Lily wasn't on birth control.

"But first you need to come." Aidan released his cock and shifted her up onto the bed, then settled between her legs.

His mouth clamped onto her clit and in what had to be no less than thirty seconds, ecstasy flooded her body.

AIDAN FLOPPED ONTO the bed beside her, his palm dropping to his six-pack, which she was a huge fan of.

"Jesus," he groaned.

Both of them were drenched with the heat of their sex and the tropical air. Despite the air conditioning, it was still damn hot.

When she didn't say anything, Aidan turned his head and asked her if she was okay.

"Yup," Lily said. She was, but every time she slept with Aidan it left her head swirling.

He moved them so she was lying over his arm.

"I'm not going to apologize because that was insanely hot, and I can't remember the last time I came that hard. But we will sort this out."

She gave him a small smile, knowing what he meant. He'd get her the morning-after pill.

"I can't get pregnant."

"Can't?" Aidan asked, lowering his brow.

"No, I can. I just can't. You know, that would be bad. Destroy my career. Life," she explained.

"Gee, thanks." Aidan laughed. "I'm not that bad of a catch."

Lily let out a half giggle. "I don't mean that."

Aidan rolled to his side and faced her. "What do you do? For a job."

"Nothing as fancy as you."

He grinned. "You know what I do? Did you Google me?"

She rolled her eyes.

"Fine. Emma told you," he said, and she nodded. "But I don't know what you do, so enlighten me, peaches."

"Can you stop calling me that?"

"Probably not,"

Lily let out a sigh. "Nothing fancy. I'm a PA. But I want to be a teacher."

She felt a little dumb talking to this phenomenally successful and intelligent man about her incredibly average career goals.

Emma had told Lily all about Aidan inventing a piece of technology that was so influential it was used in nearly every digital touch point in all their lives. She couldn't conceive of doing such a thing.

Not many people probably could.

The truth was, she'd been surprised when she met him. He was a lot goofier than she expected someone with both a science and engineering degree to be.

But that was such a dumb judgment, and she hated herself for it.

"What's stopping you?" Aidan asked.

Damn.

Lily didn't want to have this conversation with him. There was no way he'd understand what it felt like not to have the financial means to achieve a dream.

But then again, what was the point of lying? None. And she wasn't ashamed of helping out her family. Or getting a great PA job, which had been a great pay raise and promotion from her job at Martha's.

Matt appreciated her, even if he was a little inappropriate at times and worked her hard.

Okay, fine, a little more than inappropriate.

The hand sliding over her ass in the elevator last week had felt very creepy. As if on cue, her phone texted.

It was Matt.

She knew because she had a special tone for his messages. She groaned and went to move to get her phone.

Aidan stopped her. "Who is that?"

"My boss. He has poor boundaries," Lily said and was surprised to see a wild flash cross his eyes.

"What kind of boundaries?" he growled, taking her hip and turning her into him so they were facing. "Has he touched you?"

"No."

Well, not the way you do, but I know he wants to.

"Tell me the truth." Aidan sat up and peered down at her. She flopped onto her back.

"He hasn't. But he sort of tries. It's fine. I need the job," Lily said, and her eyes met his. "Look, I'm clearly not rich. I can't just walk away from the job. I'm saving to go to college and until then I just have to put up with Matt and his occasional approaches."

Aidan gripped her chin.

"You like him," he said angrily.

"No, I don't like him. He's not horrible, but he is my boss. It's just harmless flirting. It doesn't go anywhere."

"Fuck that. We'll get you another job. Go work at Dufort," Aidan growled. "I'll tell Daniel to hire you."

"I live in Chicago. Not New York."

"Fuck. That's right," Aidan growled, then he pointed his finger. "You can move. Logan will find you something in Philly at his company."

Emma bunched her lips and frowned.

If she thought he was joking, she might have just brushed it off, but she could see his mind whirling and planning her entire life out.

"Aidan, stop. I might let you dominate my body, but you are not upending me from my home and family."

Clearly, he needed boundaries, just like Matt.

"But you will let some guy finger you," Aidan growled.

She pushed at his chest. Which did exactly nothing.

"Get off me. He doesn't finger me. You're disgusting."

"He better not," Aidan said and pushed her down. His mouth inches from hers. "Not his fingers, his mouth, or his cock are going near this pussy."

Lily just stared at him.

Surely, Aidan must know how inappropriate his response was.

Their arguing stopped when his mouth took possession of hers and she found her arms wrapping around his neck, her legs being tugged around his body, and his cock sliding back inside her.

CHAPTER TWELVE

Aidan repositioned his sunglasses on his head as he walked through the lobby of the Dufort Hotel. Logan and Daniel were standing just outside the doors, looking as close to twins as any of them could.

The two were closer in age than he was with his brother, and both the same build and height.

Aidan was an inch taller than Logan and while he still had a lot of bulk on him, he was leaner.

"Hey," he said, dropping his sunglasses over his eyes. The sun would set in an hour, but it was still bright outside. "Where is everyone else?"

Tonight, there was a festival on in Waikiki and they'd all decided to head out and enjoy it. The rest of the weekend was going to be well structured, with all the wedding dinners and the event itself, so tonight was a free-for-all.

Aidan was looking forward to just wandering around the markets and listening to the local bands. Even from here, he could see thousands of people wandering along Kalakaua Avenue—the main road along Waikiki Beach.

"Liv and Fletcher, Jackson and Kristen are already out there," Logan said. "Hunter and Addy are…otherwise disposed."

Aidan smirked.

"And Emma and Harper are up to no good, I suspect," Logan said, nodding to Daniel.

"David, her security is with them, so he'll keep me informed if anything happens," Daniel said.

Logan laughed.

"You think? I'd say Harper's threatened her private security guard within an inch of his life."

Daniel crossed his bulky arms. "He's four times her size—" Then shook his head and cursed. "Goddamn it, you're right."

Aidan snorted. "So much for powerful billionaires. You guys are pussy whipped."

Daniel uncrossed his arms and slapped him on the back as they began to walk down to the beach. "Your time will come, cousin. Your time will come."

"Then you'll understand," Logan added.

Aidan doubted it.

He was surprised two powerful men had chosen such sassy strong women. Not because he thought the alternative was to have a wife who was agreeable and weak-minded, rather that he saw Logan and Daniel as individuals who, like him, enjoyed control.

Needed control.

Then he remembered seeing Harper with Daniel and how she had softened during a private moment. It occurred to him he might not have the full picture. Their intimate lives might be quite different from what others saw.

Still, while Aidan enjoyed the sass and humor of the outspoken recent additions to their family, it was Lily who garnered his attention.

Whose blushes had him adjusting his crotch and thinking of ways to get her alone.

It was her softness that triggered his dominance, made him feel alive, and brought out his protective side.

Such as finding out who this Matt was that Lily worked for and making sure the guy kept his dirty mitts to himself.

Such as finding out where Lily was right now. Logan and Daniel hadn't said she was with the other women, so she was either with the others at the festival or on her own.

Aidan wanted eyes on her, and he hoped to steal her away to get the morning-after pill at a local pharmacy. Oddly, he wasn't feeling as panicked about it as he should, but Aidan was certainly going to take responsibility for coming inside her without protection.

Lily couldn't have stopped him at that moment if she'd tried.

She hadn't, and that moment was playing over in his mind. Their eyes locked and the heat between them felt like an erotic inferno.

Then Aidan saw her.

Lily wore a long white dress with a pair of flip-flops, a crossover handbag, and her hair in loose waves down her back. She looked so damn pretty.

Relaxed

Well fucked.

His lips twitched, feeling like a caveman wanting to thump his chest and say *I fucking did that.*

"Lily," Logan called out, waving.

She turned and placed a hand on the top of the floppy pink sun hat she was trying on at one of the stalls, then smiled.

It lit up the whole fucking beach.

Jesus.

It might have been only him that noticed.

Aidan ran a hand over his mouth and then shoved his hands into his pockets as the three of them slowed to greet her.

"Hey," Lily said, still smiling. "Isn't this so much fun? I love markets."

Aidan did, too, and he wished Daniel and Logan would fuck off. He had this sudden desire to take her hand and walk around in the tropical heat until the sun dropped and the party got started.

"The bands will start playing soon. The local groups are amazing," Daniel shared.

As a regular visitor, the CEO was very familiar with all the events on Oahu and the other islands. Between him and Harper, they never needed to Google anything.

"Where's Amelia?" Aidan suddenly asked, turning to his brother.

"No idea," Logan said.

"She came down with me but got a text and had to leave," Lily said. "I thought she went back up to the hotel."

Logan turned back to him in question.

"She wasn't with me." Aidan shook his head.

"Christ, I'm glad we never had a sister," Daniel groaned. "I'd have her surrounded with security twenty-four-seven."

"Is she in danger?" Lily asked, her eyes widening.

Aidan smiled at her innocence and wanted to pull that sexy, lithe body up against his and kiss her sun-kissed nose.

"No, we're just overprotective," Logan said. "I'll ring her. Lily, do you want to join us?"

Lily glanced at Aidan, and he very subtly shook his head, quietly loving that she naturally went to him for direction.

"I'm going to keep trying on some hats. I'll catch up with you. We're meeting on the beach later, right?" Lily smiled.

"Yup, by the volleyball nets," Logan said, and the two men began to walk off.

"I'm going to grab a cap. Left mine at home," Aidan called out and, not waiting for a response, turned back to the stall and lifted a Hawaii cap off the rack.

Whether they believed him or not, he didn't care. He was staying with Lily.

Aidan shoved the cap on backward and took a step closer to Lily. He dropped his eyes to hers. "What do you think?"

"Very handsome. As always." Lily's cheeks pinkened.

"You think I'm handsome?" Aidan smirked.

Lily lifted her brows. All *you know very well you're hot.*

He wasn't oblivious to the way he attracted women, even when they had no idea what his bank account was. Unlike other members of his family who had public profiles, Aidan got away with walking around more discretely.

But hearing Lily say she thought he was handsome made him stupidly happy.

"Yes, and so do hundreds of other women—and probably men—around us right now." She sighed as if that fact was super annoying.

He leaned down and kissed a spot on her neck, then whispered. "Well, I've only got eyes for you this weekend, peaches."

Lily gave him a shy smile, then grabbed another hat.

Aidan grinned and did the same, pulling another cap down off the rack. He had plenty in his suitcase, despite his little white lie earlier.

"Excuse me," said a brunette with a chest full of assets, pushing between them. She fluttered her fake long eyelashes at him and held his gaze as she grabbed a hat.

She hadn't even looked at it.

Aidan stepped away and ignored the flirtation.

Lily rolled her eyes at him and moved away, continuing to shop.

He suppressed his grin, liking that she was jealous.

For someone who had earlier told him she thought this was only a one-night deal, she was certainly reacting as if she liked him a little more.

No one was more surprised than him that he wanted more from Lily.

What it meant was something Aidan was trying to understand. She was perfect for him sexually. But it felt more than that.

It was as if no other woman existed right now.

He had spoken no greater truth moments ago. He only had eyes for her.

Except Aidan had to wonder, when they flew home, whether the feelings he had for her were going to simply stop.

And what it meant if they didn't.

Lily's phone beeped loudly, and she reached inside her bag for it.

Aidan grabbed another cap and put it on.

"Looks hot," the brunette said.

Aidan pressed his lips together in a polite but uninterested smile and ducked down to look in the mirror. He didn't give a shit about the hat. He was watching his girl in the reflection.

"Hi, Matt," Lily said and took a step away.

The fuck?

Her boss was calling her in Hawaii. Again.

Aidan grit his teeth.

Did the guy have no fucking boundaries? With his hands or Lily's time? Irritated, Aidan pulled off the cap and turned around, ready to get her off the call.

Then he froze.

His girl?

What the hell was that?

"All of those files are in the marketing folder. Remember, I showed you," Lily said, then laughed awkwardly. "Yeah, that night we had Chinese."

Her smile dropped, and she stared at the ground.

Aidan clenched his jaw, forcing himself to stay silent and not rip the phone out of her hand.

"Sure. I'm back on Wednesday, but if you need me to, I could see how I'm feeling when I'm home Tuesday night."

What the fuck?

Aidan felt his irritation turn much darker. This time, his patience was almost at zero. Without thinking, he walked straight up to her and loudly said, "Come on, baby, let's get moving."

Her eyes shot to his as he placed a hand on her lower back.

"What? No, I'm with friends." Lily glared at him and took a step away.

I don't fucking think so, peaches.

Aidan moved closer again, and her palm went to his chest. He covered it with his own and locked his eyes with hers, firmly telling her he was taking control.

"Hang up," he hissed. "Now."

Lily swallowed.

Aidan could hear the guy was still speaking, but neither of them were paying attention. He saw the fear in her eyes but pushed her anyway.

"Three seconds or I do it for you."

"Matt. Matt. I have to go. I will talk to you later," Lily said, and then, with a few more fucking promises to the asshole, she hung up.

They stood staring at each other, his hand still holding hers to his chest.

"What did you just do?" she gasped quietly. "He's my boss, Aidan."

He tugged her hips against him and leaned down, threading his hand through her hair. It didn't occur to him to worry who might see. He just had to.

"You know what I did," he said gruffly.

He'd taken possession of her.

Not just her body. He'd taken more. He'd demanded more. And not given her a choice.

What it meant after the next few days, he didn't know. Right now, she was safe with him, and that was all that mattered. With Lily, he knew he had to go a little slow.

Hell, he needed time to wrap his head around what was happening inside his damn chest.

For now, they had something else to take care of.

"Let's go to the pharmacy. I want to make sure we take care of that."

Lily swallowed. Then, resigning to her fate, she nodded and glanced around him.

"Oh, I didn't decide on which hat," Lily said and when he released her, she walked over and picked up the three she'd been trying on.

Aidan pulled a hundred dollar note out of his pocket and handed it to the seller. Then grabbed all three of them.

"Let's go." He smirked as Lily ran after him, calling him crazy.

Yeah, about you, Aidan nearly replied.

A FEW HOURS LATER, they were all down on the beach, watching the sun go down, eating dishes they'd purchased from the food trucks, and sharing their shopping bargains.

Aidan and Lily had got the Plan B pills and then wandered around together.

He'd purchased her a few more things, and they'd argued the entire time about him paying. Which Aidan had found far more enjoyable than he'd expected.

Then, she'd surprised him with a HAWAII cap, taking him for his word earlier, and he didn't have the heart to tell her he didn't need one. She'd slipped it onto his head, and it was all he could do to not kiss the life out of her.

Instead, he'd only taken a little bit, dropping his mouth to hers and lifting her off her feet, his arms tight around her back as he spun them.

"I love it," he'd said, and the smile she'd given him in response had undone him. Before he could say something stupid, he'd shaken his head, grabbed her hand and said, "Come on, peaches."

"God, these malasadas are divine," Harper moaned.

"Don't do that," Daniel growled.

"So good," Kristen said, offering one to Emma and Logan. "Want one?"

They both shook their heads, but Addison and Hunter reached out and took one from the box. Lily declined and pushed out her legs on the sand, her white cotton dress fluttering in the light breeze.

She was glowing.

And too fucking far away from him.

Kristen and Jackson jumped up. "Who's up for volleyball?"

"I'm in," Logan said. "Bro?"

"Yeah, I'll play," Aidan said, then kicked Jacob and Blake, who'd shown up with a bunch of beers.

Thankfully, his parents had decided on a quiet night in their suite.

Aidan lifted his brows in question at Lily, who had a notebook on her lap and was sketching. He'd been leaning over her shoulder and watching her for the past forty-five minutes.

They were amazing, and he wondered if she knew how talented she was.

"I'm recovering from the SUP," she said. "I need a whole day in the hot tub."

"Girl, I hear you," Harper said.

"Same. Whose stupid idea was it?" Emma asked.

"Yours!" All the girls cried, laughing.

Aidan shared a smirk with the boys, and someone tossed the ball at him. He reached out, snapping it out of the air, and threw it at Blake.

"Drop the beer, Jacob," Logan yelled out.

"God gave me two hands for a reason," the youngest Dufort replied.

For the next few hours, they played volleyball. Family sports in this family were highly competitive, and somehow Harper had appointed herself the point scorer, and *somehow* her husband's team ended up winning.

"Damn cheats," Logan muttered as Fletcher, Hunter, and Daniel slapped each other's backs.

"We should have appointed Lily. She's neutral," Aidan said.

"No thanks. Every single one of you threatened Harper's life at some point. Even her bodyguard was starting to look concerned," she replied.

"To be fair, Daniel threatened no sex. But I think we all know he didn't mean it." Harper grinned.

"Stop talking, wife," the big guy said, kissing her on the lips.

Aidan wished he could do the same to Lily and the way her eyes drifted to his, he got the feeling she did too.

Risking some funny looks, he tugged her down on the sand next to him and let a stupid amount of happiness spread through him as everyone hung out chatting. It was the most relaxed he'd seen his family in a long time.

It also allowed his older cousins and younger ones to get to know each other better.

"Any hot tips for leading a big team?" Blake asked Daniel.

Daniel leaned his elbows on his propped-up knees and tilted his head. "Be authentic. Support your leaders so they can support their people. If you try to be dictatorial, you'll fail."

"I'd agree," Hunter said. "As a leader, your job is about identifying people's strengths and encouraging them to do a good job as they grow. Not trying to force square pegs into round holes, as the generations before us did."

Fletcher nodded.

"It means you'll lose people when they outgrow you, but while they are there, you'll get the best out of them. And people talk—your company will be known as a great place to work."

Aidan glanced down at Lily, forcing back the words *unlike your boss, Handsy Matt.*

She shot him a quick look and twirled the butterfly on her necklace. Which she did a lot when she was either nervous or sexually frustrated.

"Thanks, that sounds smart. I've had a few problems, but I'm sure I'll get it sorted." Blake shrugged.

"Do it quickly," Daniel said. "If you spot toxicity in your teams, the longer you let it fester, the more difficult it is to resolve."

"That," Aidan said.

He might not have a corporate structure, but he hired a number of people who worked remotely. Even contractors needed managing.

"I'm sure they think I'm too young to be this successful," Blake confessed vulnerably.

Daniel shook his head. "Fuck that. It's 2023. Kids on social media make ten times their parents."

"If any of them have an issue, you move them out. They're the wrong people to have in your business," Aidan said.

"Easier said than done, though. I feel responsible for them. Some of them are kind of friends." Blake lifted one side of his mouth.

Poor guy. Learning this shit was hard.

"I have a small team in the Dufort business. It's so easy to get close to your team, but at the end of the day, you're all there to do a job, so if the lines blur, just learn from it. You'll make mistakes. We all have," Oliva said.

Blake blew out his breath.

Logan and Aidan shared a look. Neither of them realized he was so stressed about it. If they'd known, they would have sat him down and helped.

"You've got this, bro," Jacob said, slapping his back.

"We're here to support you." Aidan kicked his foot playfully. "When we get home, let's catch up."

Blake nodded. "Thanks, man. It's all happened so fast."

"I think you're all amazing," Lily suddenly said.

Aidan realized she must feel like a fish out of water. They were all incredibly successful and wealthy, so not at all like the people she would normally socialize with.

"Here I am just trying to go to teacher's college. And you're all running billion-dollar businesses. God, listen to me," she said, waving her hand out. "Stupid alcohol."

Daniel smiled and looked away.

It wasn't the first time any of them had heard a similar reaction. There was no right answer here. Nothing they could say.

He knew all of them were grateful for what they had and didn't take it for granted, but at the same time, this was their life, and walking around feeling guilty about it was no way to live.

"Honey, every single one of us felt like that when we first met these guys," Olivia said. "I worked with them for a year before hooking up with Fletch. Stepping into their personal lives was a whole different ball game."

"I bet." Lily nodded.

"Remember when I phoned you from Philly, when Logan kidnapped me?" Emma asked. "I never dreamed I'd be sitting here with his engagement ring on my finger. I mean, he lives in a mansion."

"Wait. You told her I kidnapped you?" Logan frowned, then added, "It's not a mansion. And it's your home now, too."

Lily giggled.

"It has a thousand bedrooms, darling. It's not a normal house." Emma smacked a kiss on his lips as Logan shot him a look over her head.

Aidan shrugged, staying out of it.

He leaned forward on his elbows and swirled the liquid in his can and then tossed it down.

He wanted to tell Lily it was just money, that it was no big deal. That she was just as important as any one of them sitting around their group. That she would become a teacher one day if she really wanted it.

And he felt a tug to help her achieve it.

Not once had Aidan felt a need to get involved with a single woman he'd dated before. Dated. Or fucked.

He got to know some of the women from HEAT. At times, some of them would share a challenge or hardship in their life. Or the bartender might gossip.

It hadn't breached his stony heart. Okay, well, there was that one time he found out a school gym had burned down and donated money so they could quickly rebuild it. Kids needed sports.

But no one knew about that.

Yet the petite blonde in front of him who rode his cock like she belonged on it had triggered something within him no one else had.

He should be worried, but he wasn't.

Mostly because he had a strong feeling it would wear off.

He just wasn't the marrying type and, for all his father's crude words, he was right. They were chalk and cheese.

The sky erupted above them as fireworks rocketed up into the heavens. The entire Waikiki beach lit up, and the soaring sounds filled the air.

"Aloha Friday!" the girls cheered.

Around him, all the couples got cozy. Emma leaned into Logan, and he wrapped an arm around her. Harper clapped as she climbed onto Daniel's lap. His cousin surrounded her body with his powerful arms.

A tightness in his chest stirred a need. He glanced at Lily. She was lying down on her back in the sand, her hands under her head.

What was she thinking?

Was this the vacation of a lifetime for her?

Of course it fucking was.

Did she wish she had a man to snuggle during this romantic tropical moment? She didn't seem to be worried about him. She had a little smile on her lips and was looking very content.

His jaw tensed as the next question popped into his head. Did Lily secretly have a crush on her boss? Handsy goddamn Matt. Was that why she was answering his calls and why she stayed working with him?

Was she thinking about him now?

And why did he care?

And where the fuck was Amelia?

CHAPTER THIRTEEN

Lily's eyes blinked open as her phone alarm began to blare. Beside her, she heard a groan.

Shit.

Startled, she grabbed her phone and then turned to stare at Aidan. "You're still here."

He stretched his entire body—and my God, it was gorgeous—looking unfazed.

Right now, he looked like any other guy. Well, except for the expensive watch on his arm, which she'd noticed said Rolex on the face.

With subtle diamonds.

She assumed. It was safe to say Rolex didn't use cubic zirconia.

Probably.

Yeah, no, they wouldn't.

Lily mentally shook her head. There was one thing knowing he was a billionaire but another spotting things like that, which really emphasized it.

"You're very observant in the morning, peaches," Aidan said, reaching and tugging her up against him. "I fell asleep because you wore me out."

Was he joking?

She was the one who was going to be stumbling down the aisle tomorrow. Between Aidan's insatiable sex drive and that damn SUP, her legs were jelly. Before she could reply, his mouth was on hers and her legs wrapping over his hips.

"I'm sore," she said, against his lips.

"I know," Aidan replied. "I just want your mouth this morning. To be clear, on my cock."

She felt him hard against her tummy and her core immediately began to throb. Who was she kidding? The moment those green eyes of his had landed on her, the spark ignited.

After he'd thoroughly ravished her mouth, Aidan pushed the sheets off them and presented her his hard thick cock. Slowly stroking it, those green globes held hers.

"You were a good girl last night, Lily." His voice was husky this morning.

She swallowed and nodded.

"Turn around and climb over my face so I can play with your sweet pussy while you take my cock down your throat?"

"Yes… sir," she replied almost automatically now.

"Good girl," he purred.

Lily straddled Aidan's face, steadying herself on his strong, solid thighs. Then she reached and took his member in her hand.

She felt so naughty as his breath warmed her pussy behind her. A shiver of anticipation ran through her body as he took his time running his tongue over every other spot but *there*.

But once he did, she let out a loud moan.

"Mouth on my cock, Lily," Aidan ordered.

How could she concentrate when he had her butt cheeks spread like she was a bowl of ice cream, licking her clean?

She glanced down at the bead of precum leaking out and lapped at it with her tongue.

"Tease me any longer, peaches, and I'll flip you over and slide my cock inside this tight ass."

Lily let out a squeak and tried to pull away when Aidan brushed his thumb over the puckered spot, his tight grip not giving an inch.

So instead she got to work.

Her mouth stretched over his fat head and took him deep inside her mouth. Her hand stroked as she sucked him, occasionally rubbing the head when she took a breath.

When she'd gained speed and was losing her mind when Aidan shoved his tongue inside and pinched her clit, Lily relaxed her throat and took him deep.

"Fuck, Lily,"

She kept up the vigorous play, gagging a few times and then taking him again.

"Fuck, fuck, yes, baby. Oh, shit."

His cock swelled, and when she felt he was close to climax, Lily pressed down on his face.

Cursing, Aidan lifted her and pressed at least two of his thick fingers inside her. Her head came flying off his cock as her orgasm erupted. Waves of pleasure overtook her as come spurted from Aidan's cock onto her tongue and chin.

"Aidan," she cried.

Neither of them stopped until they were milked dry.

Finally, Aidan lifted her and rearranged them so they were lying chest to chest.

"You are so fucking perfect," he said, rubbing his come down her neck and onto her breasts. "The things I'd love to show you. Teach you. If we had more time."

Lily lay there, sated and wondering whether Aidan would give her that time if they lived in the same city. Or if he would lose interest in her quickly.

She knew the answer. She wasn't a dreamer.

Of course he would.

Which was fine. Aidan wasn't someone she could see herself with—not that the option was there—she wasn't interested in wearing an enormous ring and living in a mansion.

This was the furthest she'd been away from her family. She was missing her family and worried about her dad.

As for work, it barely felt like a vacation. Matt had messaged again last night, and when she had replied, she'd found Aidan glaring at her. Fortunately, they'd been in the elevator with others, so he couldn't say anything.

Then, when they stepped out onto the floor, the elevator in front of them had opened and a very upset-looking Amelia stepped out. It was obvious she'd been crying.

"The fuck, Amelia?" Aidan had said, going straight to her. He gripped her shoulders, leaning down and staring at her.

"Who did this?"

Logan was right behind him, demanding, "Amelia."

"Give her space, for goodness' sakes," Emma said, trying to nudge them away. "Sweetie, are you okay?"

"No," Amelia cried and launched her face into Aidan's chest. His enormous arms tightened around her, and Lily watched as he shared a stern look with Logan.

"Who is he, Amelia?" Logan demanded.

"I'm not telling you." Her voice was muffled. Then she lifted her head. "Stay out of it, please."

Emma shot her a cringe.

Even Lily knew that was unlikely and she hadn't known them all that long.

"I mean it," she cried. "I love him…but. It doesn't matter anymore."

Love?

"The fuck it doesn't," Logan growled.

"Come on. Let's get you to bed," Emma said, tugging her out of Aidan's arms. "Some Tylenol will fix this."

"And champagne," Amelia said.

See. Rich people. Who drinks champagne with Tylenol? Billionaires. That's who.

Logan and Emma had escorted the teary Amelia to her room, leaving Lily and Aidan standing alone. He'd looked stressed, so she'd nudged her thumb over her shoulder.

"I'll just—"

Aidan nodded. When she began to walk away, he called out to her, "Lily!"

She turned.

"I'll just check on her."

Lily shook her head. "You should stay with her."

Then she'd turned and walked down to her room. Obviously, he had *not* stayed with Amelia, but he *had* arrived at a very bad time.

Lily had been on the phone with her father.

Not expecting Aidan to return, Lily had thought the knock at her door was Emma or hotel staff, so she'd said, "Dad, hang on a minute,"

Then opened the door.

Her eyes had flown open.

"Is that your fucking boss?" Aidan had growled.

"Lily? Who is that?" her father had cried, knowing it was late and she was in her hotel room.

Jesus.

It had been a clusterfuck.

"Give me the phone!" Aidan said. "This guy has no limits. What the hell time is it in Chicago? Barely breakfast."

Lily had taken a step away, trying to catch her bearings.

"Lily Peterson, do you have a man in your room?"

Good God. *I'm not fifteen, Dad.*

"Wait. Just wait," she said to both of them. Or maybe to herself.

She held up a hand and surprisingly Aidan halted, but she could see by the darkness in his eyes that he was very close to ripping the phone out of her hand.

"No, *Dad*," she said pointedly and arched a brow at Aidan. He partly relaxed and took a step back, although she saw some disbelief. "It's the TV. I sat on the remote."

She moved further away and sat down in an armchair across the room as Aidan crossed his arms and glared at her.

That was fun.

"You scared me. Christ. I know you're not a child, but you have to be careful when you're traveling alone," Gary said.

Alone?

She was surrounded by half a dozen enormous, powerful men. She was not in any danger. Well, except for the man sending daggers across the room.

Lily knew she was going to pay it on her ass.

"I'm not alone. I'm with Emma and Logan, and their family. Anyway, how are you feeling?" she asked. "Did Mom give you the meds?"

"Every day and every night," her dad replied.

Aidan uncrossed his arms and moved to the sofa. He sat with his legs spread and she had wondered if men sat that way because of the large things between them.

Namely… well, she knew what she meant. And they were not things she should be thinking while talking to her dad.

As if he knew what her thoughts were, Aidan had smirked.

"… so I suppose we will wait for the test results, but it's nothing to worry about."

Lily suddenly snapped out of her lust. "What did you say? Dad, repeat that."

"It's mostly routine. Just because I've had a few breathing issues lately," Gary said.

A heavy feeling laced through her.

"You knew. You knew before I flew over here," Lily said, feeling the color drain from her face.

"Hey, kid. It's fine. We've been through this before."

Her stomach dropped.

"Lilypop," Gary said, using her stupid childhood nickname.

Which she loved.

"Dad," she said quietly and wished Aidan wasn't here. Sitting on the edge of the seat, she kicked off her flip-flops. "I'll come home. Tomorrow. Tonight."

"No, sweetheart. Stay. Have fun. The results will be back on Monday, so there is nothing you can do, anyway. Emma needs you. This is an important milestone for her and your friendship."

"She might get married again," Lily said quietly, knowing he knew she was joking.

"Funny girl. Lily, please, I want you to stay and enjoy yourself," he whispered.

When her eyes lifted, she knew they were full of emotion. Aidan was staring at her with such intensity, it freaked her out.

She swallowed and looked away.

"Call you tomorrow, Dad. Promise to ring if anything changes?"

"Promise, Lilypop," he said. "Love you."

"Love you, Dad."

She lowered the phone onto her lap and chewed her lip. Aidan stared at her for a long minute, neither of them saying anything.

"He's dying," he said.

"Yes,"

"That's why you aren't going to college to get your Bachelor of Education?"

Lily nodded.

"Colon cancer. He's been in remission."

Aidan shook his head.

"Aidan, he knew," she said, tears starting to fall. "He knew he was starting to have symptoms again and he let me fly all the way over here."

Aidan got up, walked over, and scooped her up in his arms. Then carried her back to the sofa and sat with her on his knee.

"I wish I could fix this for you," he said as she rested her head on his chest.

She lay there for a long moment while his hand ran over her back, and her tears flowed. It was different than her mom hugging her or friends consoling her. His muscular arms felt like protection against the world and all her pain.

Almost.

"You care about people," Lily said. "Your cousins, your sister. Your brother."

He reared his head back and when she glanced up at him, he was half frowning and half smiling. "Did you think I was a monster?"

"I don't know what to think. You're different from the people I normally meet," Lily admitted.

"Because I'm rich?"

She shrugged. "Maybe."

"Let me ask you this. If I gave you ten million dollars right now, what would you do?" Aidan asked.

Her mouth dropped open.

"Think about it carefully."

Lily ran through a list of expenses in her head. Paying off her parent's mortgage. Making repairs. Buying herself a house.

Vacations for them…

Oh.

It wouldn't change what really mattered.

She met his eyes. "You knew."

"Money might be able to help him. If he had time and with further research one day, but no one has been able to find the miracle cancer cure yet," Aidan said. "AI might be able to one day. I'm working with an advanced team on a number of medical projects."

Wow, he was?

"But money doesn't theoretically give us the things we truly want in life."

Aidan shrugged as he continued to think out loud.

"Don't get me wrong. It doesn't suck. It makes life easier. And I'm not going to lie and say I know what it's like to struggle. I don't. I was born into a wealthy family. But there are different challenges."

"Like what?"

"Like, I'm not fucking telling you because no matter how important I think they are, to someone struggling to eat or house themselves or pay for their dying loved one's medical bills, I'd just sound like an asshole."

Lily let her eyes drift across the room as she processed that. Then dropped her head to his chest. She respected his answer. It was honest, even if she didn't really like it.

"We are very different."

"Yet here we are," Aidan said.

They sat staring out at the dark Hawaiian sky for a long while until Lily wriggled off his knee.

She'd lived with her dad's illness for over a year now. He was right. It was probably one of those bumps in the road and he'd be fine.

Lily wanted to be here for Emma as her bridesmaid. She knew it would be her one and only wedding. The two were so madly in love.

Plus, in just a few days, she would be home.

"I have to pack," Lily said. "Maybe you should head off and do the same."

"Firstly, no. And secondly, why? Are you going home?" he asked.

"We're flying to Maui tomorrow, remember?" Lily said.

"Can't you do it in the morning?" Aidan asked.

"No, it will take me at least half an hour."

Aidan laughed at her.

"Lily, how much stuff did you bring?" Aidan stood and walked into the bedroom, following her. When she opened the cupboard, he turned to her. "It looks like you've moved in."

She shrugged. "I like variety. Plus, I flew first class so figured I'd just bring all the things I love."

"Okay, peaches, let's get all this shit into your suitcases and then I have plans for you in the shower."

And he did.

For much longer than she would have let him if they'd been back home. God knows what the power bill would be after the hour-long sexual marathon.

Lily glanced at her fingers now as she lay in his arms, surprised they weren't still wrinkly.

As for Aidan teaching her more sexy stuff, Lily glanced at his handsome morning face and, knowing they were halfway through their vacation, she should protect her heart.

Opening up to him last night about her dad had been very intimate. She liked the way it felt when he held her and wiped away her tears.

Way too much.

"We don't have time and live in different parts of the country so I will just have to fantasize about all the things you would've taught me," she said, kissing a line across his square jaw.

Aidan could play the part of Superman with that jaw. Tall, broad, handsome, and with a smile that melted panties. And that was before you reached his sparking green eyes.

"I have a jet." He shrugged, running his hand over her butt.

Lily froze.

What?

What did he mean?

To continue this after they left Hawaii? Surely he didn't mean that. They'd just said how different they were. It would never work, and she couldn't just let him pay for everything because she didn't have the money to do the things he could.

That wasn't a balanced relationship.

Plus, it felt…different.

"Don't do that," Lily said, moving to get off the bed.

"Do what?" Aidan asked.

"Talk about this like it's going to continue when we leave Hawaii. It won't and you know it."

His face hardened. "Why? Because of Matt?" Aidan said, then cursed. "Forget it. You're right."

Aidan dropped a hard kiss on her lips and climbed off the bed.

"I better get packed. See you at the airport, peaches."

Lily lay there bewildered as he tugged on his shorts and shirt, then shot her a halfhearted smile and walked out of the penthouse.

Just left.

Wow!

What the hell was that?

CHAPTER FOURTEEN

Aidan walked up the steps of the private jet and nodded *morning* to Logan and Emma as he made his way down the back where Blake and Jacob were sitting at one of the tables.

The others were boarding behind him, their cars still pulling up. His parents had flown over early this morning on their own jet.

Amelia climbed out of her seat and curled up next to him. Her Gucci shoes squeaked on the white leather as she tucked them underneath her.

"You going to give me a name so I can have his balls removed, or do I need to torture it out of you?" he asked, stretching out his legs and wrapping an arm around her.

Then he kissed the top of her head.

"Just leave it. I'm only here for the hugs," Amelia said into his shoulder.

Aidan frowned.

We'll find him. Blake mouthed, and Aidan nodded.

One thing all the Dufort men had in common was their need to protect the women in their lives. Amelia hated it most days, but look at her now, snuggled into him. Truth was, he'd never seen her this upset. So whoever the guy was that had broken his sister's heart, he was going to find out.

His eyes lifted when the flight attendant walked through the cabin and offered him a bottle of water.

"Thank you," he said, taking it.

"Vodka," Amelia said. "Gray Goose."

"Meel's, you can't spend the weekend drunk," Blake said, indicating to the flight attendant for another bottle and he slid it over the table that separated them all.

Aidan stopped it and positioned it in front of his sister.

"Drunk or crying. Those are the two choices," she mumbled, but grabbed the water. "Anyway, I don't care. I hate men."

Jacob pressed his lips together to stop him from smiling.

"If you became a nun, it would make life much easier for Logan and Aidan," Blake said. "It's a sound plan."

"Shut up," Amelia said, but her lips twitched. Then she sat up, pulling her knees up to her chest and uncapping her bottle.

Aidan's gaze drifted across the cabin and found Logan watching them. *She's fine*, he mouthed, and his brother nodded and returned to his conversation with Emma.

Then dropped his eye back to his drink.

To keep from finding the one set that would remind him what a dick he'd been earlier.

Instead, he wondered what it felt like to be getting married. This was his brother's second wedding, and he seemed much calmer.

Aidan couldn't imagine committing his life to one person. Sure, it sounded all romantic and shit, but one person. Forever?

His father might want that for him, but unless he couldn't live without someone—which sounded all kinds of dependent and unhealthy—he wouldn't.

It wasn't that he didn't think he could love anyone that long, it was quite the opposite. His heart was already shared among a lot of people. People he would die for. People he would kill for.

Aidan was a lover, not a fighter, but last night watching Lily talk to her dad and the panic on her face. Well fuck, he'd wanted to fly her home and fix... fix all her problems.

And yes, he would happily kill Matt.

None of this made sense.

Maybe there was something about tropical islands and love affairs. They made you insane.

After all, he'd known Lily for only a matter of days. Sure, he'd met her three months ago, but during that time she had been in Chicago, and he'd been living his life, looking forward to seeing her again.

It wasn't love at first sight.

Lust, yes.

Now here he was, throwing his toys and storming out of her suite because *she* had said she didn't want to see him after they returned home.

Like a fucking teenager.

Don't talk about this like it's going to continue when we leave Hawaii. It won't and you know it.

Why? Because of Matt?

Jesus.

Images of her back in her office with Handsy Matt leaning over her desk and looking down at her top had hit him like a ten-ton truck, and Aidan had seen red.

The only thing he could do before he said anything more hurtful was to leave.

After all, what right did he have?

None.

And why did he care so much? Because that's what he did.

His mom had once said to him, "Aidan, you act the fool, but I see you. When you love, you love with your whole heart and soul. Just make sure you choose the right people to give the pieces away to."

He lifted the bottle of water to his lips and drank half of it in one go.

They were staying at a large property on Maui that belonged to a friend of Daniel's. His cousin had sourced it for Logan and Emma when they'd announced they wanted to get married in Hawaii.

This meant they were all going to be in much closer quarters than they were in Waikiki.

Aidan needed to apologize to Lily.

He had questions about why she wouldn't want to continue seeing him, but for now, he needed to play it cool around his father.

Aidan did respect it was Logan's wedding, so he wasn't going to do anything to upset any of the family. After the confrontation yesterday, it was better to just grin and bear it.

When they got home, Aidan was going to confront him.

Lily might normally be right. Anyone else he would normally hook up with like this, and the fun would be over when their flights were called.

Not this time.

And she was about to learn he didn't give up easily. Distance meant nothing to him. If he wanted her, he was going to have her.

"All aboard," Harper announced as she entered the cabin through the main door.

"She's sober, I promise," Daniel advised and got a slap on the chest for it, while Kristen laughed.

Jackson, Hunter, Fletcher, Addy, and Olivia followed, having chosen to leave their jets on Oahu.

Olivia sat down next to Lily, who was curled up reading a book.

"Hey, oh, can I hold him?" Lily preened as Baxter gurgled.

"He needs changing," Olivia warned.

"Gimme." Lily took the baby in her arms, then scrunched her eyes and laughed. "Oh, I see what you mean."

Aidan's chest tightened.

That was when he wondered if she had taken the morning-after pill. She was going to do it this morning, and of course, he'd stormed out.

He would ask her.

Lily handed Baxter to Fletcher—who disappeared in the back to, he assumed, change him—and locked her eyes with Aidan's. For a long moment they stared at one another, and he wished his family would vanish into thin air so he could speak with her.

A nudge in his ribs got his attention. Aidan dropped his gaze to Amelia.

"What are you doing?" she whispered at him, frowning.

"Nothing." He shook his head and took a drink.

"Leave that poor girl alone, Aides. She's way too nice for you to go and break her heart."

Blake stared at him and then turned curiously to glance at Lily. "Did you—?"

"Stop. I'm not...I'm not breaking anyone's heart," Aidan said under his breath.

What would they think if he told them she had basically rejected him?

Disbelief, probably.

But here they were.

FORTY MINUTES LATER, they landed on Maui, where a Mercedes Benz bus greeted them. After taking a quick business call while their luggage was being loaded, Aidan was the last to climb on.

Which meant the only spare seat was next to Lily because everyone was coupled up.

He nudged his bag under the seat and sat down.

"Hi," she said softly, and he felt the urge to pull her into his arms when he saw how uncomfortable and confused she looked.

The bus roared as it pulled out onto the road, providing them some privacy to speak. Aidan turned his body toward her.

"I apologize," he said quietly, and Lily nodded. His hand slid onto her thigh before he knew what he was doing. "Lil, I am sorry. I had no right to say that. Or leave so abruptly."

"No, you didn't," Lily said quietly, "But you don't understand my situation. How could you?"

Right.

How could he?

Because he was sitting on a bus heading to a property that was costing them fifty thousand dollars a night and wearing a sixty-four-thousand-dollar Audemars Piguet watch?

Because today he'd already earned ten thousand dollars. Not including interest. After tax.

And it was only noon.

Because he had over a billion dollars in cash and investments and couldn't comprehend having to stay in a situation where he was being treated inappropriately by someone more powerful than him. Where he had to choose between putting up with crossing boundaries and paying for food, utilities, and medical bills for someone he loved.

Fucking hell.

Aidan clenched his teeth.

He wanted to yank her onto his lap and slam his mouth to hers and tell her there was no way he was letting her suffer or struggle anymore. Like a superhero.

He knew Lily enough to know she wouldn't accept it. Goddamn her.

Instead, he simply gave her leg a squeeze and nodded. "You're right. I can't."

Then leaned his head back and closed his eyes.

She might argue with him here in Hawaii, but that didn't mean he was going to accept it. Aidan wasn't letting her fly home and forget about him.

No fucking way.

If she thought he would carry on with his life, knowing Handsy Matt was taking advantage of her, leaving her unprotected, then she really didn't know him at all.

His mind flew back to the night they'd shared and the incredible sex. She'd been fucking incredible. Compliant, willing, and eager to please him.

Every time she called him sir, he'd just got harder.

Her petite body in his arms felt so sexy, so vulnerable, and so trusting when he used the robe to tie her wrists.

Those damn eyes of hers pleading for pleasure and rolling back when her orgasm hit.

But it was when he was sponging her in the shower, as she was half dozing, and he slid his cock inside her one last time, that her luscious globes connected with his. Like lightning, a bolt of something powerful and all-consuming had struck him.

A need to own and dominate her had cemented itself in his DNA. All he knew right now was this wasn't just a holiday fling.

Lily knew just as well as he did.

He'd seen it in her eyes.

It scared her.

Neither of them had planned this, but she had to know a man like him wasn't going to accept no for an answer.

Hell, Aidan wasn't even sure he was asking.

By the time they pulled up outside the property, Aidan was riled. He stayed seated, pretending to rifle through his bag until they were alone on the bus. Then he stood and let Lily step out.

They walked to the front of the bus when he finally snapped.

"Lily," he said, reaching for her arm.

She turned, her eyes widening.

"This isn't over."

Lily shook her head.

"I'm not going to let you walk out of my life and forget me. That's not fucking happening." His voice was gruff. "And that boss of yours is never touching you again."

"Aidan..." A little gasp escaped her, and his cock thickened. The blush on her cheeks was sending him over the edge.

"You better walk away, or I'm lifting your skirt and sinking my cock inside that sweet pussy of yours."

"My God, your dirty mouth." Lily shook her head and pulled her bag against her chest, making a hasty retreat.

Aidan smiled to himself and stepped off the bus after her. That's when he saw his father standing with his arms crossed, watching them.

Dammit.

CHAPTER FIFTEEN

The property was huge and impressive, even to him. Aidan had stayed in some incredible venues in his life, but this was prime beachfront Maui real estate.

It was fucking stunning.

They settled into their rooms and spent the afternoon moving between the pool and beach, being served lunch and cocktails. Then, when everyone had arrived, including Emma's family, they changed for dinner.

The long table was scattered with delicious dishes, wine, and brightly colored tableware and wine glasses. Plumeria flowers filled the air with their tropical fragrance as glasses were topped up and plates handed across the table.

"A toast," Andrew said. "On behalf of your mother and I, we wish you all the very best for tomorrow to be all you dreamed of and go off without a hitch."

His mom lifted her champagne flute and smiled at Logan and Emma.

"Thanks, Dad. Mom," Logan replied, and then Emma's dad stood.

"I know this is a little premature, but I wanted to say how happy we are to have such a wonderful son-in-law. Emma, you have chosen a good man. We both wish you a lifetime of happiness."

Aidan had only met Emma's brother and sister-in-law, Kevin, and Jada, briefly at the engagement party, but they both seemed nice. Lily, of course, knew them and was sitting next to Emma's mom.

More toasts were made as the champagne flowed.

After dinner, it didn't take long before they were all standing around the pool mingling, talking, and enjoying the music. Tomorrow would be a big night, so some were already heading off inside.

Blake was talking to Lily and Emma, so Aidan made his way over.

"South side? You're so badass," Blake teased her.

"I'm not badass. I'm poor." Lily laughed. "Emma grew up there, too. And her family. They've all moved now, though."

"I'm trying to get her to move to Philly." Emma nudged her arm.

Aidan was taking a drink of his Macallan when Lily's eyes met his. He might have to recruit Emma to help him persuade Lily to move.

"So, did I hear that you want to be a teacher?" Blake asked, and it took her a moment to slide her eyes away and answer his cousin.

"She is," Emma answered her. "I'll make sure of it."

No, I will.

"I will. One day. I love children," Lily admitted.

He didn't know that.

Did she want to be a mom? How many kids did she want?

Why were there so many people around them so he couldn't have her to himself and ask her a million questions? And kiss that blush right off her cheeks.

Emma turned as her name was called and tossed down her drink. "That's my cue. Night, you guys. We're turning in early."

Lily and Emma faced each other, their faces breaking out into huge smiles. "Ems! You're getting married tomorrow."

"I know. Holy shit." Emma danced on the spot. "*And* I love him. Bonus!"

Aidan grinned.

There was something about seeing a woman love your brother so completely that filled him with a sense of peace. And happiness.

Emma made her way back to her parents, hugging them and saying goodnight.

"What does your dress look like?" Aidan asked Lily when Emma disappeared into the house.

"You'll just have to wait and see." She smiled playfully at him. He liked they had a secret and that only he knew about her now fading bruises between her legs.

Well, and Emma. But she hadn't said anything more than that, as far as he knew.

"You know, you could look at college in Philly," Blake said, picking back on that conversation.

"There are universities in Chicago she can train at. Isn't that right Lily?" his father said. Aidan hadn't noticed him arrive, but the way he refused to look at him gave him pause.

What the hell is he up to?

"Yes, there is," she answered, glancing quickly at him.

"Do you have a boyfriend back home?" Andrew asked, ignoring her discomfort.

Aidan stiffened.

Even in the flickering light of the tiki torches, he saw Lily's cheeks turn pink. "No, sir. I do not."

Andrew rocked on his heels. "I see. Well, I hope you don't have your sights set on either of these boys."

Lily's mouth dropped open.

What in the actual fuck?

Aidan turned to Andrew, anger in his eyes. It was such an ambiguous statement he didn't know how to react without making a fuss. Something he'd promised himself he wouldn't do.

But this was crossing the line.

Just as he was about to open his mouth, Lily glanced at him. For a second, all he could see was the shame in her eyes. Then she blinked. In their place, she had erected a rock-solid wall.

A cool chill swept through him.

Lily steeled her shoulders and shook her head. "Absolutely not. I'll be heading home to Chicago on Monday."

"Smart girl. This family is not for everyone," his father said, pushing the dagger in further.

Mother fucker.

"Hey, w—" Aidan started, then Lily interrupted.

"You know, I think I should retire myself. I'm one of the bridesmaids, after all, and tomorrow will be a big day."

Lily awkwardly moved her drink around in front of her, looking for a place to put it.

Blake took it.

"Thanks. Um, goodnight," she said and hurried off.

Jacob and Daniel chose that moment to walk over and join them.

"What did I miss?" Jacob asked, obviously sensing the tension.

"Your uncle being an asshole," Aidan growled, glaring at his father. "You have some nerve."

"You'll thank me one day," Andrew said, tossed back his whisky and added, "Enjoy your night, boys. I'll see you in the morning."

Then, with one last glance in his direction, his father walked casually across the yard to his mother. After a quick exchange, the two of them went inside and retired for the evening.

"What the fuck was that?" Blake growled.

That was his father making a huge, irreparable dent in their relationship. One that wasn't going to heal easily.

AIDAN TOSSED HIS empty glass into the garden and cursed angrily.

"Tell me," Daniel growled, picking up that shit had just gone down.

Where did he start?

"Uncle Andrew just got White Privileged Man of the Year," Blake answered, shaking his head.

That was a good start.

"What am I missing?" Daniel's brows bunched.

"I take it you're sleeping with Lily." Blake crossed his arms.

Aidan let out a long sigh and nodded.

"Jesus, what did he do?" Daniel asked.

"Basically, told her she wasn't good enough for any man in this family and that she should hightail it back to Chicago and her mediocre life," Aidan said. "And yes, I'm fucking her."

"Aides, you just let him—"

"Don't." Aidan held up his hand to his older cousin. "It would've made things worse if I'd defended her. I did try, but she cut me off."

It was a shit excuse, even to his own ears.

"Why the hell would he do that?" Jacob asked.

"He's been on my case about getting married to a socialite or an appropriate woman who will fit into our family."

"Fuck that." Daniel shook his head.

Yeah.

"You still should've said something." Blake uncrossed his arms and slid his hands into his pockets. "I don't think she could've felt any worse than she did."

"Trust me. He wouldn't have held back if Lily hadn't got the message," Aidan said.

He knew his father. The guy was a narcissist. He didn't care who he hurt. What he wanted to know was what his end game was. That was blunt, even for him.

"Aidan's right. Both Andrew and Jonathan can be cold assholes when they decide on something," Daniel said, then narrowed his eyes at him. "You're what? Thirty-one? Why the massive urgency to get married?"

Aidan shrugged. "No idea. I need to check with Amelia. See if he's been doing the same to her," Aidan said.

He wondered for a moment if the man she had been seeing had broken up with her for reasons similar to what had just happened. Unlikely, as her father had just arrived on the island.

After Christmas, just a few weeks ago, she'd had another breakup.

Unless it was the same guy.

God, he didn't know.

Aidan might tease her about being a starving artist—which was so far from the truth it wasn't funny—but she *was* a dramatic creative soul.

She fell in love, even when she wasn't really in love. And with that came tears and heartache.

Which usually lasted forty-eight hours.

Seventy-two if she was enjoying the attention and pampering from her brothers.

He would speak to Logan and find out what the fuck was going on with their father.

Lily didn't deserve to be dragged into it and treated like a lower-class citizen because her bank account had seven fewer zeros than theirs.

If his father wanted to throw digits around, Aidan would win.

His fortune was greater than all the men in the family. His invention reached nearly every person on the planet, and money poured into his account like a rushing river. Aidan had double-digit billions and kept pretty quiet about it.

Even Logan wouldn't know his exact net worth.

Hell, even Aidan didn't.

It grew every hour with interest and investment. The latter was managed by a team of people, and they were paid handsomely for their skills and confidence.

All of that could wait. Aidan needed to check on Lily.

"Where is everyone?" Jacob glanced around at the almost diminished crowd.

"Bed," Blake laughed. "Breaking news. There is a wedding tomorrow."

"Fuck that. Let's head into Lahaina," Jacob said. "The night is still young."

When you were twenty-two, like Jacob was, the night was just beginning. The mood Aidan was in, he was on board.

"You know what? Good idea. Let's get the fuck out of here," Aidan said. "A few shots of tequila sound like a much better idea than dragging my father out of bed and giving him a black eye."

"Much," Daniel said, slapping him on the shoulder. "Have fun, boys. I'm going to take my wife to bed. Behave."

Blake and Jacob smirked.

"No more media chicks. And make sure you're home and sober for the wedding."

"Someone told me you were fun," Blake teased and ducked when Daniel threw a fake jab at him.

"They lied."

Aidan let out a laugh. His mood was lightening up already. A few more shots and things would feel a lot better. He wasn't a big drinker, but his emotions were feeling all over the place.

"Give me ten or fifteen minutes to speak with Lily," Aidan said. "Book an Uber and I'll see you out front."

CHAPTER SIXTEEN

Lily walked into her room and shut the door. She leaned against the back of it and the tear that had been threatening to spill fell down her cheek.

She wiped it away angrily.

Stupid tears.

She wasn't sad. What she was, was mad. How dare that man speak to her like that?

Lily already felt like a fraud being in Hawaii with the Dufort family. For Aidan's father to call her out like that in front of everyone was embarrassing.

Worse, Aidan just stood there and said nothing.

Because he agreed.

All the talk about seeing her again, and he saw her as nothing more than some poor girl from the South Side.

Well, fuck him.

Lily wished she were more like Harper or Emma. Or any one of the women in the house right now. They would have had some clever come back or called Andrew out for his rudeness.

She'd never been like that.

It was why she let Matt get away with the things he did. She didn't like confrontation. It was better to just stay quiet, keep the peace, and walk away.

Because it never ended there.

The person usually had some clever or harsh comeback, and her brain just didn't work that fast. This time, though, Lily wished she would have found her voice. Just for five seconds.

I hope you don't have your sights set on either of these boys.

Smart girl. This family is not for everyone.

What he was saying, and everyone knew it, was Lily wasn't good enough for the Dufort family.

Correction.

Andrew was saying she wasn't good enough for Aidan.

She'd seen Aidan's father when they got off the bus. He'd shot a dark look at his son and Lily had immediately felt uncomfortable. It was as if he knew there was something going on between them.

Had Aidan told him?

Lily had never expected anyone to say anything to them as they were hiding their holiday romance. If you could call it that.

Sex.

That's all it was.

If Aidan had cared, he would have said something to his father.

So now she knew.

If Aidan hadn't understood what she'd meant this morning, now he did. She didn't belong with these people. And sadly, that included Emma now.

Their lives were drifting apart.

When she left Hawaii, she would think about all that more. Now she had to focus on being her bridesmaid and hope that the horrible man kept away from her.

Anyway, it wasn't just her bank balance that made her feel alien among this family.

Lily had lived a sheltered life. Even her PA job only saw her travel thirty minutes from home. Unlike Emma, who had moved into the city, traveled around the country and to London and Melbourne for book conferences, Lily still went to the same grocery store, the same pharmacy, and walked the same streets as she had growing up.

Did she want more?

Honestly, she'd never thought about it. One minute she was at high school, the next she was helping her parents with their bills, and then her dad was diagnosed with cancer.

Colon cancer.

At only fifty-three.

Occasionally, when she was riding on the bus to work, Lily daydreamed about what she might do when—if—she got her teaching degree.

She imagined herself in Paris, dressed like Audrey Hepburn in a Chanel dress and hat, black pumps, and a long cigarette—well, not the cigarette—and striding through the streets swinging a beautiful handbag. Leaving the scent of Chanel no.5 behind her.

It was silly.

She always stopped there, thinking herself a fool for dreaming so big. First, the flights to France were way out of her budget and she couldn't even afford a bottle of Chanel no.5. The closest she got was sneaking a spray when she was in the Macy's department store when the retail assistant wasn't looking.

Visualize and dream it. Then you will create it.

She'd seen that on a bumper sticker once.

Good one.

It wasn't that simple, and life wasn't made of magical Lego pieces.

But then she'd see a friend on social media traveling to a faraway place, or they'd met an Australian man and were giving birth to their first child. One girl from her high school had won bronze in the damn Olympics.

If that wasn't magic, then wow.

Others had created companies and their careers were flying.

It was easy to make excuses, but all of them had come from the South Side of Chicago just like her.

Heck, even her best friend Emma had become a bestselling author and was marrying a billionaire.

Lily was still just Lily.

She sighed, walked over to the bed, and flopped down, staring at the ceiling. The only difference she could see between her and everyone else was the choices and actions they took each day.

It wasn't magic.

Although maybe there *was* a slither of luck involved.

But it couldn't show up if you just kept doing the same thing every day. Like she was.

Aidan was right.

She could've changed jobs. She could've signed up for the teacher's training and invested in her future. It would've meant she didn't have the money to help her family and because of that, Lily had no regrets.

She didn't know how much longer her dad had and both she and her mom were as prepared as they could for the day when it came.

It would be sooner rather than later.

He didn't have years.

It might be months.

So perhaps there was something serendipitous about this vacation. Perhaps Andrew Dufort had just given her a gift.

Delivered harshly, yes, but it was giving her the motivation to really reach for her dreams.

One day—and she was in no hurry—she would pursue her dreams and become a teacher. And dammit, she was going to go to Paris and sip coffee in a café while watching the beautiful French women in their Chanel and Karl Lagerfeld dresses go about their fabulous French lives.

So fuck Andrew Dufort and fuck Aidan for not standing up for her, but she was pretty sure they had both done her a favor and one day she would thank them.

Just not this weekend.

And not to their face.

Lily pushed off the bed and had just walked toward the bathroom when she heard a knock at the door.

"Lily," Aidan called out in a loud hush.

"Go away," she replied, standing in the doorway of the bathroom, which was only a few feet from her door.

"Open the door," he ordered.

She groaned.

She had known he would come to her eventually, whether it was tonight or tomorrow. He was so bossy there was no point in ignoring him.

Lily whipped open the door and put one hand on her hip, the other hand she used to wave out in front of her.

"Well, come in. Say what you have to say." She sighed.

Wow. Maybe she did have a little sass in her.

Aidan gave her an odd look, then stepped inside and closed the door. "Are you okay?"

"No. But I will be," she replied. And that was all he needed to know.

When he stepped forward to touch her, she stepped back.

"You have one minute, Aidan. Then you need to leave. I have to call my dad and then get some sleep," Lily said.

When her phone beeped, Aidan's eyes drifted over to the bed where it lay.

"I think we both know that isn't your father."

CHAPTER SEVENTEEN

Aidan's patience was wearing thin.

Which was ironic, given he had no right to be possessive of the woman standing in front of him. Yet fucking Handsy Matt and his constant messaging were pushing him right to the edge.

But he had to focus.

He was here to apologize for his father's abhorrent behavior and make sure Lily was okay.

Which she clearly wasn't.

"If my boss wants to message me while I'm on vacation, that's none of your business," Lily said, crossing her arms.

A physical barrier.

In other words, she didn't want him touching her.

Aidan didn't blame her after what Andrew had said. But not touching her wasn't fucking happening.

He tugged her arms apart and growled softly, "Lily."

Her barriers began to crumble.

"You said nothing," she cried. "Nothing, Aidan."

"I should have," he admitted. "I thought I'd make it worse. Honestly, he caught me by surprise."

A crappy excuse, but true, nevertheless.

"Yeah, well, so was I. So was Blake," Lily said. "But the message was received loud and clear."

Aidan flinched. "Listen—"

Lily shook her head. "You don't need to say anything. I know this is just sex. I never said I wanted to be a part of your life."

He clenched his teeth.

Neither had he asked her to be, but Lily was making it very clear she didn't want to see him once they left the tropical islands.

Aidan wasn't sure he believed her.

Hell, he was mature enough to know not every woman wanted him, but then again, he also had enough life experience to know the difference between wanting to dominate and own a woman. Whether for a few hours or a night.

With Lily, he wanted to fold her up and slip her into his back pocket and keep her.

What he wanted to know was if she was reacting from hurt, after what his father had said, or if she truly didn't have any other feelings developing for him.

Because he fucking did.

And this wasn't over because Andrew had made some remarks that frankly didn't align with anyone else in the family.

Aidan glanced at his hands circling her wrists and felt the sudden desire to bind them and push her up against the wall with them above her head, then rip up her skirt and fuck her.

Claim her.

"I never said I didn't want you to be in my life, Lily," Aidan said.

What was he saying?

Did he want her to be his girlfriend?

Okay, I haven't thought this through.

"Stop. I'm here for Emma as her bridesmaid. That's it," Lily said. "You are an intoxicatingly handsome man, Aidan Dufort."

His nostrils flared.

"The way you look at me like you want to eat me for dinner is incredibly arousing. I've never met anyone like you. Never been desired by a man like you do."

Oh, baby, you have no idea.

He took a step closer, her back pressing against the wall.

"Keep talking," Aidan said, lifting her hands above her head. "And keep these up here."

She shook her head.

"Forget my father. Forget what he said. He's an asshole," Aidan said, running his hand across her collarbone and down the side of her breast. "I want you, Lily. More of you. Here. And when we get home."

Her breath hitched as he circled around and ran his knuckles over her nipple.

"Don't you feel this?" His gaze lifted to hers.

"You make me feel so…sexy,"

He reached under her short sundress and reached inside her panties.

"Naughty," she groaned as Aidan pressed his body against hers and his fingers slid through her wet, warm flesh.

"Aroused," she added.

The heel of his palm rubbed against her clit as his middle finger entered her. Then Aidan tugged down the top of Lily's dress, exposing one needy puckered nipple.

He pinched it, and her body quivered.

"Here, I thought you were a good girl. I was wrong. You're a bad girl, Lily. I think you want me to do lots of bad things to you," he rasped.

"Yes." She closed her eyes, moaning and arching into him.

She was soaking, and he wasn't going to waste it. Aidan pulled out his hand, spun her, and ripped her panties down her leg.

"Spread your legs," he ordered harshly and pushed his shorts down.

His cock sprung free.

"I'm going to fuck you, peaches. Hands on the wall."

"Oh God, oh God, Aidan," she cried with her face squashed against the wood.

In one thrust, he was inside her.

"Jesus fucking hell,"

Once again, she felt incredible. Her pussy tight, clenching his cock as he continued to go deeper.

Aidan took in her tiny body, with his enormous one enveloping her, and felt an animalistic need to protect. It was a predator claim, one he knew he couldn't stop.

Lily was his.

And no one was going to get in his way.

"Baby, it's just you and me," Aidan said against her neck, licking along her warm, tanned skin. "No one is going to hurt you again, you hear me?"

Thrust.

"Yes," Lily gasped.

"This pussy is mine. Your heart is mine," he heard himself say.

What?

He slammed into her, pounding harder and faster, their flesh slapping together. "And then I'll steal your soul."

"Aidan," she cried out.

"Give me your orgasm, Lily. Scream for me. Let them all fucking hear that you belong to me."

Only mildly aware he was out of control, Aidan didn't care. Right here, right now, he needed his semen inside her, to mark her so no one tried to harm her again.

Not Handsy, Matt, or his father.

"Mphfphknoof, my God," she cried out as he sunk his teeth into her neck.

Heat sped down his spine as his balls tightened and his seed rushed from his thick cock, filling her as he climaxed.

Aidan pressed against her, both of them panting, until she nudged at him.

"Sorry," he said, realizing he was squashing her, and then felt his come leak as he pulled out. Scooping her up, he went to the bathroom, grabbed a cloth, and began to clean her.

"Stop. I need to shower."

Aidan used the washcloth and wiped himself as Lily turned the shower on and tugged off her dress. When he went to pull her into his arms, she shook her head and wouldn't look at him.

"Lil…"

The hell?

"Nothing has changed, Aidan," she said, her voice laced with regret.

"Bullshit. Look at me," he ordered.

Her eyes lifted to his.

"This is something. You know it is."

More fucking shaking of her pretty little head.

"I have a life in Chicago. My dad. My dreams. You know I don't belong in your world," Lily said.

The fuck she doesn't.

Okay, maybe she doesn't…

Aidan cursed.

She placed a palm on his chest. "I need to sleep. Go. We can talk when we get back to Oahu on Tuesday."

Two fucking days. She expected him to just stand back and leave her alone for two days?

"Tomorrow. After the wedding," Aidan countered. "I am not staying away from you, Lily. If you think I'm a man who will just give up, then you don't know me."

She smiled at him knowingly.

Oh, right? She didn't know him. That was the point.

Shit.

He turned away and slammed his hands down on the bathroom counter, letting out a frustrated growl. Then he spun back around and gripped her face.

"One day," Aidan said. "I'll give you one fucking day, Lily. Then you're mine."

Aidan didn't wait for her response. He knew she had doubts and concerns. Well, she could keep a hold of them for twenty-fucking-four hours. Then he was going to blast them all to smithereens.

Because once his brother was married and they were on their own back on Oahu, they were going to have a talk about their relationship.

Jesus, was he the only man on this planet forcing a conversation about feelings?

Fucking felt like it.

Aidan slammed his mouth done on hers. "Sleep well, peaches. You will need it tomorrow night."

Her hand went to her mouth, her eyes full of confusion, as he backed away.

Then he tugged up his shorts and left.

FOUR STEPS DOWN the hall, he came face to face with his brother.

Crap.

Logan lifted his brow.

"Nice acoustics." Logan put his hand on his hip and lifted a brow as he leaned against the wall.

Ignoring the dig, because yeah, he'd known people would hear, Aidan said, "Thought you were retired for the evening."

"My bride is in bed. My job was to make sure she got there before midnight. Mission accomplished." Logan shrugged and pushed away from the wall. "I was heading out for another drink with my little brother and instead heard him praying to God."

Aidan let out a snort.

"I haven't been little since we were kids, and yeah, shit went down tonight. I had to make it right," he said, pushing past him.

Logan followed. "By fucking our bridesmaid."

"Yes. As a matter of fact," Aidan said, grabbing his wallet and phone off the kitchen counter as they walked past.

Logan continued to follow him through the house and then slowed as he saw Blake and Jacob outside, waiting for him. "Are we going somewhere?"

Yeah. They were. He needed a stiff drink more than ever now.

Aidan turned and lay his hand on his brother's shoulder. "Come on. We'll update you in the car. We're going into Lahaina."

"And here I thought I wasn't getting a bachelor party." Logan smirked.

Oh boy.

He might be apologizing to Emma tomorrow.

CHAPTER EIGHTEEN

That wasn't how Lily saw the conversation with Aidan going. Then again, nothing with that sexy man seemed to go the way she expected.

Certainly not meeting his father.

Andrew Dufort hadn't spoken to her at the engagement party three months ago in Philadelphia, but then again, it had been a much larger affair.

Tonight had been a small family event and for some reason he had clearly felt it necessary to let her know she wasn't welcome in their family if she had her sights set on his son.

Had she?

Lily stepped out of the shower and felt her core muscles twinge. A reminder that said son had just well and truly fucked her.

And told her she belonged to him.

She didn't bother arguing with him. First, he'd been drinking, and secondly, everyone knew men like him—rich, attractive men who got what they wanted—didn't like being told no.

She was going home to Chicago, and they both knew he'd lose interest after a few days. He'd get on with his life, meet a new challenge, and be sleeping with someone else way before she'd gotten over him.

Lily wasn't going to lie to herself. The way he made her feel was incredible.

She'd never orgasmed so hard or so much in her life. And the way he stood and walked beside her in such a protective manner was intoxicating. Even his kisses made her feel like she was the most precious thing on earth.

It was addictive, and she'd be a fool to say she didn't love it. And want him.

She did.

But Lily was pragmatic.

The entire thing was messing with her brain. She knew she was right, that Aidan would move on, and yet as she'd sat on the beach wearing one of her new hats last night, he'd shot her a wink. One that said, *I fucking bought that for you and I'm proud as punch.*

Despite his immeasurable wealth.

Later on, back in her hotel suite, Aidan had lifted on and asked her if it was her favorite.

"They all are," she said, leaving out *because you got them for me.*

He was such a contradiction.

Lily had no idea why Aidan had singled her out and wanted her. She was just a girl from the South Side of Chicago.

She didn't even own a car.

The most valuable thing in her life—except her family— was her sketches. They might not be worth anything, but she'd been doing it all her life, and they were her way of expressing herself when there was no one else to share her feelings with. And capturing moments that meant something to her.

Like she had last night on Waikiki Beach. Drawing the scene in front of her, and when Aidan finally stopped watching her, she'd outlined his incredible profile.

So, she had nothing of value besides her easel pencils and paints. And her butterfly pendant her dad had bought her for her twenty-first birthday.

One she would wear forever.

Reaching for a towel, she patted herself down and then twisted her hair up into a wet, messy bun. Then she straightened her necklace, so it sat perfectly on her collarbone and headed back out to the bedroom.

Lily located her phone, flopped onto the bed, and scrolled. Then pressed send on her dad's number.

After a dozen rings, she pressed end.

Then she tried her mom's phone.

The same thing happened.

Weird.

She chewed her lips. It was early morning in Chicago, so unless they were having a sleep-in, which they'd never done in her life, something was wrong.

Lily called the housephone, and it just rang.

A chill crept down her spine.

She flipped her legs over the bed and stared at the wall, her heart pounding.

It's fine, it's fine. They are probably sleeping.

"Fuck," she muttered, knowing they weren't.

Counting to thirty, she tried her mom's phone again. Finally, she answered.

"Mom. Jesus. You frightened me." Lily smiled. "I've been calling. God, I was freaking out. I know, *calm down, Lily.* But you know. I'm here in Hawaii. Freaking out."

"Hi, Lily." Her mom's voice was quiet.

No.

"Mom?"

"It's okay, darling. We're at the hospital with your dad."

Lily stood up abruptly. "What? When?"

Her mom began to speak, but she interrupted, her brain exploding with the worst-case scenario.

"When. Why? What… is what happened?"

"Breathe. I'm here with your dad. We had to call an ambulance during the night."

Oh, my God.

"Why didn't you call me?" she screeched, her voice breaking like a teenage boy.

There was silence.

"Mom…" Tears filled her eyes. "Is he dead?"

"No, baby girl. No. But it won't be long, they think. I'm sorry, I wanted you to enjoy your holiday."

Lily almost vomited.

Her legs gave way underneath her, and she collapsed back on the bed.

"You don't get to make that decision," she cried as Emma came flying into her room, blinking awake.

Lily figured she'd made a lot of noise.

More than before.

"What is it?" Emma asked quietly.

"Dad's in the hospital," Lily said, sobbing.

Emma took the phone and put it on speaker. "Mrs. Peterson, I'm here with Lily. What's happened?"

"Hello, Emma sweetheart. It's his liver. His body is giving up. Lily, it's time, and I'm sorry I didn't call. I wanted to save you this pain and guilt, being so far away."

Her heart broke.

Oh my God.

The doctors had told them when this first happened that it could be a matter of hours, days, or at best, weeks.

Her father was dying.

"How long does he have?" Emma asked.

She could hear her mom crying.

"Oh, Mom, I'm sorry," Lily said, falling against Emma as she wrapped her arm around her.

"A day. Maybe a couple more. They don't know, but he won't be coming home."

She began to sob.

She hated that she was here in Hawaii worrying about what stupid Andrew Dufort thought of her while her father was dying, and her mom was all alone with him.

Well, fuck that.

There was no way she was staying here while there was a smidgeon of a chance she could get there before he took his last breath. She jumped up and started packing, throwing her things into her suitcase.

"Mom, hang up. I'm coming home. I need to use my phone to book a flight," Lily said as she tossed her clothes, toiletries, and shoes haphazardly into the black case.

"Lily, no."

"Forget it. He's my father. Tell him I will be there as soon as I can and to hang on for me," Lily cried, tears falling down her face. "Please, Mom."

There was a moment of silence, then her mom said, "I'll tell him. But, Lil, he might not be able to and that doesn't mean he loves you any less."

Her eyes shot to Emma. A guttural cry left her throat as tears poured down her cheeks.

"Have a beautiful day tomorrow, Emma," her mom said.

"Thank you, Mrs. Peterson," Emma replied. "I'll get Lily home safely."

Lily looked up as Emma ended the call.

God, she'd totally forgotten. But there was no question what she had to do here. "I'm sorry, Em. I just have—"

Emma held her hand up. "Don't even say it. He's your dad. You have to go. Let me get the jet ready for you."

Lily shook her head. "Oh, God. No,"

"It will be faster. And more private. You don't want to be crammed in with hundreds of other people feeling like this. If I could, I would go with you." Emma said, halfway out the door. She stopped in the doorway. "Finish packing and I'll organize everything."

Lily let out a sob.

"We will get you there to see him one last time," Emma said and pulled her into a tight embrace. They both knew she couldn't promise anything, just as her mom couldn't, but Lily appreciated her friend trying.

Ten minutes later, a shirtless Daniel was standing in the living room, his hand rubbing the back of his head. He was staring at her while speaking into the phone.

Lily sat on the sofa, her luggage packed and ready, while her leg bounced up and down. Harper and Emma were on either side of her, rubbing her arms.

Daniel hung up and frowned at Harper. "Baby, put some clothes on."

Lily glanced down and saw Harper had a very lacy and sexy blue nightie.

Harper waved at him. "You're half naked. So, what's happening?"

"The jet will be here in an hour," Daniel said. "I'll organize a car. They will need to do a few things before they take off, but you should be home by early evening in Chicago."

Eight or nine hours.

Lily nodded. "Thank you. I'll—"

She was going to offer to pay for…um something. But let's face it, there's no way she could even afford the food aboard a Dufort private jet.

"Nothing," Emma interrupted. "Just get home and focus on your dad. Draw him a picture."

"Sketch," she muttered.

"Yup, that." Emma smiled.

Lily wondered where Logan was. He was likely asleep, and Emma hadn't wanted to interrupt him. Aidan hadn't come out, and while nothing mattered except getting home, she thought he'd have heard her cry and ventured out.

Lily lowered her face into her hands. What if she couldn't get there fast enough? She didn't regret coming to Hawaii. It could have happened at any time, but damn Murphy's Law.

For a brief moment, she wished Aidan was holding her, and wondered if she should wake him.

At least to say goodbye.

She realized then just how safe and wanted he made her feel. That damn protective and over-possessive way he had about him would feel really nice right now.

She glanced at her phone, which was tucked tightly in her hands in case her mom phoned, and considered going down to his room. But then realized that was a bad idea.

While she was overwhelmed with fear and panic about her dad, a slither of sadness slipped in. It was over between them.

What she and Aidan had shared—it was over.

She'd never feel his mouth, his body, or those dominant green eyes on hers again.

This was how it was meant to end.

Her Hawaiian romance was over.

CHAPTER NINETEEN

"Dude, it's mahalo, not *well hallo there*." Aidan snorted and tripped on the step as they made their way back into the Maui beachfront property. "It means thank you."

Blake grabbed his arm and steadied him. Which was about as useless as the glass of water he'd had to sober himself up.

Completely useless.

Oops.

He'd had seven shots of tequila in a row and wasn't sorry.

"I would've thanked her very much if she'd invited me home," Blake shared. "All of that long, dark hair would wrap nicely around my fist."

Aidan shot him a smirk.

"Praise kink much?" Aidan teased, and Blake shrugged.

Yeah, he did.

"Guys, keep it down," Logan said, tripping over the same step he had. "Fuck,"

Jarod, Blake, and Aidan laughed.

They pushed open the door and walked inside the house. It was dark and quiet.

"I think those two would've been up for a multi," Jarod said, flopping down onto the sofa. "Couldn't you have pushed the wedding out a day, Logan?"

"Sorry to disrupt your sex life, asshole," Logan drawled and tossed them all a bottle of water from the fridge.

Most of them landed short and on the floor.

More laughing.

"If I have a hangover, you'll be apologizing to my bride."

"Take some vitamins and toughen up, old man," Blake said, twisting open his cap.

"So you two multi?" Aidan asked, far more interested in that conversation.

"No. We don't," Blake said firmly. "I don't want any cocks belonging to my family near me when I'm fucking."

Jacob shrugged. "There are ways. You need to explore more."

Aidan shot a humorous glance over at Logan, who was shaking his head.

"My exploring is going just fucking fine, thanks, bro. Just keep your dick to yourself." Blake scowled.

Aidan laughed loudly.

"You into group stuff?" Blake asked.

"Nope," Aidan replied with a pop. "I'm way too dominant for that. I want my girl all to myself."

Lily.

Not any girl.

Being away from her tonight, even for a few hours, had created a yearning inside him he'd never felt before. She was special. He was really beginning to accept it.

Would she?

Aidan had nearly messaged her twice in the first half hour, so he'd turned his phone off. Drunk texting Lily would only scare her off.

Was she dreaming of him right now?

Aidan wondered if she was sore after slamming his dick into her tonight. He hadn't prepared her enough. In a sadistic way, he hoped she was aching. Thinking of him while she tossed and turned in her sleep.

God, he wanted to walk down the hall and take that petite body of hers in his arms and sink his hard cock inside her again.

Tomorrow was Logan and Emma's wedding. He would let her sleep. She had a job to do.

But then afterward, as promised, she was his.

"What girl? Lily?" Blake smirked.

Aidan used his bottle to point at his cousin. "You stop talking. I'm going to bed."

"About fucking time," Logan said, joining him when he stood and walked out of the room.

"Aides," Blake called out. "She's a nice girl. Andrew might've been an asshole, but he might not be completely wrong. This is a different world from hers."

Aidan turned and glared at Blake.

"Let it go," Logan growled quietly.

He had. He'd been thinking about it all night. In between every tequila shot. In between every girl who tried to flirt with him.

In between every moment, he reached for his phone and then made true on his promise to leave her for tonight.

"Maybe I don't want a girl who fits in. Maybe I want one who stands out," Aidan replied.

"Go to bed," Logan called out and nudged him into the hall. They stopped outside their bedroom doors and stared at one another.

It wasn't always obvious to others, but he and Logan were close. Really fucking close.

"Don't get divorced again. I don't want to have to drag your ass back to the club." Aidan did a little wobble.

"Fuck you," Logan replied. Then they grinned at each other and man-hugged.

"Go get your beauty sleep. You look terrible." Aidan slapped him on the back and then walked to his room.

And face-planted his bed.

His last thought was of the pretty submissive blonde down the end of the hall and how he was going to make her scream like a goddess tomorrow night.

He wasn't letting her get away.

He wanted the whole damn peach tree.

Well...he'd work on a better line when he was sober. That probably wasn't as romantic as it sounded in his head.

FIVE HOURS AND thirty-three brief minutes later, Aidan stepped out of his room and headed straight for the coffee machine.

There were way too many voices in this house.

He'd already taken a few Tylenol tabs, but it was going to take a lot more than that.

"Hello, sweetheart," his Aunty Samantha said, kissing his cheek.

"You fly in this morning?" Aidan asked as Amelia fought him for the coffee jug. "Aimes. I swear to God, not today."

His sister stepped aside, and he stared at her while the rich dark liquid filled his mug. Then frowned.

It wasn't like her to give up so easily.

"Yes, I flew overnight," his aunt said and began to explain why she had been delayed, but he was barely listening.

"Morning kids," Andrew announced loudly.

Fucker.

"Dad," Aidan replied, not bothering to look at him. "Is breakfast still being served?" he asked the room, not caring who answered.

He added some cream and sugar, stirred it, and then Amelia rubbed his back and gave him a small smile.

What in the fuck?

The next minute, his mom walked in from outside and waved her hand in front of her face. "Lord, it's hot outside already. I'm going to check on Emma. The poor dear."

Why? Because she was marrying his brother?

Amused with his own private joke, Aidan took a long sip of his coffee, then headed outside. Everyone was seated around the table while the wedding planners set up the rest of the yard.

Servers were still clearing the table and delivering plates. Thank God.

"What can I get you, sir?"

"Everything. Eggs. Bacon. Mushrooms. Tomato. More coffee. Toast. A roast chicken. Everything," Aidan said.

Jacob and Blake burst out laughing across from him.

"Sir, I'm not sure we have chicken," the server explained, confused. "But I can check,"

"I'm messing with you. Just a full breakfast, please," Aidan said, smirking at his cousins.

Young fuckers.

They didn't look hungover at all.

Daniel stretched out his arms, yawning, and tossed his napkin on top of his plate. "What a night. That's one way of getting out of being a best man."

Aidan narrowed his eyes.

"I'm not *that* hungover. I'm still going to do my job," Aidan shot back. "Logan was with me, so he's half to blame."

Daniel stared at him and then laughed. "Not you. Me. Although you do look like shit."

Rude.

But fair.

"Why are you not standing up today?" he asked, wondering if he'd woken in an alternative universe.

Amelia sat down next to him.

"With Lily gone, Emma only has one bridesmaid, so she said I could sit this one out and when Logan finally gets up, he'd agree."

What?

"I offered, but Lily took the dress with her," Amelia said, rubbing his thigh affectionately under the table. "I liked her. She was nice."

What?

Aidan glanced from face to face.

"Gone where?" Blake asked.

"Chicago," Daniel said. "She flew out in the middle of the night on my jet."

The fuck?

His father walked out and sat down with a platter of fruit.

Finally, his brain began to pick up speed, and he blinked, clearing away the fog of confusion.

Lily was gone.

Fucking gone.

"I'm sorry. Did you say Lily packed up and left in the middle of the night? And flew home in your jet? The one that was parked on Oahu. And she flew home to Chicago?" Aidan asked slowly.

Was that what his cousin was saying?

No.

No fucking way.

"Her father is dying, Aidan. Of course I did," Daniel replied, as if he was completely unreasonable. "I wasn't going to send her home in coach, for God's sakes."

Aidan pushed his chair back, and it grated against the outdoor tiles.

Amelia turned.

Lily is gone.

"Aidan," his father began, but he ignored him and raced inside the house, looking for his phone. It was in his jeans lying on the floor. Powered off, and the battery was dead.

Mother fucker.

He plugged it in and waited a long minute for it to do its thing and finally turn on.

No messages.

"Fuck!" he cried, slamming his fist down on the bedside table and shit went flying. "Fuck, fuck, fuck."

She hadn't even said goodbye.

And he couldn't leave.

CHAPTER TWENTY

Lily closed her eyes as the jet landed on the runway. The bumps almost jolted her out of the nightmare she was in.

Except this was her life.

Her dad was dying.

For over ten hours, since leaving the Maui beachfront property, Lily had been in transit.

She'd said goodbye to Emma, then traveled to the airport with Daniel and Harper, who had got her settled in on the plane.

The waiting to take off had been painful.

Now, after an eight-hour flight, directly from Maui to Chicago, she was home.

It was already after two in the afternoon in Chicago, and it looked freezing outside. Because it was. There was snow on the ground. Thankfully, Emma had reminded her to pull her winter coat out before she left the house.

Daniel had booked a car to collect her and take her directly to the hospital. Or his secretary did. Right now, she was on track to arrive by four p.m. and was hoping like hell her dad was still alive.

Hang in there, Dad.

It was nine a.m. back in Hawaii. They'd all be excitedly preparing for the wedding. Lily couldn't believe she'd gone all the way to Maui only to have this happen.

It was something to consider another day. Right now, she was bone tired.

Lily had tried to sleep during the flight, and she had. Sort of. Thoughts of Aidan and her father merging together in a confusing movie had played in her dreams.

She'd awoken with tears in her eyes at one point.

One fucking night, Lily, and then you are mine.

She reminded herself he hadn't been sober, and he was a wealthy, gorgeous man who wasn't used to being told no.

Aidan would soon forget her.

After watching his father intimidate and humiliate her, his reaction last night was one of guilt. Nothing more.

Still, Lily wished they'd had the opportunity to say goodbye. Despite her cynicism, she had enjoyed their time together and was realizing with every mile now between them, and every hour that passed, just how much she liked him.

They had connected. She couldn't deny that.

But it didn't change the fundamental barriers and differences between them.

Lily's mind was way too full, and her emotions were raw right now, knowing she had to say goodbye to her dad. When she'd caught her breath, she would text him to say goodbye and wish him well.

Even if something deep inside her curled up in a little ball and felt a much bigger loss than she was ever expecting.

Today, nothing mattered except getting to the hospital to see her dad. Everything else could wait.

Everything and everyone.

Well, except Matt.

Lily had messaged her boss to let him know it was unlikely she'd be back at work on Wednesday because her father was in hospital.

Matt knew her dad was ill. He'd replied, asking if she needed a ride from the airport and if he could do anything.

Lily thought that was very nice.

She'd thanked him and declined.

She couldn't afford very much time off, but there was no way she was going to work and leaving her dad's bedside. Or the day after he died. Her mom had said it would happen anytime, so Lily would dig into her savings and use the rest of her leave.

Lily pulled her bag onto her shoulder, collected her carry on, and thanked the flight crew as she descended the Dufort jet.

As her feet hit the tarmac, she glanced back at the black aircraft and let out a long sigh, taking in the last of her incredible Hawaiian adventure and farewelling the lavish lifestyle and extravagant travel.

It was safe to say she would never fly first class again. Or on a private jet.

Goodbye, Aidan.

What a wild few days it had been.

Perhaps one day she would meet another man like him. Someone successful, who came from humble beginnings.

Someone who would sweep her off her feet and stick up for her if anyone tried to make her feel less than she deserved.

Maybe that man would be in Paris when she finally visited.

First, she had to get her bachelor's degree in education. Then she could start planning her wedding to Pierre or Francois, or whoever her future husband might be.

Aidan's dark eyes came flashing into her mind.

If you think I'm a man who will give up, then you don't know me.

Lily shivered and watched her luggage being loaded into the SUV. She wrapped her coat around her tightly, shaking off Aidan's words.

But they wouldn't fade away.

He hadn't meant them.

Had he?

"This way, please, ma'am," the driver said, and she climbed into the back seat. The heat was very welcome and was a reminder she had left the tropical island breezes behind. And with them, the tall, dark, handsome man who kissed like a God.

An hour later, Lily was walking into her father's hospital room. Her mom leaped up and enveloped her in a tight embrace and began to sob.

"Is he still alive?"

CHAPTER TWENTY-ONE

Aidan considered his hangover a blessing in the end. If he hadn't been feeling so dehydrated and groggy, he knew he would've started drinking early and made some poor decisions.

He wasn't a huge drinker.

Like most of the Dufort men, Aidan loved a good drop of Macallan. Even a nice cold vodka.

Today, though, after learning Lily had left and not messaged him, he was furious with her.

Worse, he was angry with himself for not being home. Then he blamed his father for causing his angst the night before and going to Lahaina in the first place.

If he'd been at the house, he would've heard what happened and been able to…

What?

Go with her?

That wasn't an option. But he could've said goodbye and told her he would be with her in Chicago after the wedding.

Except it was bluntly obvious Lily didn't want that.

Not one fucking message.

Aidan let that sink in. Lily didn't need him.

He stood staring out the window as Logan did up his shirt behind him.

"Just call her, Aidan."

"No." He turned. "She needs to focus on her father. Dealing with me is the least of her problems."

Obviously.

He got it. He did. But that didn't mean it didn't sting.

Aidan could have taken care of her. He could have arranged the jet and paid for her to get home.

Instead, another man had done it while he was off in a bar drinking merrily.

What an asshole.

Lily was his.

Aidan didn't know how or why, he just knew. Like he knew the day of the week, he just knew.

In the past, he fucked women and moved on.

With Lily, he'd bought her silly sun hats, soothed her bruises with Arnica cream, got her medical care—the morning-after pill but whatever—and then failed to be there when she needed him the most.

God damn her father for choosing this exact moment in time to leave his life.

Hey, asshole…

"Call her. Your face doesn't match your words," Logan said, turning to check his wedding attire in the floor-length mirror. "I don't want you snarling in our wedding photos."

Aidan snorted.

Then he looked in the mirror himself and was shocked. Staring back at him was a man ready to commit murder.

"It's okay to care. It's okay to like her," Logan said. "Blake was right, though. Lily isn't like Emma or even Harper. She doesn't fit in our world, Aides. Call her. Say goodbye. Wish her well. Then get back on the horse."

Fuck the horse.

"I'm going to check on Emma. I'll give you ten minutes," Logan said.

"Wait. It's bad luck to see the bride before the wedding," Aidan warned him.

"We just had lunch together." Logan laughed. "Plus, it can't be any fucking worse than my first marriage." Logan stilled and pointed at him. "Repeat that to Emma, and I will kill you."

Aidan smiled for the first time today.

"Go. I'll make the call, so your wedding photos don't suck."

Logan shot him a smile and walked out.

Shit.

What did he say? He wasn't saying goodbye, that's for sure. But hearing her voice might help, so Aidan pulled his phone out of his pocket and snarled at the blank screen.

Still no messages from her.

It was nearly three in the afternoon in Maui, making it almost nine in Chicago. Late.

Stop looking for excuses.

He scrolled to her number and pressed the green button. His stomach lurched as it rang.

He nearly hung up, realizing he hadn't figured out what to say. He could hardly get mad at her for dropping everything to race to her father's bedside.

This wasn't the time.

Did she really need to hear a heartfelt set of well wishes from him right now?

Hope your father is okay.

He's not.

Then I hope he will be okay.

He won't be.

Then I hope that when this is over, I can fucking see you again because I don't like the idea of never looking into your rich brown eyes. Of never tasting your sweetness. Or never hearing your soft pleas of having my cock inside you.

"Hey. Oh, crap," Lily answered, sounding flustered.

"Lily?" Aidan said, his heart thumping excitedly just hearing her voice.

"Damn. Missed the call," she said. "Just hold this for me."

Who was she talking to?

"Lily," he called out as a rustling noise filled the speaker. "Lily!"

More rustling.

"Oh. Hi. What are you doing here?" Lily asked someone.

"I—" Aidan started, then realized she wasn't talking to him.

Then he heard it. Or rather him.

"I had to come. To see if you needed anything," the man's voice said.

Aidan's jaw tensed.

"That wasn't necessary," Lily replied quietly.

That fucker. Aidan knew who it was.

"Have you eaten?" the man asked and Aidan's teeth ground painfully.

"Just a muesli bar from the machine," she replied.

"Lily, Jesus. Come here," the man said, and Aidan could almost see his outstretched arms.

"Fuck! Lily!" Aidan yelled. "Pick up the phone!"

"Let me get you something to eat," Handsy Matt said.

He knew in his bones it was him.

"Matt, honestly, I'm not hungry," Lily said.

Bingo.

He couldn't listen to another word. Aidan ended the call and threw the phone onto the sofa beside him.

Then let out an animalistic growl and threw his head back.

"Fuck!"

If it was any other goddamn day of his life, he would jump on a plane and fly to Chicago right this minute.

The last thing he wanted was Matt taking advantage of Lily's vulnerability right now.

Maybe he had no right.

Hell, maybe Lily didn't need him or even want him, but there was no way he was going to sit back and let that creep manipulate her.

Aidan made a call to his assistant and had his jet fly to Maui, ready to head to Chicago tonight. After the wedding, he was heading to the Windy City.

AN HOUR LATER, Aidan stood beside his brother, watching Emma walk down the aisle in a fitted mermaid dress. The silver fabric was scattered with shimmering diamonds.

Harper, her one remaining bridesmaid, wore a deep blue strappy short dress. Was Lily's the same? Was that why she was worried about her bruises showing?

Before he knew it, the bride and groom had said their vows.

"I promise to honor and respect, love and cherish you for the rest of my life," Logan finished.

"You better," Emma teased.

Everyone laughed.

Then the rings were slid on each other's fingers while Harper wiped a tear, and Logan scooped up his bride and planted a huge, really inappropriate kiss on her lips.

Good on him.

Jacob let out a whoop and everyone stood and applauded. Music started and servers suddenly appeared as Logan dropped Emma to her feet and they were surrounded by their family.

Aidan didn't drink much knowing he'd be jumping on a late flight, but the champagne flowed enough for him to relax and enjoy his brother's big day.

"Congratulations, bro," he said, hugging Logan a few hours later.

"Thanks." Logan grinned. "She's the best thing that's ever happened to me."

He didn't disagree.

Emma had saved Logan from himself. He might have had his life back on track, or at least his business, but he'd been full of anger, convinced there would be no love in his future.

Aidan had never thought about it much.

He was a scientific man and loved to solve problems. He knew when the time was right, he would find love. Or it would find him.

His father's attempt to hurry him into it with *the right woman* was nothing more than an irritation.

He wanted Lily.

And that was that.

Last night he recalled saying he wanted someone who stood out, not fit in. Ironic really, given Lily was such a wallflower.

But to him, she was as bright as a sunflower.

A sexy submissive and addictive little thing that he wasn't going to let get away.

He hated using the word compliant, but the truth was, it made him fucking hard. Lily was compliant, obedient, and soft. But she also made him think and feel in ways no other woman had, and they barely knew each other.

He had visions of ordering her to sketch while he spread her legs and lapped at her juices. Of her tossing it aside as he flipped her over and fucked her senseless.

Of trying different toys, teaching her pleasures beyond what she knew was possible.

Aidan wanted someone who would stand beside him at events, while he received awards, and also pursue their own career goals.

Someone who would spread their legs and let him take complete control for her pleasure and his.

Someone who looked at him as though he were a God, while playing with her butterfly pendant, and with such intense desire that it took his breath away.

Aidan was sure that someone was Lily.

"You chose a good one this time, brother," Aidan said.

Logan nodded, and they both watched Emma laughing like the blushing bride she was.

Aidan wondered if he was crazy.

Was it just that she'd rejected him?

He didn't really know her.

How could he be so fucking sure in only a few days? Yes, he knew her body. Yes, she made him hard, made him smile, made him do things he wouldn't normally do.

But Lily had also packed up and left, leaving him hanging after he'd told her he wanted her.

If this was his ego, Aidan needed to check it before he went flying across the continental US and demanded she be his.

Then he remembered Matt and his heckles raised on his neck once more. His teeth clenched.

"So, you didn't get hold of her?" Logan asked, sipping his champagne.

"Who?" his father asked, joining them.

"Lily. I didn't get to say goodbye." *Thanks to you.*

Asshole.

If his father hadn't caused the trouble he had, Aidan would have been in her room. He would have been there for her and been able to say goodbye.

Then he'd have clarity.

"Yes. Very sad," Andrew said flippantly. "I'm sure the girl is happy to be by her father's side. That was very generous of Daniel to send her home in his jet."

Aidan lowered his brows and shook his head. "Jesus, Dad."

"What?" Andrew asked. "You know the cost of flying those things."

"Her father is, was—" Fuck, he didn't know. "—Dying. The flight wouldn't have made a dent in Daniel's bank account," Aidan growled.

"Don't be obtuse. You know what I meant," Andrew said.

"Fuck's sake, Dad. Drop it," Logan said.

"I've already transferred the money into his account," Aidan said, and he had.

"Clearly you've fucked the girl," Andrew said.

Exactly how bad would it be to punch my father at my brother's wedding? On a scale of one to ten?

"Hey." Logan poked Andrew in the shoulder with his finger. "Lily is my wife's best friend, so watch what you say."

"Fine. She's a nice girl. I will give her that. But I don't want to see my other son end up with her because she's good with her mouth."

Ding.

He didn't care anymore.

Aidan moved like lightning, but Logan was faster.

He'd barely grabbed his father's shirt before his brother shoved him off and stood between them.

"Dad, get the fuck out of here right now. Or I won't stop him a second time," Logan growled, glaring down into Aidan's face.

"Fight at my fucking wedding and I will never forgive you."

So, a ten.

Aidan stepped back, cursing.

"Go walk it off," Logan said as Emma walked over and joined them. She had her dress scooped up in her hand and a glass of champagne in the other.

"What's going on?" Emma asked as Andrew walked away.

Aidan shook his head. "What the fuck is his problem?"

Logan turned and stared after their father. It looked like their mother was having a go at him about something now. She shook her head and then stormed into the house.

"Should I go?" Emma asked.

"No." Logan held out his hand to stop her. Then turned to him. "Something's not right. I know Dad can be a prick at times, but this is crazy."

Amelia wandered over.

"Aimes, has Dad started on at you about getting married?" Aiden asked.

She nodded and tossed back her champagne.

"Oh yeah. I got a whole lecture two weeks ago, and he tried to set me up on a date with that McKenzie guy. You know, Dad's lawyer's son."

Wow!

"The five-foot-three guy?" Aidan asked.

Amelia nodded slowly.

"Already receding hairline at twenty-seven and... *and*," she emphasized, "he's an accountant."

"Oooh, no." Emma shook her head in disgust. "No, Amelia, you need someone way more dynamic than that."

They were getting off track here.

"My point being, he's been doing the same to me," Aidan shared.

"Parents do that," Emma said. "When they start getting older. Plus, with us getting married, it triggers all the wedding and baby conversations."

Babies.

God.

He needed to think about whether he wanted kids. Lily would. She said she loved kids.

Hell, why hadn't he thought about all this before now? She'd want to know.

"Who does he want you to marry?" Emma asked him.

"Not Lily, that's for sure," Logan said, and as Aidan's eyebrows shot up, he saw the moment his big-mouthed brother realized what he'd done.

"Lily?" Emma asked, laughing, and then her smile faded.

"Oh, boy," Amelia said and began to walk backward. Aidan glared at her. "Gotta go powder my nose and stuff." She disappeared.

Fucking chicken.

"What about Lily?" Emma asked again.

Aidan ran a hand down his face.

"You know what? Why don't we cut the cake and do all the speeches?" Aidan said, trying to step around them.

Emma moved into his path.

"Aidan. Did you sleep with my best friend?" she asked incredulously. "When we told you to stay away from her."

Well.

Yes.

"She's a grown woman, Emma. Lily can make her own decisions," he said, ignoring the dark look Aidan sent him.

"No. I don't think she is." Emma shoved her glass into Logan's hands as he tried to stop her. The next minute her hands were on her hips, and she was taking steps toward him. "You Dufort men do not know how…"

"Handsome?"

"Intoxicating you can be."

"Intoxicating?" Aidan asked, his brows raised and a smile forming.

"Dominant. Pushy. Impossible to say no to."

"Well, that's not true. Women have said no to Logan before." Aidan smirked.

"When?" Logan frowned.

Emma turned and glared at him.

"Sorry, but honestly, never happened." Logan shrugged.

Aidan giggled silently, then shut it down when Emma turned back and glared.

"Listen, Em. Lily was…"

"Innocent," Emma replied firmly.

Hardly.

She might've been quietly inexperienced, but she sure knew what to do with her mouth. Really damn well. And she took direction like a pro.

So not innocent in the least.

"I mean, not completely." Aidan squinted.

"Gross. I didn't mean like that. I meant she's an innocent kind of person. Kind. Not worldly like other women you would normally date."

He didn't date.

Occasionally he'd have someone accompany him to events. Or take someone to dinner because he wanted to fuck them. But he didn't date with the intention of having a relationship.

He just never considered it.

Until now.

"I think you underestimate Lily," Aidan said, sliding his hands into his pockets. "She's smarter than you think."

Emma let out a sigh and dropped her hands.

"I'm not questioning her intelligence. Or her heart. I love that girl. I grew up with her. But she's lived a sheltered life. Coming here was a big deal."

Aidan nodded and stared down at the grass they were standing on, considering her words. Maybe he had been the naive one? Maybe he'd seen what he wanted to see.

"I like her, Em," he admitted when he lifted his eyes. "I'm going to Chicago."

"Don't," she said, shaking her head.

Logan cursed.

"Please don't, Aidan," Emma said. "You will destroy her life when you're done with her."

Who said he would be…

God.

Was Emma right? Would this all fall to bits, and he'd just end up hurting Lily?

"Handsy Matt is with her," he said, as if that explained everything.

"Who?" She frowned.

"Who the hell is Handsy Matt?" Logan asked.

"Wait. Her boss, Matt?" Emma asked, and he could see the clogs in her brain turning and working it out.

Aidan nodded.

"He was at the hospital when I rang. Don't worry, she didn't hear me. Long story." He waved his hand out, knowing that was too hard to explain. "I'm leaving later tonight. I need to know the guy isn't taking advantage of her."

Logan moved closer to Emma and wrapped his arm around her lower back. He had concern in his eyes.

Funny how your spouse's friends became a part of your life. And Aidan realized that no matter what happened between him and Lily, she would always be a part of their extended family.

You're going to be Emma's brother-in-law.

Clearly, Lily was much smarter than he was.

"That guy is a creep," she admitted. "The timing of this is terrible. I should be there with her."

Aidan shook his head.

"Enjoy your honeymoon. Enjoy the rest of your special day. I will go to Chicago and sort this out."

Emma shook her head.

"This is so wrong. I'm her best friend. You shouldn't be anywhere near her."

Aidan felt his chest tightening.

"Yeah, well, that might be true. But right now, I care about her and I'm not walking away. I told her that last night and she ran away without telling me," Aidan said, then held up his hand when Emma began to interrupt.

"I know her dad is dying. But she could've texted me."

Logan rubbed her arm. "Babe, I think Aidan likes Lily a lot more than he realizes."

Oh no, I realize, I'm just confused as fuck.

But she is mine.

And she sure as hell wasn't ending up with Handsy Matt. Aidan was going to make sure of that.

"Two rules," Emma said, pointing at him. "Don't fall in love with her. And do not let her fall in love with you."

"Fine," he lied.

CHAPTER TWENTY-TWO

Lily brushed her teeth with vigor, spat, and then rushed out to her bedroom. She pulled on her coat, grabbed her bag, and then left her apartment.

When she stepped outside, her boots skidded on the ice, and she grabbed the railing.

Shit.

The Uber pulled up, and she climbed inside. She didn't care it was blowing her budget. She had to get back to see her father.

Her mom had kicked her out eventually the night before. Her father had been sleeping when she'd arrived, and while he'd woken a few times so she could tell him she loved him, he wasn't very alert.

But it had been worth it, flying for hours to see him open his eyes.

She'd bawled silently, shaking, holding his hand.

Afterward, Lily was exhausted and agreed a few hours of sleep would benefit her.

Matt, who had shown up that evening, offered to drive her home. In the past, she'd been careful to never let him near her residence, even though, as her boss, he had her personnel records. She saw it as a healthy boundary, given his behavior in the office.

But he had surprised her by picking up some dinner and walking her to the door, handing it to her, and then dropping a light kiss on her head.

He'd been really lovely, actually.

But he wasn't Aidan.

He didn't make her heart sing and thighs press together with need.

Lily had lain in bed after eating two or three mouthfuls of the Thai takeout and scrolled through her phone. Emma had posted wedding photos on her social media.

She looked so beautiful.

A tear had slid down her cheek, sad that she'd missed the important day, but without regret for flying home to see her dad.

Try as she might, Lily had not been able to look away from the photos of Adian. After all, he was the best man.

God, he was handsome.

She'd nearly reached out and touched the screen before catching herself and realizing how dumb it was.

Then she remembered someone had phoned just as Matt had arrived. That and seeing her father lying in his hospital bed with all the wires and tubes. The machine beeping. Her mother's tear-stained face.

She went into her missed calls and her eyes widened.

Aidan.

Oh, my God.

She had smiled, seeing his name, but stopped short of replying. She figured he hadn't left one, and it was just a courtesy call to say goodbye.

If he'd really wanted to, he would have texted.

Before her eyes had closed, Lily decided she'd message Aidan when she was back at the hospital and had caught her breath today.

She would.

Despite the seriousness she was facing in losing her father, Aidan had continued to be on her mind.

She needed closure.

It was time to say goodbye.

The Uber flew through the streets of Chicago, and Lily stared out the window, wondering what he was doing. Sleeping, obviously. It was four a.m. in Maui.

He'd probably drunk too much Macallan and gone skinny dipping in the ocean like he'd threatened to do with her. Sad they never got the chance, Lily pressed her lips together.

But at least she'd been brave and said yes to him, so they'd had a couple of incredibly sexy nights together. She would never regret them.

Aidan was an amazing lover.

He was a force of nature.

Last night when Matt had shown up at the hospital and pulled her into an embrace, she had felt two very conflicting feelings. The hugs were nice, and it was comforting to know her boss cared.

But the stronger and more surprising thought was that she was cheating on Aidan.

So ridiculous.

Lily was a loyal person, but they hadn't promised each other anything.

Look at me. This is something. You know it is.

She drew in a breath and wondered. What was it? How could it have been anything when he stood back and let his father say those things? When they'd only known each other a few days.

When he hadn't left a message saying he missed her or even a goodbye.

What could it be when she came from the South Side, and he had never worried about where his next paycheck was coming from?

She knew the answer.

Great sex and a rich boy wanting it all.

Well, Lily wasn't a toy.

Maybe it was a good thing she'd had to leave so suddenly. There had been no long goodbye. No chance for him to talk her into seeing each other again, as Aidan had already been attempting, only to have her heart broken weeks or months down the line when she figured out what she had now.

Decision made, Lily promised herself she would text him later today and wish him well.

She climbed out of the Uber and headed inside the hospital. Her mom would still be there. She'd refused to leave.

Lily had picked up a bag for her on the way home last night. Matt had been kind enough to stop.

Gosh, he really had been nice.

Not only had he fed her and driven her home, but he'd also waited outside for her to pack a bag for her mom.

But he'd also taken liberties.

"Take as much time as you want," Matt had said, reaching out a hand across the console and squeezing her leg.

Lily had flinched.

Instead of moving his hand away, Matt squeezed tighter and smiled at her. "Hey, it's okay."

No, it wasn't.

She didn't want him touching her.

It had been wrong before, but after being with Aidan and having the memory of his touch on her skin, she didn't want anyone else touching her.

Yet Matt's smile, almost condescending, had made her feel like she was making too big a deal about it.

"I'm here for you," he continued, rubbing his hand on the spot. It was not high enough to be inappropriate, but it was borderline.

"Thanks, Matt," she said, then when she turned to climb out of the car, he grabbed her hand.

"Come here," he said, tugging her closer and hugging her.

Lily had just frozen and stared out the window as he held her. She hadn't known what to do.

When Matt released her, she forced a smile onto her face before going into her mom's place. "Thanks, again. I won't be long."

Because she needed her job.

Lily let out a sigh as she made her way through the maze of corridors to her father's hospital room.

"Hey, Lilypop," he forced out when she walked in the door.

"Hey, Dad."

Her mom was curled up in the armchair in the corner. He lifted his finger to his lips, looking like it took all his strength, and went *shhh*.

"Let her sleep," he whispered.

Lily nodded and put the bag down on the ground. Then sat on the side of his bed.

"How was Hawaii?"

"Dad. We don't have to talk about that." She smiled.

"Baby, I want to hear about your life. I don't have much longer. Tell me everything." He gave her a wobbly grin, and she brushed away a tear, nodding.

So she did.

She told him about the SUP boarding and flying first class, and how she had met the brother of Emma's new husband, and that she liked him.

Because why not?

He was her dad, after all, and who better to give her advice about men? If only for one more day.

A FEW HOURS later, Lily's dad was sleeping, so she convinced her mom to leave so they could get a bite to eat.

"Lily, I've heard about people who step away and their loved ones choose that moment to pass," her mom said.

"You need to look after yourself. It's good you had a shower, but you need a break. It's been nearly two days," Lily said, pressing her hand on the back of her mom's arm and guiding her down to the hospital café. "Eat a sandwich or something, then we will go back."

Her mom let out a sigh.

"You're right. It could be days and I need to keep my energy up for him. And what lies ahead."

And what lies ahead.

The words hung heavy between them as they ordered coffees and very average-looking cabinet food. They sat at a small table and played with their sandwiches. Lily took a bite, then her mom did the same. They both cringed and shared a little laugh.

"Is your back sore from sleeping in the chair?" Lily asked.

Her mom shrugged. "Yes. No. My heart hurts more."

Lily smiled.

"What?"

"You're lucky, you know. Not everyone finds love like you and Dad have."

"I know. We both know that. And you were our little love child."

"Gross."

Her mom shot her a grin. "I wish we could have given you a brother or sister, but we were blessed to have you."

Lily shrugged. "I got you all to myself all these years. I'm not unhappy about that."

"Having a sibling is nice. I love your Aunt Sherie. She's on her way here."

Lily nodded.

"That's good. I take it Uncle Freddy will stay behind?" Lily said.

They lived in California, and Freddy didn't fly. He had a fear of it and so when they visited—which had been only twice in her life—it was a big deal.

They had driven across the country and stayed for two weeks.

"Yes." Her mom nodded, stared into the distance, and sipped her coffee. Then her eyes darted back to Lily's. "Thank you, Lily. I needed a break. I just couldn't give myself permission to step away."

Lily reached out and squeezed her hand.

"It's going to be okay, Mom. We're going to be okay."

She was pretty sure she was talking to herself as much as her mom. Lily let her mind drift back to the night she told Aidan about her dad's illness. How he'd listened and comforted her. It had been nice.

Really nice.

It would be nice to have him here with her. In reality, it would be significantly more complicated than that. But the thought of having Aidan's big powerful arms around her, to feel his powerful presence supporting her so she could let go, even for a moment, and stop being strong, would be incredible.

And just a dream.

Yes, Matt had been comforting last night, but he was her boss, who she couldn't say no to. What would happen if he asked more of her one day?

Emma had warned her, and Lily had brushed her off. Last night in the car, the way he'd really given her no choice but to let him hold her, she didn't like that.

Aidan would have hit the roof.

But Aidan wasn't here.

Except she couldn't stop thinking of him. Goddamn it, she didn't want to never see him again.

Never kiss him again.

Never not feel his body against hers.

Ugh.

Lily didn't want to feel like this, but she did. She regretted not running down to his room and waking him up. Even just for one more kiss.

Hindsight was a shitty thing.

At the time, she'd been in a state of panic.

God, maybe he had heard and didn't want to get up and do an awkward goodbye. Perhaps that was what he was ringing to say last night?

It was driving her insane not knowing.

She tapped her phone and saw it was now nearly one in the afternoon. Aidan would be awake in Hawaii.

But no message.

She let out a sigh.

"Are you all right, sweetheart? I know this is tough. Shall we go back?" her mom asked.

"Yeah," she said, finishing her cold coffee and placing her cup on the saucer. "Mom, how did you know Dad was the one? How did you know you were in love?"

Water filled her mother's eyes as she smiled.

"Oh, that's easy. When I knew that I didn't want to live a single day without him. That I *couldn't* live a day without him. At least not as happy as when I was with him."

Lily didn't know what made her ask that.

Okay, she did know.

Aidan had moved into her head and wouldn't evacuate. Surely, she hadn't fallen for him in just a few days.

That was insane.

Seeing the teary smile on her mom's face brought her back to what was important.

"But you'll have to," Lily whispered. "How?"

"Yes, but I'm also a mother," she said, standing and placing her hand on Lily's cheek. "Your dad knows I have a life ahead of me, being your mom. Then a grandmother."

Grandmother.

Lily's eyes widened and her mom let out a soft laugh as they started walking back.

"When you have a child one day, you will understand. A love with a man is special, but so is creating a tiny little life. You are both important to me."

Lily hugged her mom's arm.

"But it was also terrifying," her mom continued.

"Terrifying?"

"Oh yes. When you were born, you were so little, and I thought you were going to die every day for at least twenty years."

Lily let out a small laugh.

"It drove your father crazy." She smiled. "Choose a powerful man, Lily. They're your rock. When your hormones are zooming around your body, he will ground you."

Lily felt her cheeks warm.

When she went quiet, her mom slowed. "Have you met someone? Is that why you asked me about falling in love?"

Oh, shit.

"No, I just—"

"Is it Matt? Your boss?" her mom asked. "Are you in love with him?"

"Are you?" a dark voice from behind her asked.

Lily whipped around and came face to face with a six-foot-three wall of hotness.

Her mouth fell open.

God, he looked incredible. Dressed in a pair of dark jeans, a black shirt, and a black coat hanging over his arm, he looked every bit the billionaire she knew he was.

His hair was slightly mussed from the weather outside and his eyes were dark as they bore into her, waiting for an answer.

Lily was still taking in the fact that Aidan was standing here.

In Chicago.

Looking like something out of a magazine.

And presumably, he was here for her.

"Answer the question, Lily," Aidan demanded.

"Oh, my," her mom said.

Yes. Oh, my.

CHAPTER TWENTY-THREE

Aidan waited for Lily to answer, but she was just staring at him. His eyes drifted to the older woman standing beside her, and he dropped the macho act.

"Aidan Dufort," he said, reaching out his hand. "I'm sorry about your husband."

"Thank you. Angela Peterson," she said, shaking his hand.

"What are you doing here?" Lily finally asked.

"I think I will just—" Angela thumbed over her shoulder. "Go check on your dad."

"Okay," Lily said, not taking her eyes off him.

"Nice to meet you, Aidan."

"You too, ma'am," he replied and watched her mother disappear down the hall and into a room, which he assumed was where Lily's father was.

Emma had told him the man had hours or maybe days left. Which meant Aidan was staying in Chicago for a while because he wasn't leaving Lily's side.

Unless she answered in the affirmative.

If she did love Matt, Aidan would need to walk away. He'd assumed Lily was being a compliant employee, answering all his calls and messages in Hawaii. It hadn't occurred to him she might have feelings for the guy.

Until he had overheard the conversation with her mom.

"She hates being called that," Lily said. "Ma'am. She thinks it makes her feel old."

Aidan took a step forward. "Do you know what I hate, Lily?"

Lily shook her head and glanced around them.

"I hate waiting for the answer to an important question." His voice was rough.

"I can't believe you're here."

Still. Not. Fucking. Answering. Him.

He tugged her down the hall until he found an empty room and then closed them in there.

"What are you doing?" she gasped.

He dropped his bag on the floor, his coat on the chair beside them, and took her face in his hands.

"Two seconds, peaches. Are you in love with Handsy Matt?" Aidan growled, his thumb sliding over her cheek.

"No," she finally answered quietly.

With a deep growl, Aidan dropped his mouth to hers.

Hard.

Then she let him in, and Aidan thrust his tongue inside, tasting that sweet heaven once more. They eagerly lapped at one another, smooth lips moving together greedily as Lily turned to rubber in his arms.

When he felt her wobble, Aidan slid an arm around her, palming the small of her back and tugged her against him.

"Easy, baby," Aidan said, steadying her as she drew in long breaths.

Hell, he was doing the same.

His heart swelled with happiness just having her back in his arms. And that she wasn't in love with her boss.

He'd never expected to feel like this about her. What *this* was, he still wasn't sure. Only that with every mile he'd flown overnight felt like it had taken a year.

Aidan had opened his phone and scrolled through the photos he'd taken of her. Some she knew about, most she didn't.

He more than liked Lily, and he sure as hell wasn't letting her boss put his fucking hands on his girl again.

Because she *was* his and now, he had to convince this sweet submissive peach of his that despite their differences, this could work.

Couldn't it?

"Why didn't you just answer me?" He frowned.

Lily shook her head and dropped her eyes. He took her chin and lifted them right the fuck back up to his.

"Aidan, stop."

"Try again," he growled softly.

"It was a private conversation with my mom."

"Try harder."

She scoffed and tried to pull away. In the hallway, he could hear the sounds of the hospital and knew they didn't have much time. When Lily began to squirm, he let her go. She took a step away and lifted her pretty eyes to his.

"You can push me away, Lily, but I didn't fly all this distance to roll over. That's not who I am."

Crossing her arms, she nodded. "I know. But why are you here, Aidan?"

"For you. Isn't that obvious?"

"No."

"Well then, I better try harder."

"I NEED TO get back to my dad," Lily said, still in a state of shock that Aidan was here in Chicago.

He'd flown all this way for her.

"I'll go check in at the hotel," Aidan said, picking up his bag and coat. Then he closed the distance between them and wrapped his arm around her lower back, tugging her up against him once more.

Her heart fluttered—*fluttered*!!—and her face lifted, taking in his strong, handsome features.

"I missed you," he said, and the fluttering turned into an almighty tornado. It must have been obvious, as his smirk spread across his face. Then he kissed her softly.

"I'm glad you are here," she said reluctantly. Because it was true, even if it was confusing.

"I know." He kissed her again and then guided them back out into the hall.

Lily watched the nurses take in the tall, powerful man beside her, his hand on the small of her back, and a small sense of pride and…wow, what was that?…ownership came over her. She turned and Aidan cupped her face.

"I'll be back in a few hours." His voice was deep and husky.

Oh lord, her lady bits were going to react very inappropriately if he didn't leave soon.

"Okay." A warmth filled her chest.

She wasn't going to say no to his support when her father was close to passing. That he was here when she'd been craving those muscular arms around her was a miracle.

Thankfully, Aidan hadn't pushed his questioning any further about the conversation with her mom. Explaining that she wanted to know what it felt like to be in love because her feelings for him were… strong was definitely not what she had in mind.

He had caught the tail end of the conversation and assumed she loved Matt.

She was most definitely *not* in love with Matt, but she did still work for him, and Aidan would need to understand that.

"How long are you staying?" she asked.

"As long as it takes." He kissed her cheek. "See you soon, peaches."

As long as it takes.

What did that mean?

Lily was sure she'd soon find out. Meanwhile, her face heated as she watched Aidan walk away.

God, he was beautiful.

His strong back, dark wavy hair, perfect ass—she knew it was perfect as she'd had a handful of it in her hands a few times—and powerful arms. He walked with the confidence of a man who knew his worth and was willing to confront anyone who challenged it.

As long as it takes.

Lily really wanted to unpack that. What did he think was going to happen?

While he'd taken her by surprise and it was a little romantic, especially his kiss, she was still confused by his presence.

Nothing had changed.

I hope you don't have your sights set on either of these boys.

Was she right? Was Aidan on a rich boy's path of rebellion? It would be irresponsible of her to read too much into his arrival. Aidan had money. Lots of it. Flying across the world wasn't as significant as someone else doing it.

Did she want him to leave? No.

Did she want to melt into his arms and let him take care of her? Oh, boy, yes, she did.

But that was leading him on.

When Aidan returned, she would speak to him and be honest. She didn't love Matt, and there wasn't anything romantic between them, but she needed her job.

And she wasn't available for anything more than what she and Aidan had shared in Hawaii. His being here gave them the opportunity to say goodbye properly.

Then she could turn her attention back to her father and wait until he took his last breath.

And grieve them both.

CHAPTER TWENTY-FOUR

Aidan handed his credit card to the man, checking him into the Dufort Hotel in Chicago.

The uniform-clad man frowned, then glanced up.

"Ah, this…"

Aidan lifted a brow, then realized he'd noticed the Dufort name on the black card. "Oh. They're my cousins. I'm still paying. So charge it up."

"I need to check," the man said.

"You need to check to take my money?" Aidan laughed.

"Yes, sir."

"Okay, well, please hurry. It's goddamn cold in this town," he said, shivering in his coat despite the heat in the lobby. Chicago was fucking freezing and coming straight from Hawaii just made it ten times more so.

He'd showered on the jet but was looking forward to another one. Then he would organize more winter clothes to be sent to the hotel and any other necessities while he was here.

"How long are you staying, sir?" the man said when he returned.

Good question.

"Let's say two weeks," Aidan replied. If he couldn't convince Lily to fall in love with him by then, he was off his game and needed a kick in the ass.

But he'd seen it in her eyes.

Perhaps she wasn't in love with him yet, but she would be.

Heck, maybe *he* wasn't completely and utterly in love with Lily yet, but he knew he was falling. Just seeing her beautiful face in the hospital today had sent a charge through his heart.

The moment she'd clarified she wasn't in love with Matt, he'd begun to formulate his plan. First, he would be by her side as her father passed. No demands, just that she let him support her.

Then he would tell her she was not going back to work.

Aidan rested his hip on the counter and looked around the luxurious hotel lobby.

Whoever Handsy Matt was, Aidan was going to enjoy meeting him. Aidan was one of the wealthiest men in the world. Matt Whoeverthefuckheis would soon find out he was Lily's man.

And never touch her again.

HE BALANCED THE phone in his hand and punched the combination on the door of the hotel suite.

"I'm on my honeymoon," Logan groaned.

"Then make sure you have pants on when I'm talking to you." Aidan smirked and his brother laughed as he tugged on his shorts.

"How was the flight?" Logan asked.

"Long. But I'm here. You can tell Emma Lily's dad is still with us."

"Did you meet him?" Logan asked, surprised.

"No. I met her mom, though. She's an older and pretty version of Lily."

There was a brief silence, then Logan said, "You really like this girl."

Yeah, he did.

"Obviously. I could have fucked any number of women in Hawaii. Lily was the only one who had my attention. Then and now," he replied.

"Emma isn't happy."

Fuck Emma.

He wasn't going to say that out loud.

"Tell her my intentions are pure. Again." He rolled his eyes as he dropped his bags on the bed and zipped open his suitcase.

Then propped the phone up on the table and began to unpack. His last-minute booking meant he didn't get a penthouse suite, but the executive room was big enough for now. If he ended up staying longer, he'd pull some strings.

"She doesn't believe you," Logan replied.

What if I said I wanted to spend the rest of my life with her?

And why was it so hard for everyone to believe he might actually like a woman?

"Okay well, good talk," Aidan said, putting his bag of toiletries in the bathroom and eyeing the shower. God, he couldn't wait to be warm. "How's Aimes?"

Maybe I'll have a fucking bath.

There was a bunch of noise over the phone, and Logan and Emma began giggling. Fortunately, he couldn't see, as he had his back to them.

"If you two are doing sexual things, I am hanging up," he said, walking back out and planting his hands on his hips.

This time, Emma's face was on the screen.

"My plan is working." She grinned.

"Amelia," Logan said. "You saw her yesterday. She seemed okay."

Yeah, he had, but he'd also seen her glancing at her phone and tossing back far too many glasses of champagne. She was pretty drunk by the time he'd left and had even asked him to take her with him.

Any other time and he would've said yes.

"I'm not going to Philly, Aimes. I'm heading to Chicago." He'd kissed her cheek as he stood by the door of the Uber.

She'd nodded and wrapped her arm around herself.

"Who is this guy?" Aidan had asked.

"No one. An asshole."

There wasn't a lot he could do to take away her heartache. Not when she wouldn't tell them anything.

"I'll call you in a few days." He'd hugged her one last time and then climbed in the car.

"I asked Blake to keep an eye on her. They all flew back to Oahu today," Logan said.

Great.

There was a fifty-fifty chance he'd get distracted or get Amelia in more trouble. It went either way with Blake.

"What about our NYC cousins?" Aidan asked.

"They've flown directly back to New York."

"Okay, family time is over. I want my husband back now," Emma said. "Husband. I have a husband."

Aidan smiled.

"Have fun, you two. Don't terrify the staff and spend the entire time naked."

"Spoil-sport." Emma laughed.

Aidan ended the call and stared for a long moment at the bed and then the bathroom.

"Fuck it. I'm having a bath. This place is goddamn freezing."

Aidan ripped off his shirt, turned on the taps, and ordered some room service. Then he began formulating his plan to win Lily's heart.

CHAPTER TWENTY-FIVE

Lily's mom was holding a cup and straw to her dad's mouth when she walked back in. Predictably, she gave her that knowing-mom smile but didn't say anything.

Lily knew it wouldn't last.

"Hey, Dad," Lily said, walking around to the other side of the bed.

"Lilypop, will you please put your mother out of her misery and tell her who the young man was?" he said, winking at her.

He'd obviously kept their conversation secret and she kind of loved him for it. Even if she would tell her mom everything, anyway.

Her mom gasped. "Gary, I told you not to say anything."

She loved watching her parents tease one another. They'd done it for as long as she could remember. Perhaps that's why she liked…no. She wasn't going down that path. Yes, she liked Aidan, but no, he wasn't the right man for her.

Thinking anything else was a recipe for disaster.

If she couldn't be clear on that in her own mind, she wouldn't convince Aidan.

"From the look of his tan, I'd say he was someone she met in Hawaii," her mom said. "Does he live here in Chicago?"

Lily bit her lip. "No,"

"Aidan is a lovely name. He's also a very handsome man, Lily."

She wasn't going to argue with that. "The way he was looking at you… My goodness, it reminded me of your dad."

"I never looked at you in any way." He lowered his brows but shot Lily a wink.

Her mom blushed. "You most certainly did. And you still do."

Lily sat down in the seat behind her and let them keep up their little flirtation. Who knew if it might be their last.

Her chest tightened.

What a gift to have this moment with them. Just over a day ago, she wasn't sure if she was going to make it here in time to see her father one last time. Now, while he might seem to be in good spirits, his movements were slow, and he was gray around the gills.

"He's Logan's brother," Lily said in an almost defeated tone when they turned to her for more details. To her, it was explanation enough.

"What a shame you didn't meet him earlier. Double wedding." Her father winked.

Oh, I did. He put his hands inside my panties.

And there was no way she was sharing that naughty bit of information. Also, there would be no wedding. That's not what this was.

Even if Aidan thought it was.

It wasn't.

She was very clear about that.

"Wait. Aidan Dufort? Oh my God. Lily. Logan's brother," her mom said, finally clicking.

She pressed her lips together, puffing out her cheeks, and nodded. All like *yup, never going to happen.*

"Aidan Dufort. Right. What did I miss?" her father asked, his eyes darting between them.

Lily rolled her eyes and crossed her arms. "He's a billionaire, Dad. A. Billionaire."

"So?" he repeated. "My girl is good enough for some rich man. Who told you to think like that?"

"No one. He's just…different from me," she snapped.

"Because his bank account is fatter than yours? Lilypop, I taught you better than that." He coughed.

"Darling, you know what she means." Her mom patted his chest.

Then he started coughing harder, and the machines began beeping.

God, please no.

Lily jumped up. "Dad!"

Please don't take him because we were fighting over Aidan. Oh, my God.

"Dad!" she cried as the nurses came flying in and moved them away so they could do their thing.

"He just needs a drink," her mom said, and Lily frowned.

A drink? He has cancer and mom thinks he needs a fucking drink?

"Clear the room, please," one nurse said, nudging them out of the room.

Her mom started crying and Lily put her arm around her, steering her out into the hallway.

"Clear the hallway please," someone called out and her mom began to sob as Lily pulled her into her arms.

"It's okay, Mom," she cried, wishing Aidan was there even though it made no sense.

They walked down to the waiting room, and, after a few hours, they were eventually allowed back in. It was clear things had then changed.

There was no more teasing and flirting. But there was a lot of handholding and softly spoken words.

Lily wrapped her cardigan around herself and sat quietly after telling her dad she loved him about ten times.

He patted her hand. "Forget the money, Lily. Follow your heart."

She smiled and kissed his cheek, then dozed for a few hours in the chair, feeling like the ground beneath her was crumbling.

What was she going to do without her dad?

He'd been her rock all her life.

CHAPTER TWENTY-SIX

Aidan pulled on a pair of blue jeans.

Prada's.

He wondered whether Lily would have a point of view about them. She'd made a comment about him wearing a Prada T-shirt in Hawaii, and he figured it was the price tag.

Well, she'd just have to get used to nice things because he intended to treat his girl to a lot of pricey things.

He pulled on a long-sleeved T-shirt, added a Tom Ford merino and cashmere sweater, and slid his feet into a pair of…Aidan had to glance inside to look.

What do you know, Prada shoes.

Sliding his phone into his pocket, he added his Piguet watch and grabbed his coat and wallet on the way out.

The soak in the tub had warmed him up. He had a full tummy and even caught an hour's sleep.

He checked the time again. Five thirty.

Aidan didn't want to be any later than this, but he had waited until after work hours to see if Handsy Matt would turn up.

Aidan stopped just inside the doors to pull on his navy coat. Two women walked into the lobby and their eyes roamed over him from head to toe.

They both wore well-tailored suits, had their hair pulled back with a reasonable amount of makeup, and carried large tote bags.

Corporates. Either visiting or here for a business meeting.

The type who usually caught his attention unless they were dominant in and out of the boardroom.

Many female leaders enjoyed a dominant lover so they could drop the more masculine side of their personality and step into the feminine.

He'd lost count of how many women told him they got sick of having to be so strong and in charge.

It's why he was so attracted to Lily. There wasn't that hardness most women had to have these days. She was soft and compliant. Vulnerable and trusting.

Yet she had her own mind and goals.

For him, it was an intoxicating mix that got his cock rising ready to fuck her, and his hand thumping his chest to protect her.

If that made him a caveman, then hand over the rocks. Because he was falling for her hard.

Aidan gave the women a smirk and nodded *ladies* to them as he walked out of the hotel. They'd have to find someone else to play with as he was taken.

A short Uber ride got him to the hospital just as the snow began to fall. He pulled on his woolen beanie and climbed out of the vehicle. Then ducked his head as he ran inside the main entrance.

Shaking off the snow, he pulled off his hat and tucked it into his pocket, finding his way back to the ward he'd been in earlier today.

He got as far as the elevator before his phone rang.

Blake.

Aidan had tried him multiple times while in the tub—not that he was going to share that piece of knowledge with his cousin—and it had gone straight to voice mail.

"Aides," Blake said when he answered. "Sorry, I missed your calls. We were swimming."

"Asshole. It's freezing here."

"Well," he said, sounding completely void of pity, "that's what happens when you chase tail back to winter."

He was going to hammer the little shit next time he saw him for calling Lily *tail*. "I'll let that go for now."

Blake laughed. "What's up? Cocktail hour is starting soon."

Aidan frowned. "It's only lunchtime in Hawaii."

"Exactly. Hurry up." Blake laughed again.

"Is Amelia with you?" He got straight to the point because, obviously, they had important things to get to.

Fuckers.

There was a long silence. Aidan even checked his phone for coverage, then put it back in his ear. "Blake?"

"Hang on," his cousin replied.

Muffled sounds.

"She's gone back to Philadelphia," Blake finally said as the elevator doors opened. Aidan took a step away and waved the people on.

"When?"

"When we arrived back at the hotel. A friend of hers was waiting for her," Blake said. "I thought she was coming back with us."

Aidan rubbed his jaw. The only friend Amelia had on the island was the guy who had broken her heart.

"Did you meet this friend?"

"No. Well, we saw him. She seemed happy to see him. Let out a little cry and ran over to him," Blake said. "More than friends, obviously, as there was snogging involved."

Jesus.

"Blake. That was the guy who broke her fucking heart," Aidan cried. "You let her go with him?"

Silence.

"Dude, she's a grown woman. And he wasn't a small guy."

"Neither are you!" Aidan said louder.

"Fair."

Lord help him.

Blake wasn't wrong, though. Amelia *was* an adult, and both he and Logan were way too protective of her. But he'd never seen Amelia so upset over a man, and now she was flying back to Philadelphia with him.

Aidan still had a weird feeling about this.

He would try ringing her tomorrow. Right now, he needed to see Lily and hold her in his arms.

The need to make her his was growing strong.

TEN MINUTES LATER, Aidan finally found the ward. The hospital was like a damn rabbit warren, and while he'd only been there a few hours earlier, he'd been jetlagged and honestly still a little topped up on champagne and whisky.

He knocked gently and opened the door. The room was dark with a small light coming from above the bed. Aidan saw her mom first, her head lying on the bed. She didn't move. He glanced around and found Lily curled up in the large armchair.

God, she looked so precious.

He was just about to back out of the room when he heard her small voice.

"Aidan?" Lily whispered.

He walked to her as she sat up and rubbed her face.

"Hey," he said, crouching and running his hand over her hair. "How are you so beautiful, even in this state?"

She gave him a shy smile. "Liar,"

His hand flew to his chest, all faux wounded. Then he stared over at her dad on the bed.

"He's in a coma now," Lily said, and tears filled her eyes.

Fuck.

Aidan pulled her down into his arms, and they just sat on the hospital room floor while she silently wept. After a few minutes, he lifted her chin. "Do you want to get some fresh air or stay here?"

Lily wiped her face and glanced over at the bed.

"Go, Lily. I'll stay with your dad. I'll text you if anything happens."

Oh. Wow.

Her mom had been awake the whole time. Aidan figured she was in a state of complete grief just holding on to the last moments with her husband.

What would it feel like to be that in love?

"I should stay," Lily said.

Adian nodded. "Okay. Do you want me to stay with you or out in the waiting room?"

She climbed off him, and he stood. Without a second thought, he wrapped his arm around her back and Lily leaned into him.

"Sweetheart, go. Take a break," her mom pressed.

Lily took a moment, then agreed. "Okay,"

He grabbed her coat and took Lily's hand. Then they headed down the long hall until they reached the waiting room. The bright lights felt harsh under the circumstances.

"It's snowing outside," Aidan said. "But there's an atrium downstairs if you want to get a drink and some cold air."

He'd seen it on his way in earlier.

Lily nodded. "Yeah, sounds good."

God, his heart was aching seeing her so sad, but this was a part of life, and Aidan was just happy he could be here for her.

"Aidan, this can't be fun for you," Lily said when they had two cups of steaming hot coffee. "I appreciate you coming to Chicago, but perhaps you should go home, and I'll call you after the funeral. I promise."

Aidan frowned and kept walking, tugging her along with him. Clearly, she'd chosen to ignore everything he'd said to her. To give her the benefit of the doubt, given the stress she was under, he didn't bite.

"Not going anywhere, Lily."

They walked through the doors that led out to the atrium and tugged their coats around them. Snow fell on the glass roof and the fake grass and concrete block seats looked deceitfully appealing.

Still, they sat on them anyway and shivered together.

"This is a far cry from Hawaii," Aidan said, sipping his coffee.

"Yeah." Lily shot him a small smile. Then she turned to him. "My dad wanted to meet you."

He pulled back. "Me?"

She nodded, a small smile on her lips.

"I told him all about you. Well, not all of it, obviously."

Aidan's lips stretched into a smile. Lily had told her dying father about him. That was a big deal. Did she realize that or not?

"You explained how charming and good-looking I was, right?"

Lily shook her head at him, and little pink splotches appeared on her cheeks.

"Mom did that," she said, then leaned her head on his arm. "There were some complications this afternoon, and then we had about two hours with him before he drifted into a coma."

Jesus.

"He said he wanted to meet you, to make sure you knew how lucky you were to have me."

Aidan put his coffee down and wrapped his arm around her. Lily slid hers around his waist and gripped a handful of his coat. His heart swelled despite the bittersweet moment.

"I wish I could've met him. I would've told him I know I'm lucky, and that I can see the doubt in his beautiful daughter's eyes, but I'm going to fight like hell to win her heart."

She was quiet.

"You don't believe me. I realize that. But you will."

Her face lifted to his. Aidan lowered his mouth to hers, feeling her tremble against him. Was it her grief, the cold, or the way he made her feel?

Because his own heart was thumping, like crazy.

"I wish I could wrap you up in my arms and steal you away from all this pain," he said, caressing her lips.

"Why me?" Lily asked.

"I don't know. Why me?" he challenged back.

"Aidan. You have women throwing themselves at you. You're gorgeous, wealthy, successful."

True, but when it came to Lily, it was irrelevant. Aidan knew she wanted an answer. One he didn't have, because while he'd never searched for love, he also wouldn't have put *rich chick* on his search criteria.

He liked to think he had a bit more soul than that. Plus… well, he had enough fucking money. What he wanted, when he thought about it, was someone who made him think, made him smile, made him hot as hell.

Lily was the winner in all those regards.

Was he going to tell her that right now?

Fuck no. She'd likely run a mile.

"Maybe I like you because you don't throw yourself at me." He shrugged.

"So, I'm a challenge?"

"No Lily. You were not a challenge. I was in complete control from the moment I laid eyes on you. Don't tell me you don't know that."

She swallowed.

"Then you left Hawaii and took a piece of me with you. I don't know how or why. But there was this hole where you'd been."

Okay, fine, so maybe he wasn't going to hold back. The words just kept falling out.

"I'm going to marry you one day, Lily Peterson. Trust me, no one is more surprised by this than me. But I'm not going to live without you."

Fucking hell.

It was like a dam had broken inside him.

Lily jerked back in shock.

"Aidan, that's… no. You just…"

Then her phone rang, and now he'd never know what she was going to say.

"Mom?"

"Lily, come back now."

Shit.

Her face broke, and he tugged her to her feet.

"Let's go, baby." Then they raced upstairs, and he stood in the doorway as Lily went to the other side of the bed and gripped her father's arm.

Fifteen minutes later, he was gone.

I promise you, Mr. Peterson. I will love your daughter as much and for as long as she lets me. That's my promise to you.

CHAPTER TWENTY-SEVEN

For over an hour, Aidan sat in the armchair in the corner, waiting as Lily and her mom grieved. At one point Lily rounded the bed and hugged her mom, the two of them just standing there staring down at her father.

It wasn't comfortable being there, but Aidan refused to leave. If Lily needed him, he wanted her to know he was there.

So, he would wait for as long as it took.

A while later, Lily glanced around and spotted him. "Aidan?"

"Yeah, babe."

"You're still here," she said, surprised.

"I told you I'm not going anywhere," he said gently. "When you're ready, I will take you both home."

Angela wiped her eyes and began to chat with one of the hospital people who entered the room.

Lily walked over to him. He opened his arms, and she fell into his chest. "I knew this was going to happen, but it still feels like my heart has been ripped apart," she cried.

Aidan nodded, even though she couldn't see him.

It made him reflect on how angry he'd been with his father. None of them lived forever and while Andrew had been completely out of place, if the man dropped dead, Aidan would regret not clearing things up.

Were they close as father and son? Not really.

But they hadn't been at war like it felt they were right now. Not just him, either. Now he knew their father was doing the same to Amelia. It was pretty clear the man was going through something.

Perhaps Emma was right, and it was their nuptials that had triggered it.

Or something else.

Financial maybe? Was he having troubles?

Aidan promised himself he'd call his dad and have a chat. Right now, his time belonged to Lily.

And his heart, apparently.

She's mine.

She lifted her face to his. "Thank you for being here."

Aidan tugged her against his chest again and rubbed her lower back. He wanted to get her home so he could look after her properly.

Over the top of Lily's head, he saw her mom nod at the hospital woman. Then her eyes lifted to his, and she smiled warmly at him as he continued to embrace her daughter. She glanced down at her husband once more, leaned down and kissed his head, and then straightened.

Slowly, she moved the sheet over her face and turned away.

Jesus.

He wished he could take their pain away. Aidan couldn't imagine losing someone you loved that damn much.

"Let me take you both home," Aidan said as her mom walked over to them, placing a hand on Lily's shoulder as tears poured down her face.

When she nodded, indicating she was ready to leave, Lily pulled out of his arms, and they grabbed their bags and walked slowly through the hospital.

"The Uber will be two more minutes," Aidan said, glancing at his phone.

"Lily!" a deep voice called out.

Aidan glanced up and his eyes narrowed.

You have to be fucking kidding me.

"Matt?" Lily said in surprise, still tucked into his side.

It was half past fucking eight at night. What was Handsy Matt doing here?

With one glance, Aidan took in his professional suit. He was middle class at best, with his slightly scuffed shoes, off-the-shelf pants, and worn-too-many-times coat. The man was good-looking, in an average kind of way. Short blonde hair, which indicated he might have been military once upon a time.

He was shorter than Aidan's six-foot-three and had a slimmer build.

"Hi," Matt said, slowing his approach, his eyes taking in the entire situation. As in the part where Lily was in his arms.

That's right, asshole. Lily belongs to me.

Well, not yet, but soon she would.

"Matt Harris," he said assertively, thrusting out his hand. "Who are you?"

Aidan ignored his hand and took another look at the screen.

"Lily's father has just passed. I'm taking them home," he said instead. *Let me translate: Put away the testosterone and get the fuck out of my way.*

Matt dropped his hand.

"I'm so sorry, Lily," he said, reaching for her.

And she fucking went to him.

His arms went around her, and Aidan grit his teeth. When Matt lifted his eyes over her head and shot him a look every man recognized, Aidan wanted to rip his damn head off.

He was challenging him. Confirming what Aidan had sensed all along. He was attracted to Lily and wanted her.

Bad news, asshole, she doesn't want you. She just wants her job and paycheck.

But I'm about to change that.

"Well, look at that, the Uber is here," Aidan said, smiling at Lily's mom, who looked nearly as unhappy as he was about Matt manhandling her.

Fine, hugging her.

Lily *finally* left Matt and pulled her coat tighter around her, and Aidan didn't waste a second moving closer and placing a hand on the small of her back.

Mine.

"Lily will be on bereavement leave for the rest of the week," Aidan announced, letting Matt know two things: one, he knew who he was and two, he was making decisions for her.

"I don't need that long," she said softly.

Fuck, Lily.

"Take the week, Lily," Matt smiled at her, then shot Aidan a dark look.

Good boy.

Next, you'll accept her resignation. But one thing at a time.

"You know I've got my car." Matt pointed over his shoulder. "I can take you ladies home."

Lily pressed her lips together.

Jesus, this guy doesn't give up.

Aidan pointed outside. "The car is right there, Matt. Sorry you didn't hear that before. Have a good evening."

He wasn't going to give the guy an inch. Aidan knew men like him. They tried to manipulate and coerce people.

They didn't like being called out and, as it turned out, that was Aidan's specialty.

"Thanks, though." Lily smiled.

My sweet, naïve little peach.

Aidan widened his arms and guided Lily and her mom outside as Lily said a quick goodbye.

Letting them run ahead through the falling snow, to climb in the vehicle, Aidan halted, then turned and held Matt's gaze for a long moment.

"The name is Adian Dufort," he said coldly. "Lily has told me all about you."

"Funny, because she's never mentioned you," Matt said, sliding his hands into his pockets, smiling.

Aidan grinned.

"Google me." Then he jogged to the waiting car.

If Matt had any brains, and he was a lawyer so he must have, then once he learned who he was, he'd realize Lily was now under his protection.

With money came power.

It wasn't something he very often played with, because, unlike his brother and cousins, he didn't run massive conglomerates, but he would pull any string he had to. To protect Lily.

Matt would never touch her again.

AN HOUR LATER, he stepped into Lily's apartment and handed her the keys.

"This is my humble home," she said, tossing the keys on the kitchen bench. Which was about two steps from the front door.

It was small.

And in very average—which was being generous—condition.

God, he wanted way more for her, but saying anything of the sort would just prove the stark differences between their lives that Lily was already uncomfortable with.

Thanks, Father.

"Do you want to take a shower?" Aidan asked, pulling off his coat.

Fuck, it was freezing. He found the heat and walked to turn it on, then found Lily staring at the wall.

Right. She was still in shock.

He led her to the bathroom and turned on the taps.

They'd pulled up at Lily's mom's place at the same time her aunt arrived in a cab from the airport. Aidan asked Lily if she wanted to stay with them or have him take her home.

In the end, Angela told her to go home and get some rest.

"The next few days are going to be exhausting. Your Aunt Sherie is here, and you have this nice young man looking after you. I'm here if you want to ring."

At first Lily wasn't sure about leaving her mom, but when he reassured her, he would bring her right back if she changed her mind, she climbed back in the Uber with him.

Aidan tugged her clothes off and when Lily stepped under the water, her pretty eyes looked pleadingly at him.

"I'm not going to take advantage of you, Lily. I'm here to take care of you. That's it."

Unlike Handsy Mike.

"I need you," she said, reaching out her hand. "Please."

Dear lord, I'm not that strong a man.

Off came his clothes, and Aidan stepped under the water, wrapping his arms around Lily. The feel of her pert breasts again on his chest felt like a piece of heaven as her hands ran up and down his back, over his ass, and back up again.

She pulled back, tears glittering in her eyes. "Touch me."

Christ.

"Lil, your dad has just died."

"I know," she croaked out. "And I don't want to feel it anymore. I need you to take away the pain."

Fuck.

"I think you—"

"Aidan, please." She reached between them and wrapped her hand around his erect cock.

Not. That. Strong.

Cursing, he lifted her up, so her legs wrapped around his body and pressed her into the wall. Her little butterfly pendant sparkled as the water splashed on it.

"You know I'm a dominant lover, baby. I don't do soft."

She nodded, biting her bottom lip.

"Play with your pussy. I want you wet before I thrust into you." His voice was gruff.

It had been days since he'd fucked her and, yes, he wanted his cock inside her wet, tight channel, but not if she hated him for it afterward. So, he watched her slide her hand between them again and circle her clit with her fingers.

"That feel nice?"

"Hmm mm." She nodded.

"Is your pussy feeling greedy? Does it want my thick cock, Lily?"

"Yes," she moaned, closing her eyes.

"Don't you take your eyes off me. I want you to know who's pleasuring you,"

She tilted her head at him. "Well, it's me, right now."

His lips stretched into a smile. "Is that so?"

Aidan understood Lily's need for relief from her pain, but if she thought fucking him hours after her father died meant she could regret in the days following and use it as an excuse to end what they had, she was wrong.

"Are you going to give it to me?"

"Are you going to regret this?" he asked, and her eyes dropped. "Look at me,"

"I just want to feel you. To feel safe and full of you," Lily said, meeting his eyes once more.

Jesus.

It wasn't possible for him to deny this woman. She arched into him, her breasts teasing him with their stiff nipples. And when she moaned, Aidan knew she was becoming needy.

"Hold my shoulders," Aidan instructed her.

Then he lifted her an inch so he could line his cock up with her core, and then thrust inside her.

Sweet Jesus.

Lily's tight pussy sheathed him just as she'd done in Hawaii.

"Oh, God!" she cried.

"Fucking hell," He slammed her back against the shower wall again and slapped a hand on the plastic.

"Aidan, fuck," Lily cursed. "You're bigger. I'm sure you're bigger. Thicker."

He laughed as he thrusted. "You do this to me, baby."

His other hand gripped her ass, feeling her juices surround him, and he began to pound fast. Real fast.

"This what you want, baby?"

"Yes, harder."

Jesus, he wasn't holding back.

Slam.

"You want me to fuck the pain out of you, peaches? Like this. Hard. Deep. Thick."

"Yes,"

Her nails dug into his skin as his cock pounded her over and over. Tits bouncing, their mouths gasping as they tried to kiss, but it was all too messy and wet and needy.

Then Lily's core clenched around him, her climax near, sending an electric jolt through him.

"Come. Lily. Come on my cock. Fuck," Aidan cried.

"Ohmygod, ohmygod," her sweet voice cried as she trembled in his arms and his seed shot into her like a cannon, claiming her, filling her, and taking all of her.

Panting, their mouths crushed together as he held her pressed against the wall.

God damn.

Aidan pulled out, sliding her down his body as their mouths remained connected. He leaned down, lapping at her tongue, neither of them wanting the pleasure to end.

God damn, he never wanted to let this woman go.

Lily placed her hand on his cheek and, holding his gaze, said, "Thank you."

A dark dread threaded its way through his chest. Call it an omen, but Aidan knew Lily thought she was saying goodbye to him.

Fuck that.

He wasn't letting that happen.

They quickly washed and dried each other, then climbed into bed. For the rest of the night, Aidan held Lily while she cried and dozed.

By morning, Aidan knew, without a shadow of doubt, that he was completely in love with Lily Peterson.

CHAPTER TWENTY-EIGHT

Her dad was gone.

She'd known this day was coming, but really had no idea how hollow she would feel. The man who had been her protector and biggest fan all her life had just gone.

Life made no sense.

As if to not leave her alone and unprotected life, God, the universe, or some magical being had given her Adian.

At least for now.

And the beautiful man was lying in her bed—her bed—right here in Chicago. Watching him sleep peacefully, with not a single cheeky or dark expression on his face, was a gift. He always woke when she did, but it was likely she'd kept him awake with her tossing and turning.

The way he'd fucked her in the shower had been the outlet she'd needed. It was like she was sad and angry all at once.

Aidan had shouldered it.

She hadn't missed how protective he'd been when Matt turned up last night. Lily knew she should care if Aidan had offended him, and if she still had a job, but the truth was all she cared about right now was her broken heart.

And she was still creeped out by the hug in the car a few nights ago. There was no way she was telling Aidan about that.

Still, she did need her job, and so she would ring Matt after the funeral and apologize.

After that, she would have to make some decisions. Lily knew she couldn't stay working there. Emma and Aidan were right. Matt was a creep.

Right now, she appreciated the comfort Aidan was giving her. His arm was under her head, his hand resting gently on her hip and his breaths steady.

Lily lifted her hand and softly ran her finger over his lips. He had beautiful lips. Full and plump, and his jaw was perfect.

So was his nose.

Even his eyelashes were long, dark, and thick.

She smiled to herself.

His cock was pretty perfect, too.

Wow, she really did like this man. Was this how her mom felt about her dad when they fell in love?

Lily didn't want to read much into Aidan's words, but his being here was making it hard not to.

She'd expected him to slip away when her father had taken his last breath. Instead, she'd found him patiently waiting for her and then he'd taken her and her mom home. To be honest, he was a far more thoughtful man than she'd been expecting.

But long term, she knew this wasn't a relationship that would last.

Surely, he knew that.

In a few days, they would bury her father and then she'd have to return to work. She didn't want Aidan to leave. But she also didn't want him to stay. She had nothing to offer and would hate herself if she used him during her grief and then ended it.

It was almost laughable to think she might break his heart. Despite her dad berating her, she still found it crazy that a man like Aidan would want her.

Lily let out a sigh and her fingers dropped away.

"Morning, beautiful," Aidan said, his voice sleepy.

"Hey," she said, as he pulled her against him and gently kissed her.

Lily's heart fluttered.

I need you to go. I don't want to hurt you and I can't have my heart broken twice if you decide you don't really want me.

That little voice in her head was still not sure Aidan wasn't being a rebellious billionaire despite how amazing he'd been.

She hated herself for it, but couldn't he see how different they were?

"How long have you been awake?" he asked, his husky voice.

"A few minutes," Lily answered.

"How are you feeling?" His fingers brushed a few strands of hair from her face.

She shrugged. "Sad."

And horny.

Lily wasn't sure why she didn't want to talk to Aidan about her dad. She just wanted him to hold her. To fuck her.

Perhaps allowing him into that part of her soul was going a little too far.

Lily lifted her leg over his hip, and Aidan let out a groan. "Do that and I'll slide inside you."

Then, to her surprise, he shook his head and rolled onto his back. He turned his head. "What do you usually have for breakfast?"

What?

She was hoping he was on the menu.

"Hot billionaires," she said, climbing on top of him. He let out a short laugh but grabbed her hips.

"Lily, your dad just died. I understood the need to fuck last night, but I'm not here to distract you."

"Then why are you here?" she asked, sliding back down on the bed and letting out a huff. She immediately regretted the words, but maybe she was vying for an argument.

When he didn't give her one, she turned her head and glared at him.

"You know why," he said, slowly turning his face to her. "I'm patient, Lily, but don't push me. The dynamics between us are still the same."

Her heart began to pound.

"Oh yeah? What are they?"

Jesus, even she knew she was playing with fire.

Aidan climbed over her, his cock hanging thick and heavy between them, and he planted his arms on either side of her head.

"Stop. I'm way too dominant to put up with any bullshit. You like me. I like you. The timing is crap, I agree, but I'm not leaving. I am here to support you," he ground out. "But I am not a fuck toy."

Her heart thundered, his dominance flowing through her, making her wet.

"No sex. Got it," she said, biting her bottom lip.

"I didn't say that," Aidan replied, and his eyes roamed over her face.

Then, thank fucking God, he reached between her thighs and pushed them wide, moving his legs to accommodate her. Lily arched, and a moan escaped. He found her wet folds.

"Fuck me, you are moist," Aidan groaned as he slid down her body, palmed the inside of her thighs, and lapped at her.

She almost came off the bed.

Again, his tongue swept through her, then it felt like his entire mouth consumed her pussy as he began to eat her.

Lily cried out as, lap after lap, nibble after nibble, Aidan devoured her.

Until she exploded.

"Oh, my God." Her orgasm struck with such speed and strength, she screamed.

His face appeared from out of the covers as he wiped his hand over his mouth. "Peaches."

Lily blushed, and she squealed as Aidan pulled her up against him and kissed her. A moment later, he settled next to her.

"Now that my girl is pleasured, answer my question. What do you usually have for breakfast?"

Lily blinked and shook her head, waves of ecstasy still rolling through her.

Was he serious?

"Toast and coffee," she said, clearing her throat.

"Do you drive to work?" Aidan asked.

She ran her hand down over his hard abs. "Bus."

He grabbed her hand.

"Who are your friends?" Aidan asked next.

Lily frowned. "Emma. And my parents. And I have a few friends from work I hang with."

Aidan took her hand and let it creep south until it was on his cock. She wrapped her hand around it while he retained control.

Of course he did. Aidan Dufort never lost control of anything.

"Favorite food?" he asked.

"Mexican. Tacos, to be exact. And chocolate," Lily answered, licking her lips.

"Is chocolate actually food?" Aidan asked, and his cock twitched as she ran her thumb over the head. "Easy, baby."

She really wanted him inside her. Like right, damn now. But she figured this was a game he wanted to play, and they both knew he was in charge, so she had to bide her time.

And play a little herself.

"My pussy or my mouth?" she asked him.

"Neither. Yet," Aidan said. "Ask me a question."

She forced back a groan as he guided her hand up and down his cock, stroking him.

"Where is your office?" Lily asked.

"Inside my home in Philly. My employees work remotely all around the country," Aidan said. "Football or baseball?"

She grinned. "Chicago Bulls, silly. Basketball."

He smiled. "Did you play?"

She lifted her shoulder. "On the local courts, but I'm not sporty."

He increased the speed of their strokes.

"I'm going to come soon, peaches. Ask me another question."

"How many women have you slept with?" she spat out and then silently cursed.

His hand stilled.

"Try again. When I'm in bed with you, it's us and only us, Lily. Don't even do that again," Aidan growled.

Her cheeks heated.

Suddenly, she wanted to know everything. Had he been in love before? Had he had been married before?

He might have.

She knew nothing about him.

"Ask me another question," he said, beginning to stroke his cock once more with her hand.

"Sports. What did you play?" Lily asked.

"With this body? Take a guess," he said.

"Football," she answered, and he nodded. "So you're an Eagles fan."

"Yeah, baby," he said, reaching closer to lap at her mouth. "I want to know everything about you, but right now, I need this hot mouth on my cock."

His hand pressed her head down onto his groin and Lily took him down her throat.

"Suck me tight, baby. I'm ready to shoot."

Lily gripped his base and licked the head as she pulled back, and he growled at her, pushing her back down.

Then she suctioned her mouth around him and took him deep and fast. Over and over. Then underneath her, Aidan's hips lifted, and he let out a loud moan as his hot semen hit the back of her throat.

"Let me see," he said, lifting her head as he gripped her hair and stroked his cock with his other hand into her open mouth. "Fuck you're sexy,"

Then he moved them, pushing her down on the bed.

"Spread these legs."

A moment later, Aidan thrust inside her, his cock still deliciously hard.

"Sexy, beautiful, submissive Lily," he moaned, sucking one of her nipples.

She felt him thicken inside her as he lifted her hands over her head. "You have distracted me this morning, little peaches. I'm going to fuck you hard, then we will talk."

Lily swallowed, excited.

Not so much for the talking, but definitely the fucking.

"Hold the headboard. Let go of it and I'll introduce you to spanking."

She smiled.

"Your pussy."

Oh.

"That's what I thought," he growled lightly and sucked her nipple harder.

Oh, lord, he was amazing.

Aidan slammed into her, fucking her with an eagerness and vigor that had her arching and tossing her head, wanting him to own every inch of her.

"Yes, yes, yes," she said as she felt her body demand more of his seed.

"Lily, fuck," Aidan cried, before collapsing on top of her.

This man.

He made her feel things no other man had. They were still strangers, and from different worlds, yet when they were skin to skin, it meant nothing.

Then she caught sight of his kabillion dollar watch lying on her dresser, and his Tom Ford coat he'd carefully hung on a hanger on the door, and remembered who he was.

That he would one day realize she wasn't the woman he wanted. Aidan was expected to marry someone of influence and money. His dad wouldn't allow them to be together, no matter how rich or independent Aidan was.

What your parents thought mattered.

Every day it would be harder for her to say goodbye if she let this continue.

Lily just needed to find the right way to tell him she didn't want to be with him.

Even if it was a lie.

"TOAST," LILY SAID, sliding the plate over the kitchen bench. Then did the same with the mug. "Coffee."

Aidan sat on the stool, flicking through his phone. He glanced up.

"Peanut butter. That's what you eat every morning?"

Lily shrugged. "Let me guess, you have someone cook you a full breakfast every morning?"

When he simply bit into the toast, she shook her head. "I have twelve minutes from the moment I walk out of my bedroom until I have to walk out that door." She pointed at the front door. "Or I will miss my bus. You have someone cook your meals and you walk down the hall."

"Up the stairs and down the hall," he corrected.

She sipped her coffee and stared at him. "We are like chalk and cheese."

"That doesn't change anything," Aidan said, mirroring her with his own mug.

Her phone beeped.

It was her mom checking she was okay. She replied, letting her know Aidan was with her. Not that she normally kept her mom up to date with her love life, but it would calm her to know she wasn't alone.

"Do you want to go over there?" Aidan said. "I'm going to rent a car, so wherever you need to go, I can take you."

Lily felt her barriers melt. She walked around the counter and sat next to him on the stool. "You are amazing, you know that? I wish my dad would have met you."

Tears fell down her cheeks. For the seventh time since she woke. Aidan was taking them in his stride and honestly, Lily wasn't able to stop them. Little things kept reminding her of her dad.

The doorstop he'd bought her to stop it slamming closed. The Chicago Bulls keyring he'd surprised her with when she was younger. Which was almost unrecognizable, but she kept it because she loved it so much.

Just stuff.

Memories.

"Me too," he said, taking her hand and squeezing.

"I just want to rest today. Unless Mom needs me. Is that okay, or do you have things to do?" Lily asked.

"I have some work to do, so I'll go hire the car, grab my laptop, and then come back," Aidan said.

Lily nodded, noticing he didn't ask, simply told her. Some women might not like that, but she found his assertiveness very sexy.

Even if she only got to enjoy it for a little while longer.

"Back soon, peaches." Aidan kissed her goodbye and closed the door behind him.

His absence hit her immediately as she stood in the middle of the room and dropped her face into her hands.

How on earth was she going to let him go?

CHAPTER TWENTY-NINE

Walking back into Lily's apartment and having her jump into his arms was not something Aidan was going to forget in a hurry.

His mouth had found hers, his bags dropping to the floor, as he wrapped his arms around her lower back, crushing her mouth to his.

God, why wouldn't she just admit her feelings?

Surely the entire world could see but her.

Aidan was giving her space and time. Hell, her father had just died, but he wasn't a patient man.

Not when it came to Lily.

And he could see her struggling with her emotions. One minute she was all heart eyes, the next she was chewing her lip and playing with that damn butterfly pendant.

Worrying.

That's what she was doing.

He'd settled on the sofa, laptop on his knee, and tapped away while Lily curled up next to him, watching TV.

From time to time she snoozed, her small feet pressing into his thigh. When the light dimmed outside, Aidan tugged the blanket from the back of the sofa over her and ordered some food for them.

While he was waiting for the delivery, he packed up his computer and pulled her feet onto her lap, taking control of the remote. Then began to flick through the channels.

"Hey, I was watching that," her small voice said.

"Your eyes are literally still closed," Aidan replied, smirking.

He stopped on a sports channel and tickled her foot. She tugged it away and blinked open her eyes with a smile.

"How long was I asleep?"

"Three days," he teased.

She snort laughed, then her smile faded, and her grief returned. As her face contorted, Aidan pulled her up into his arms and made a whole lot of comforting sounds while he rubbed her back.

"I can't believe I'll never see him again. Never speak to him again," Lily cried, wiping her eyes and slumping back on the sofa.

"He's out of pain," Aidan said, knowing how he'd suffered after Lily had shared details of his disease earlier in the day.

"Yeah." She nodded.

"Are you religious?" he asked.

Lily shrugged. "I want to believe. I'm scared not to, but I don't go to church."

"I'm about the same. I believe in something. I just don't know what," Aidan admitted.

"Maybe he's watching us," Lily said, staring at the ceiling. "If you are, Dad. This is Aidan."

He smiled. There was something childlike and sweet about Lily, which never failed to warm his heart.

How could he not love this woman?

"Hi, Mr. Peterson," Aidan said. "Thank you for trusting me with your daughter."

"He died. He didn't hand me over like an asset," Lily huffed.

"You don't know that. He might have sent me a message."

"Did he?"

"Yes. I heard a voice," Aidan said, nudging her down on the sofa. "It said take care of my daughter and love her as much as I do."

That shut her up.

"I take my responsibilities very seriously." He kissed along her jawline, the corner of her mouth, then finally a slow and arousing kiss on her lips.

"You do." Lily opened to him, and their tongues grasped at one another, demanding more.

When her hands slid down his back, and then his ass, Aidan felt excitement flare deep within. He'd bought some toys with him. A parcel which had arrived with his other orders.

If she wanted to use distraction as a tool to get her through this, he was at her service. That and he'd been dying to show her more of the things he enjoyed in—and out—of the bedroom.

Aidan slid his hands under her sweater, his palm on her flat stomach, moving up and over her small breast. Lily let out a moan and arched into him.

"You want me to make you feel good, baby?"

"Yes,"

"Then lie back and let me take full control. Can you do that, peaches?"

As she bit her lip, Aidan pushed onto his knees and reached for his bag. Then pulled out a silk tie and a purple vibrator.

"Oh," she said, pushing up on her elbows, looking curious.

"Have you played with toys before?" Aidan asked, taking in her wide eyes.

Lily shook her head.

"I'll be in control, but you will have the ultimate say. No is no," Aidan clarified.

"Okay,"

"Remove your top and bra," he instructed and shoved off the blanket, then removed her sweatpants.

Underneath, she wore a pair of white cotton panties. No lace, just plain cotton panties. And yet they made him hard as fuck. Aidan couldn't wait to watch her enjoy every second of this while he fucked her with these toys.

"Lie back and spread your legs," he ordered and suppressed a moan as her cotton-covered pussy was exposed to him.

Aidan ran a finger through the center of her core.

"Mmm, God," Lily moaned.

He reached and tied the silk die around her wrists. "Arms above your head and they don't move."

Getting to his knees, Aidan leaned down and placed a kiss on her clit.

Lily arched.

"Now I'm going to show you the type of pleasure I enjoy, my sweet peach," he said, grabbing the vibrator and turning it on. The room filled with an electric buzz as he ran his hand over her abdomen and up over nipples.

Then pressed the vibrator to her other nipple.

"Jesus," Lily cried.

They'd only just got started and already his cock was twitching, wanting her.

Moving to her other breast, he circled the vibrator and rubbed his cock a few times as she writhed. Then he slid his hand between her legs, stroking her clit, then tugging the cotton to the side.

"This is going to feel good, baby." He glanced down and felt his mouth water as her pink flesh came into view. Her clit was swollen, waiting to be pleasured.

"More," she begged.

"Who's in charge?" he growled.

"You, sir."

Aidan nodded, then removed her panties and his own clothes. Slowly. Leaving her spread wide and waiting. Bound, wet, and eyes begging.

"Jesus fucking Christ." Aidan rubbed his mouth. "You're so fuckable, Lily. Look at this cunt."

"Touch me,"

He nearly did, but she knew the rules. He lifted a brow.

"Aidan, please," she tried again. "Sir, please touch me."

"That's my girl." He kneeled between her legs and stretched out his tongue. "Let me taste you. Fuck…"

One long lap of her wet pussy and Aidan was back in paradise. He let out a ragged groan. When he lifted the purple toy and placed it on her clit, Lily shot off the sofa. Hand on her tummy, he said, "Easy baby."

"Oh, my God, oh, oh," she said as he held it there for long moments.

His finger moved to her entrance and spread her glistening moisture around her folds.

"Sparkle for me sweetheart, God you have a wet pussy." Aidan leaned in again and flicked his tongue on her clit as the toy moved further around her cunt.

"You're going to fuck this toy when I say," He glanced across her tanned tummy as Lily was writhing in ecstasy.

Aidan flicked a nipple as he returned the vibrator to her clit. Her flesh began to swell as he slid the vibrator around her core, circling so it was covered in her juices, and then nudged it in.

Lily's body tensed.

"Relax, baby, it's not as big as me."

"Ohohohoh,"

"Take more of it." He increased the vibration.

Aidan watched Lily fight and crave the purple member. Fuck, his cock was full of envy.

"Open this pretty cunt for me. I own your orgasms from now on."

Lily tossed her head, moaning as, with a few more quick pulses, her body relaxed, and Aidan thrust the toy inside her.

She cried out with a pleasure-soaked groan, Aidan fucking her as he worked his hand up and around his cock, watching her arching and begging for more.

Lord, she was an orgasmic sight.

In and out of her pussy, the toy slid, her juices making a delicious mess on her thighs. Aidan leaned, sucking her clit, and then it was all over.

Lily screamed.

He held it like a succubus, demanding she give him all of her as the vibrator pounded into her pussy.

"Beautiful girl, come on the toy."

"Oh, fuck, fuck, Aidan," she cried again.

This. This is what he wanted with her. To see her spread, wide, vulnerable, and submitting to all the pleasure he could give her.

To come while he took complete control and then filled her with his every inch.

Slowly, he removed the toy, then licked her pink flesh as her body convulsed and thighs twitched. Wiping his mouth, Aidan lifted Lily onto his lap as he sat on the sofa.

"Put your bound arms around my neck," Aidan told her. "Then lower your hot pussy on my cock."

"I can't, oh God, I can't take any more," she cried, and he just hardened further at her resistance.

Submission he loved.

Her resistance he fucking loved.

Dominating her was heaven.

"You can, and you will," Aidan ordered, their eyes locking. "Sit down like a good girl."

With a pathetic, unbelievable groan, Lily moved over his cock and greedily took his head inside her channel.

"Fuck. Fucking hell. Yes. Jesus." His groans were deep and raw.

Aidan gripped her waist, her arms hung over his shoulder, and then he began to move her up and down his cock. Her tits bounced, giving him the best show in the world.

"Such a good submissive."

"I'm n—" Lily frowned at him, but he grinned and gave her a harsh kiss.

"I want you to come for me again. Clench that pretty cunt around my cock and suck me dry, baby."

And fuck, he was ready to shoot inside her as she bounced eagerly, speeding up as he lifted the vibrator and pressed it against her clit.

This woman.

He wanted to fuck her for life. And no one else.

Fire shot down his spine, tightening as his cock swelled.

"Come, Lily. Come right goddamn now."

"Aidan…" She held his eyes as her mouth began to gape, and when he felt her muscles contract around him, he let go.

Shooting his heart inside the woman he was in love with.

LILY TOOK THE warm wet cloth from Aidan and wiped herself.

Wow, that was… incredible.

It always was with him, but this was beyond anything she'd done before. Of course, she knew about sex toys, but none of her previous partners had ventured into anything like that. Even tying her wrists had been a first for her the other night.

She did love it, but it also scared her a little bit. What if Aidan was into things that were outside her comfort zone?

Then again, they wouldn't be together long enough to find out. Time was nearly up. Lily knew it.

She watched him pull on his jeans and she wrapped the blanket around herself and tucked up her knees. Putting her chin on top of them, she took in his gorgeous, tanned chest and strong arms.

He was so sexy.

She let out an audible sigh.

"Like what you see?" He winked.

"Yes." Lily tipped her head to the side, wondering about something. "Aidan, why do you call me a submissive?"

He pulled on his sweater and tugged up the sleeves. God, even his forearms were hot.

"Because, baby, you are." He leaned forward and kissed her lips, and she scrunched up her face. He laughed. "It's not a bad thing. In fact, I think it's the best damn thing in the world. I'm a Dom, so you're exactly my type."

His type. Like she was his favorite brand of milk?

Lily didn't like that idea. That wasn't exactly how love worked.

It just made her one of many.

"So you sleep with subs?"

Aidan turned from the bag he was putting the toys away in and his eyes held hers. "I sleep with you, Lily. Don't turn this into anything it's not."

A slice of anger threaded through her.

Was she not allowed to ask questions? Did he think she didn't have an opinion? Or a voice? Did he think she was so *submissive* she'd let him decide she was his and that was it?

Well, no.

"Is this the sort of thing you like to do every time you have sex?" She waved at the toys.

He stood and planted his hands on his hips. "What's wrong?"

"I just don't like being called submissive."

"You are."

"I'm not."

He stared at her for a split second.

"Open your mouth," Aidan ordered and, for the love of God, her mouth parted.

She slammed it shut.

"That doesn't mean anything," Lily said, standing as she tugged the blanket with her, hating she was naked underneath.

Aidan's phone beeped, and there was a knock at the door. When Lily raised her brows, Aidan said, "I ordered us some dinner while you were asleep."

"I wasn't asleep, I was thinking." Lily shrugged.

Aidan shot her a look, then walked to the door, tipped the delivery man, then took their meal into the kitchen.

"Lily, what's going on? Five minutes ago, you were screaming out my name. Now you're arguing with everything I say," he said, placing the bags on the bench.

"I don't like you thinking you're in charge of my whole life," she said, raising her voice. "You just showed up here and have forced your way in."

"Forced?" Aidan repeated calmly.

Too calmly.

"Yes. You were rude to Matt and who knows if I have a job now?"

He crossed his arms. "Carry on."

She swallowed, her eyes falling to the floor. "I'm just overwhelmed. My dad is gone—"

Aidan had his arms around her a second later. "Don't push me away, Lily. Tell me how you feel, even if you're scared, but don't fight me."

Her eyes lifted. "I am scared! I'm terrified. But do you know why?"

"Tell me."

Her heart pounded, the words on the tip of her tongue. She knew it was going to destroy everything, but it was better now than a month, a year, or ten years when Aidan finally figured it out himself.

"Because I do like you. A lot," she said more quietly.

"You more than like me, Lily."

Tears pooled in her eyes, and she shook her head to stop him from talking. "And I know you like me."

"Lily," Aidan warned.

"No. Let me get this out. You may not see this clearly, but I can." Her voice shook with emotion. "Your dad doesn't approve of me. You don't like that. I think your feelings for me are exaggerated in a type of rebellion to him."

He physically reacted, pulling his face back.

"So now you're dating the poor girl from the block. To rebel against his attempts to control you," she explained.

"First, he doesn't control me," Aidan growled, releasing his arms and moving an inch away. Lily's heart began to pound harder, and she could hear every damn beat.

She was losing him.

Wasn't this what she wanted?

Free from the pain of eventually losing this beautiful man when he'd one day wake up and see her for what she was: someone who didn't fit into his world. A woman without a qualification, without money, without any accomplishments in life.

"I won't live knowing one day you will look at me and realize I'm not who you love. Because when you do, Aidan, it will break me."

"Lily, stop. You're wrong," he growled.

"Look at this place. Look at me," she cried, waving her arms out. "A torn rug. The TV is two decades old. My God, I shop at Old Navy, and you're wearing stupid Prada socks."

"Jesus. You and Prada. I'll throw out every fucking Prada thing I own if that would make you happy!" Aidan cried.

They stared at each other, panting out their anger.

Lily shook her head slowly and sat back down on the sofa.

"You know that I'm right. This would never work. I'll fall in love with you, and you'll throw me away."

He crouched down in front of her, and she couldn't help but appreciate the way his strong thighs looked in the denim. She might as well take her last look at all his powerful beauty.

Taking her hands, Aidan looked her straight in the eye. "This has nothing to do with my father. I'm fucking in love with you, Lily."

She gasped.

"Aidan, don't. I can't."

For a long moment he watched her, and she saw the pain creep into his green eyes, his face shift.

"Jesus, Lily. I'm telling you I love you and you're shoving it back in my face."

He stood.

"My father just died. I don't even know how I feel one minute to the next, let alone tell someone I love them."

"But it's okay for you to tell me I'm *not* in love with you and that I have daddy issues. Right. Great. Nice one."

Lily stared at the floor.

"This is a lot. The submissive sexual stuff. You're a billionaire—"

"You say that like it's a disease." Aidan shook his head.

He didn't understand. How could he? It was intimidating. Especially after his father had made her feel, in front of others, that she was not acceptable.

How many others would do that if she stepped fully into his world?

Would his friends tell him he was crazy?

Would he expect her to suddenly change everything and wear Prada shit and bathe in champagne? Okay, a slight exaggeration, but Lily didn't know how to be the woman he wanted.

And she wasn't going to enter his world when this was all because he enjoyed dominating her and proving to his father he was in control.

After all, that was Aidan's thing. Control.

Lily sighed. "It's not a disease. I'm proud of your success. You are an amazing man. But our lives are different. Your dad was right. I won't fit in with your family and people. I don't want that life."

"You did okay in Hawaii," he snapped.

"I wasn't comfortable," she lied. She was until Andrew Dufort had told her she was basically a leper. "Your father made me feel like a loser because of my bank balance. He won't be the only one who does that. Do you want me to be treated like that all my life? Is that what you want for me, Aidan?"

"Of course it's fucking not," Aidan yelled, "Fuck." He spun around and cursed again. "So that's it?" he asked, glaring at her. "This is over."

Tears stung her eyes.

"I—"

"No. Answer the question. You've just told me you don't like me because I'm wealthy. That my father has made you feel uncomfortable once, so my life would be intolerable for you. You've told me that my feelings are not my own and that I'll break your heart, so you won't even give us a chance."

Lily stared back and then slowly swallowed.

"Did I miss anything?" he demanded.

"No." Her voice was weak.

It sounded really bad when he said it like that, but she knew she was right. This wasn't a Cinderella story. Aidan couldn't save her from a life of poverty.

He couldn't bring her dad back.

She could never let him pay for her education and pull strings so she could become a teacher. It would be meaningless if he did.

Aidan rubbed the back of his head. "Lily,"

Her heart began to crack like a shattered windscreen. She dropped her face into her hands. He was there in an instant, pulling her into his arms. She wrapped hers around him and began to sob.

After a few minutes, she lifted her face, and he wiped her hair away and kissed her nose.

"I'm going to go," he said, and a sob escaped her. "I'll be here for another forty-eight hours. Then, if I don't hear from you, I'll leave. Forever."

"Aidan, I—"

"Don't say any more. I love you, Lily. I know this is real. But if you don't, then that's not something I can force. I realize that now."

Aidan's lips pressed to hers and held there for the longest time. Then he stood, grabbed his bags as her heart physically shattered, and he gazed down at her one last time.

His bright beautiful eyes were gone, replaced with angry hurt dark globes.

Then Aidan Dufort walked out of her life.

Forever.

He just wouldn't know that for another two days.

CHAPTER THIRTY

Aidan tossed his bags onto the bed and let out the curse he'd been holding since he left Lily's apartment.

"Fucking mother fucking fuck!"

He kicked the sofa.

After parking, he'd gone for a long walk in the snow, trying to make sense of everything, and it hadn't helped at all. In fact, the more he came to terms with everything Lily had said, the more fury and pain flowed through his veins.

He'd lost her.

He knew it in his bones.

She might not be an overly confident woman, but Lily knew her own mind. Aidan wanted to blame her grief, but instead of clinging to him for comfort, she had pushed him away.

His father had done so much damage that night on Maui. More than he'd realized.

She said he'd made her feel like a loser.

Jesus.

Hate poured through him for the man who'd destroyed the greatest thing to ever happen to him. Because fuck the money, fuck his success. Without Lily, he didn't want any of it.

Without thinking, Aidan grabbed his phone and dialed his parents' number. His father could issue her a fucking apology.

He might be angry and full of pain right now, but he wasn't giving up.

Forty-eight hours was a long time.

"Dufort residence," his mom said, answering the phone in a chirpy voice that grated at him.

"Mom. It's me. Where's Dad?" he demanded angrily.

Silence.

"Hi, darling. Nice to hear from you."

"Yeah, hi. Are you okay?" Aidan said, trying to pull back his mood. His mom didn't deserve it.

She laughed. "Yes, I am. Thank you."

For the love of God.

"Mom. I need to speak to Dad. Urgently."

"You left things poorly in Hawaii," she said, and he rolled his eyes. "Why don't you give it some time?"

Time? Fuck. Time he did not have.

"Which is why I need to speak to him. Do you have any idea what he's done? The way he spoke to Lily. He's messed everything up. I need to speak to him. He's going to give her an apology. For God's sakes. Put him on!" he growled, dumping it all out.

Silence.

"Mom!" Aidan cried.

"No."

Aidan's head shot up. "What? Did you just say no?"

His compliant and agreeable mother had just said no. What in the hell?

"Yes. I said no," she replied, and her calm voice was beginning to make him lose his mind. "You sound angry. When you've calmed down, you can speak to him."

He drew in a deep breath, so he didn't say something he'd regret. And as the oxygen reached his brain cells, Aidan started to wonder if he was in an alternative universe.

Or he was missing something.

"What's going on, Mom? Dad loves a good argument," Aidan said, then repeated, "Go get him or tell me what the hell is going on?"

There was some rustling noise, then he heard a door close.

"Aidan," Christine Dufort sighed. "You must keep this to yourself for now."

His heart sunk knowing, almost instinctually, what she was going to say.

"Your father is not well. Four months ago, your father had a stroke. A minor one, but the doctor is worried."

"Why didn't he tell us?" Aidan cursed, dropping his head.

"Everyone reacts differently when facing their maker, darling. Your father thinks it will destabilize our finances," his mom replied. "I know, I know. I've been trying to talk sense into him, but I think he's scared."

Jesus, they were one of the richest families in America.

"Mom, that's crazy."

"Well, you know what he's like. He's preparing to die and nothing I say will change that. He wants to see you and Amelia married and secure."

Aidan shook his head.

He wasn't going to pretend he understood what his father was going through, but none of this was based on facts or common sense.

And didn't justify what he said to Lily.

Not for a second.

Copyright Juliette N. Banks 2022

"Mom, I'm a billionaire and I can find my own wife. In fact, the woman I love refuses to love me back because of his actions."

"Lily?" she asked.

"Yeah." Sadness spread through him, knowing she was in that damn apartment on her own. Aidan knew she would be hurting and grieving for her dad.

The man in him needed to protect her. To love her. To care for her.

"Are you sure you love her?" she asked and his heckles raised.

"Mom, do not start."

"You *are* very different. That might not mean anything to you, but it will to her," she said. "However, if you love one another, *truly* love one another, then it won't matter."

Aidan stared at the carpet as her words sunk in.

"How will I know?"

"You listen to your heart."

CHAPTER THIRTY-ONE

The next day, or rather twenty hours and forty-five minutes later, Lily was at her mom's place picking at the food in front of her.

"You don't have to eat it," her Aunt Sherie said.

"It's nice. I just don't have an appetite at the moment," Lily said.

"It's understandable. You'll feel like this for a while. Saying goodbye to your dad tomorrow will be hard, but it does give closure of a sort," Sherie said. "But you do need to start eating and sleeping. Both of you."

"I'm sleeping. That's all I'm doing," her mom said.

"Grief is exhausting." Lily sighed. She felt like she was grieving two men. What terrible timing. She felt guilty, like she should only care about her dad, and not some guy she wouldn't remember when she was old and gray.

Right?

She would forget about Aidan. Right?

"Where's your lovely man?" her mom asked.

Ugh.

"He's not mine. He's a friend." Lily shrugged and pushed the pasta into her mouth, chewing so she didn't have to explain more.

She swallowed the lump of what felt like concrete.

"That's not what you said at the hospital," her mom pressed.

"I was in shock." She shrugged.

"Lily. What happened? He seemed so nice. Not many people would sit waiting for hours like that. I saw his eyes. He cares for you."

"He was very nice. And very handsome," her aunt replied.

Yes, well, he was handsome.

"He's gone home," she lied. Unless Aidan had given up and decided to leave, anyway. Lily didn't blame him if he had. It was the right thing to do.

It was over.

"We're from different worlds. I told you that, Mom. He is nice, very nice, but it would never work."

I love you, Lily.

She felt her stomach lurch. This morning she'd actually thrown up. Not surprising given she'd had cried ten years' worth of tears in twelve hours.

Lily pushed the plate away and chugged some water.

"Is this about the fact he's wealthy?" her mom asked and shot her aunt a look.

"Don't, Mom. Please. Look at what happened to Dad because of this stupid topic. He died."

The room went quiet.

"Is that what you think?" her mom asked incredulously.

Lily rubbed her forehead, sweat beading. She hadn't meant to say that out loud.

"Lily?"

"No. But the whole thing is just wrong. I'm not going to see him again. The end." Lily felt seedier the more she spoke.

She chugged some more water.

"You're looking for excuses because you like him," her mom annoyingly observed. "So it's not about the money then."

"It's not *not* about the money. How would you feel if some billionaire turned up in your life and claimed to love you?"

Her mom's eyes widened. "Aidan told you he loved you? Lily, that's huge."

And more water.

"He has daddy issues." She waved her hand around.

"I'm confused," her aunt said, darting her eyes between them.

"Honey, is this about him having money? Then perhaps this is a good time to have a talk. I was going to wait until after the funeral."

Lily waved her hand in front of her face, fanning herself and glancing at the snow outside on the front lawn.

"Is it hot in here?"

God, maybe she had a stomach bug.

"Yes, tell her," Sherie prompted.

"Your father had life insurance. We never stopped paying it despite how tight things were after we learned he was sick," Angela said. "You can never be sure how these things will turn out, so we decided not to tell you."

What?

Lily stared at her mom and completely blanked out.

"I talked to your dad about this before he died. We talked in depth about it, in fact."

Lots of swallowing.

"Mom, I—"

"No, let me get this out. I know it's crude to discuss money when he's not in the ground yet, but under the circumstances, I think you need to know."

Lily stood and puffed air over her face, wiping her forehead.

"Honey, the insurance people are paying out two million dollars. Your dad and I want you to have half of it."

Shit.

Her stomach lurched.

"Excuse me," Lily said and bolted to the bathroom.

TWENTY MINUTES later, Lily finally came out holding a towel to her face. Her mom was standing on the other side of the door, and she walked straight into her arms.

One million dollars.

She had one million bloody dollars.

It was a far cry from Aidan's billions, but she was now an independently rich woman.

"If you pushed him away because you felt inferior, now you are going to have to think up a new excuse," her mom said, smiling down at her. "I saw you two together. You reminded me of your father and I."

She was just projecting; Lily was sure of it.

Then her mom handed her a small box and Lily's eyes shot back up to hers.

"This might not make you feel better right now, but at least you'll know."

Oh, shit.

CHAPTER THIRTY-TWO

Blake lowered his phone and glanced across his office, thinking. Aidan had already given him shit for allowing Amelia to leave Hawaii with this mystery man, so he wasn't about to let her wander around Penn Museum on her own.

She sounded weird on the phone.

The relationship had probably ended again already. No offense to his pretty creative cousin, but she didn't have much luck in the romance department.

While all the men in the Dufort family ran away from commitment, Amelia chased it.

Some of them had succumbed to the institute of marriage, but Blake was decades from that himself. He thought forty seemed like a good age to finally settle down.

He had plans.

His success was just starting to take off and dealing with a woman, and all that entailed, sounded exhausting.

Fucking them?

That was different.

Seeing a pretty brunette on her knees as his cock slid in and out of her wet, hot mouth was worth his time. A sexy and talented lover deserved to be praised for making him come.

Blake might be a powerful man, but he was a gentle dominant, seductively making the women he fucked feel appreciated.

Even if only for a night or a weekend.

But as for Amelia, he needed to make sure she was okay. If only so Aidan didn't kick his ass if he learned Amelia spent an entire Friday afternoon sat staring at a fucking painting on her own.

Joking aside, they were a close family, and he wanted to do his part, so Blake pushed his executive leather chair back and walked over to the coat rack.

Tugging on his woolen jacket, he said goodbye to his PA. "I'm off. See you on Monday."

"Oh. Have a good weekend, Mr. Dufort," she said, sounding a little surprised. It wasn't like him to leave the office early.

By the time he stepped outside, his car was pulling up.

"Hey, boss," Gerald, his driver, greeted him as he opened the door.

"You still working on the weather?" Blake asked.

Gerald laughed. "Yes sir, still working on the weather. Summer is just around the corner."

It was their daily joke.

They pulled out into the traffic and made it to the Penn Museum in ten minutes. Not bad for a busy Friday afternoon while snowing. Blake sat in the car staring at the entrance for a long moment and formulated a plan.

He had dinner plans at eight, so could spend a bit of time with Amelia once he found her. Maybe take her for a cocktail, get her smiling again. Then be home in time to change and meet up with his friend Taylor and the two women he'd lined up for them.

Taylor was interested in Rhonda, but they worked together, so breaching that friend's barrier had been hard for the guy.

After spotting a holiday snap on her desk, he'd messaged Blake a photo saying, "Double date this chick with me, and I'll let you take the Ferrari for a weekend."

Blake had laughed. He could buy his own if he wanted one, but he'd play along. Plus, he'd heard enough about this Rhonda the past few months. Who was he to cock block the guy? So he'd said yes.

The next minute, Rhonda thought she was double-dating to hook him up with her friend, Bella.

Bella looked boring. Like she worked in a library and her idea of a good time was reorganizing her shelves and drinking hot chocolates.

She looked like she could do with a good fucking and, who knew, if she was hotter in real life, he might see if she sucks cock.

Blake tucked his coat around him, and exited the vehicle, walking with conviction toward the entrance.

Damn, I haven't thought this through, he realized as he paid some money and stepped into the vast museum.

For over forty minutes, Blake walked through the museum, going from room to room.

"Fucking hell," he said when he saw his four hundredth Egyptian statue.

Someone cleared their throat.

Whatever.

He turned to go back the way he'd come, and then a flash of blonde hair caught his attention.

Amelia? Spinning, Blake went to head around the corner—*Smash.*

"Argh!" a female voice cried.

Blake felt the small body slam into his chest and before he could steady her, she fell on her ass, papers flying everywhere.

He glanced down at the mousy woman and forced back his curse. God damn, now he was going to lose Amelia.

Blake took a quick step and reached—*Crunch.*

"Oh my God, stop. My glasses. You idiot," the mousy girl yelled at him, her hand covering her face in distress.

Idiot?

Blake stood back and raised a brow.

"Just in case you're having trouble seeing, I am staring back at you like *you* are the idiot," he helpfully shared.

"Me? Why am I the idiot?" The girl twisted around and started grabbing the paper around her.

Blake took in her ugly blue tights and pinafore dress that looked like it had been a school uniform once upon a time. He still hadn't seen her face clearly as she was ass up—and actually it was quite a nice ass—gathering all her scattered belongings.

Help her, asshole.

Blake let out a sigh.

"You shouldn't run in museums," he scoffed, crouching to pick up a folder. "There are rules."

She spun and faced him.

"I know the rules. I work here and I wasn't running."

Blake froze.

Not because he cared she was a Penn Museum employee, but because she was the woman he was supposed to be double dating tonight.

He smirked.

Well, this was going to be fun.

"Blake?" He spun his head around and right ahead of him stood Amelia with her arm threaded through a man who look very fucking familiar.

And she didn't look miserable at all.

"Oh my God, you're Blake," Bella said with a gasp.

"Yes," He winked at her, though it was unlikely she could see him. He stood and pulled out a bunch of hundred-dollar bills from his wallet and handed them to her when she climbed to her feet.

"For the glasses."

"About tonight—"

Blake cut her off, leaning closer, and said, "Be a good girl, and wear something sexy."

Then he walked away.

Taylor owed him big time. He wanted the Ferrari for a fucking month.

CHAPTER THIRTY-THREE

Aidan stood beneath the trees and pulled the collar of his black coat up around his ears, then plunged his hands into his pockets.

The coat was Prada.

Lily would hate it.

He wished she would look up and see him, but she was standing at her father's grave as they lowered him into the ground. Around her, a dozen or so black-clad bodies did the same thing.

He watched her mom hold a handkerchief or maybe tissues to her face—he was too far away to tell—and turn her head onto Lily's shoulder, sobbing.

What the hell was he doing here?

You love her.

He did. He loved her with his entire body and soul. For two days, he'd been walking around like his heart had been torn from his chest and stomped on.

Well, forty-six hours, to be exact.

The jet was fueled and ready to go because Aidan hadn't heard a word from Lily. Yet here he was, standing in the fucking cold Chicago weather, hoping she would look up.

Hoping she would love him.

Hoping that despite his father's harsh words, Lily would want him anyway and find a way to navigate a world where they could be happy together with him.

To trust him.

To know that he'd never let anyone in their world hurt her like that again.

She had no reason to. He hadn't spoken up that night as he should have, but he knew he'd never freeze again.

Aidan thought hiding their romance was more important that night. He'd been wrong. He hadn't known he was in love with her.

He hadn't spoken to his father personally yet, promising his mom he would take a breath and calm down before he did.

If he left Chicago without Lily, it would take a while before he could forgive him. But after seeing Lily lose her father, Aidan knew he had to get over it. If Andrew died suddenly, it would be just another regret to live with.

He glanced around the park, taking in all the graves.

Fuck, life was short.

He didn't want to live with regrets.

Aidan was just about to take a step toward Lily and let her know he was there when he saw another familiar face.

He froze.

No fucking way.

Matt moved in beside Lily and put his arm around her. Then he pulled her into his chest and began rubbing her back.

She went, and that hurt more than anything.

That should be me. That should be fucking me!

Anger blurred his vision.

I'm done. I'm fucking done.

"Not one fucking call or text, Lily," Aidan ground out, even though he stood alone. Pain, unlike any he'd ever felt before in his life, lanced through every inch of his heart. Stabbing him every second, he stood watching. "Message received loud and clear. Goodbye, baby."

Aidan took one last look as Lily pulled out of Matt's arms, and when she didn't move far, he spun on his heels, walking back to his waiting car.

The forty-eight hours were now up.

LILY WIPED THE tears from her eyes and turned back to her mom. She was exhausted and depleted in every way imaginable.

Goodbye, Daddy.

Her mom tossed a yellow rose down on his coffin and Lily said a silent prayer and dropped hers down next.

Returning to her mom's side, she watched as the other mourners, friends, and colleagues of her dad began to do the same.

"Lily, would you—" Matt started to say, but his voice drowned out when something caught her eye.

Aidan?

The man was walking across the grass toward a waiting vehicle. Even though he was a distance away, she knew that body. Knew that powerful frame and large shoulders.

Oh my God, it *was* Aidan. Her body was moving before she knew what she was doing.

She began to walk fast.

Then she ran.

"Aidan!" Lily called as he reached the car and opened the door.

No!

She kept running across the grass, dodging gravesites.

Sorry, sorry.

Aidan climbed in, leaving one leg out as he arranged his coat. Then it lifted, and the door began to…

"Aidan!" she screamed.

Nooooo.

The door opened.

Oh, thank…Lily began to stumble, falling hard on her hands and knees.

"Lily?" Aidan cried, and she looked up just as he reached her. Tears poured from her eyes.

She scrambled to get up as he pulled her to her feet.

"I thought you had left," she panted.

Oh God. She had to tell him. It had changed everything. Or rather, it had given her the clarity she had needed.

None of the other stuff mattered anymore.

Not in the scheme of things.

Looking back, it was as if both of them had blinkers on and wanted this. They hadn't been careful.

She hadn't taken…

"I said forty-eight hours," Aidan replied, and Lily saw the pain in his eyes. Heck, she felt it in her heart.

She should have messaged him, but the past twenty-four hours had been a blur and she truly had thought he'd left.

Lily lifted her hand to his face and cupped his cheek. Her heart was pounding so hard, knowing this was a key moment in her life. What happened next would change the course of her life.

Not just *her* life.

"Do you really love me?" she asked, desperate to know.

"No, I was just joking. I thought I would stand out here in the cold, wishing like hell you would love me back, because it's fun." Aidan's lips twitched, but his eyes were glistening with unshed tears.

"I want to tell you I love you, but—"

"God damn it, Lily." Aidan shook his head and took a step closer. He gripped her hips, and she could see his impatience in the lines of his face.

"No wait. I do. I just. I don't know what order to do this in," she said, shaking her head.

She wrung her hands as Aidan's brows lifted.

"Then can I recommend you don't teach English, sweetheart, because there are only three words?"

She smiled, her heart beginning to melt.

God, she had missed those beautiful green eyes and his gruffness.

Aidan brushed his thumb across her cheeks. "You're killing me, peaches. Tell me."

Lily put her hand over his. "We're pregnant."

AIDAN STARED AT Lily for a really long time.

"What?"

She nodded. "Also, yes, I love you."

He kept staring.

Pregnant.

He was going to be a dad.

Oh, my God.

"Wait. Say that last bit again," Aidan insisted, the fog beginning to clear.

"I love you, Aidan Dufort," Lily said, and his entire chest burst open. He lifted her off her feet and spun her around like an idiot.

"Wait. Sound check. Because you're pregnant?" he asked, knowing the answer, but he had to ask.

He lowered her to her feet.

"No, because I realized our love is so much more important than social standing and money and worrying about what anyone thinks of where I came from. We created a life, Aidan. A baby. A BABY!"

"Yeah, I got that bit. Holy fuck." He grinned.

She nodded but grinned back at him with eyes sparkling full of happy tears.

Had she been this beautiful before? Because he was sure that in two days she had become at least ten times more so.

Or maybe this was love.

"We're going to be parents," Aidan said as Lily nodded, not moving her eyes an inch off his."

"I don't expect—"

"Never finish that sentence, Lily Peterson. Never ever think it or say it," Aidan said firmly. "I love you. We are doing this. You, me, and this kid."

He caught the tear as it slid down her face.

"Say it again, Lily."

"I love you."

"She loves me!" he cried, throwing his arms in the air.

"Aidan, this is a graveyard." Lily giggled and turned around. They saw her mom and aunt hugging one another, watching them.

Aidan was sure he spotted a smile.

He knew he should curtail his happiness. He really did, but the woman he loved, loved him back.

Finally.

And he'd promised her father he would love his daughter forever.

Aidan kissed her gently but with force. "I swear if we weren't standing near your father's grave, I would get on my knees and ask you to marry me right fucking now."

"Do it," she said, shocking him.

His eyes widened. "No. Lily."

"If you want to propose to me, then do it. Here. With my dad present," Lily insisted. "He's at peace now, and why not make this day something beautiful to remember?"

Was she insane?

"Jesus. Are you sure?" he asked, glancing around and rubbing his face.

"Aidan Dufort, if I only get to boss you around once in my life, then I'm telling you, get down on your damn knees and ask me to marry you."

He forced back his snigger.

This woman was full of surprises, and he knew there was a lifetime more of them to come.

His lips stretched into a huge smile, and he cupped her face. "Peaches, consider that your one pass."

Lily might be submissive, but Aidan was seeing a new side to her. She was going to be an incredible mom. One that would protect her cubs, and damn that was incredibly sexy.

Aidan expected her to challenge him through their life and he would enjoy bringing her to her knees.

Right now, though, it was his turn.

The one and only time.

Aidan lowered to one knee and took Lily's hand.

"Lily Peterson, I love you. I want to create a new world with you. One we both love. With this child and many more. So please do not leave me on this sacred and cold ground for a second longer, and please say yes to being my wife."

"You have to ask, not tell me."

"That's not how things work in our marriage," he said.

"One time, Aidan. One time."

He grinned. "Lily, will you fucking marry me?"

"Yes, Aidan. I absolutely would love to be your wife."

He tugged her down onto his lap and kissed that cheeky mouth of hers until she was breathless.

EPILOGUE

Aidan tugged his jacket and held his hand out. Lily took it and stepped out of the car.

Fuck, she looked gorgeous.

He tugged her against him, and she planted a hand on his chest. He let out a growl. "Lily, kiss me,"

"I will kiss you *after* we say our vows. I'm sure it's bad luck beforehand."

"I had my cock inside you an hour ago." He shook his head.

"You're late," Logan said, standing on the steps of city hall behind them. Emma came running down and the two women hugged when he released his soon-to-be wife.

"Ring first," Emma demanded, and Lily lifted her hand.

It had been a battle to get Lily to choose a sizable diamond. She didn't want anything flashy. He told her it was part of fitting into the billionaire's life, and she'd slapped his arm.

But Aidan knew she was smart enough to work it out. In the end, they'd settled on a five-carat square diamond on a plain gold band.

Big enough to scream money.

Simple enough to say I'm not trying to impress you or anyone.

"I just wanted something small," Lily said, poking her tongue out at him.

Aidan rolled his eyes. The Tiffany diamond was worth over a million. Fortunately, his soon-to-be wife didn't know that. There may have been some fake price tags involved and a bonus to the manager of the store.

"It's exquisite," Emma said, then glanced down. "Now, let me see your tummy."

Aidan narrowed his eyes and glanced at Logan. It had been two weeks. There was nothing to see.

Logan shrugged and shook his hand. "Congratulations. Can't believe you're going to be a father before me."

"Thanks, man."

"You ever coming home?" Logan asked. "Everyone is going to be mad as hell when they find out you two eloped."

Aidan shrugged.

Lily's mom was inside waiting for them, but aside from his brother and Emma, they'd kept it a secret.

Aidan has insisted they marry quickly. Not because he was concerned Lily would change her mind. He wanted their child to have his name. Right from the start.

He wanted Lily to have his name.

He wanted the world to know she was his and to start creating their new life the way they wanted it.

Starting with a small ceremony.

The baby had fast-forwarded everything. Looking back, Aidan was sure they'd have found a way together, regardless.

Lily was deciding on what college she wanted to study at, and that would dictate their home state. For now.

He couldn't wait to create a home with her. One where they would raise their children and have Christmases and Thanksgivings.

Hopefully, with his entire family.

His family knew they were engaged, and the one phone call he'd had with his mom and dad on speaker, Andrew had made a snide comment.

He was a work in progress.

Aidan was clear, though, Lily and their child were his priority.

"We'll visit. When Lily is ready," Aidan said, turning to take in his bride in her white dress. She called it a tea dress and the weird big sleeves were *billowing*, apparently.

He just called it hot.

In fact, that was why they were late. Aidan had nudged her over the sofa, flipped her dress up, and slid down her pretty white panties. After tasting her, he'd unzipped and plunged straight into her wet pussy.

Lily knew her safe word.

But he'd yet to hear her say it.

"Come on, I want to marry this woman," Aidan said, reaching out his hand. When their name was called, they rushed in nervously and stood grinning at one another.

"I now pronounce you man and wife," the judge said.

"I love you, Lily Dufort," Aidan said and crushed his mouth down on hers.

"I love you," Lily replied, and he knew he'd never get sick of those three beautiful words.

Want to find out what happens on Blake and Bella's not-so-blind date in **WICKED PRAISE ?**
Get ready for this praise kink romance.

www.books2read.com/wickedpraise

Curious about Amelia's mysterious man then read **NAUGHTY FESTIVITIES** and prepare for a **steamy Christmas with the Dufort family.** Turn the page for the blurb…or get your copy at:

www.books2read.com/naughtyfestivities

NAUGHTY FESTIVITIES

A CHRISTMAS NOVEL

Amelia

There I was, glass of Cristal in my hand at an art gallery, minding my own business. Next minute I'm in his bed. Those ten days over Christmas were the happiest, most romantic, and without doubt the most sexually intimate of my life.

My heart bursting with love. My body alive with his touch.

Jack Rutherford. The sexy and powerful bachelor, and US senator, had stolen my heart. Until the truth slid to the surface destroying everything in a single moment.

Jack

I should have told her the truth but the moment I laid eyes on Amelia I knew I had to have her.

Own her. Consume her.

My dark secret, one I wasn't ready to face head-on. Yet. I'm a powerful and influential man, a threat to the institution. My enemies are behind this, I'm sure of it, but I need proof.

I thought I had time. I was wrong.

Now, I must decide what's more important. Amelia, or exposing generations of corruption. And with it a truth that will impact my future forever.

Naughty Festivities is book seven in the steamy Dufort Dynasty series. It's part billionaire, part romantic suspense, and will appeal to readers who like spicy books with a strong storyline, sexy powerful heroes, witty dialogue, heart-clenching moments, and a delicious happy ever after.

GET **NAUGHTY FESTIVITIES on 28 November!**

www.books2read.com/naughtyfestivities

Blake Dufort is not new to immense wealth; his entire family are billionaires. His success is new and still stabilizing. Still, he's powerful, influential, and handsome. Therefore, beautiful naughty women are regularly on the menu.

Agreeing to go on a double date, so his best friend can hook up with his crush, Blake bumps into the mousy-looking girl hours before. Underneath Bella's glasses, worn tights, and nervous blush is a woman ready to be broken and praised. Her plump lips and long lashes would look beautiful on her knees in front of him.

When he finds out who she really is, the power play between them in the bedroom blurs, and Blake must navigate a dangerous, corrupt world, and his heart.

Wicked Praise is book seven in the steamy Dufort Dynasty series. Part billionaire, part dark romance, it will appeal to readers who like steamy books with spice, a strong storyline and characters with witty dialogue, heart-clenching moments, and a delicious happy ever after.

Get WICKED PRAISE now!
www.books2read.com/wickedpraise

Also, if you love steamy mafia romance, try **The Darkest King FREE!**

www.books2read.com/thedarkestking

Turn the page for chapter one….

1

CONNOR

Here we fucking go again.

Another gala event. Another speech. Another night spent with strangers who schmooze me for my money and power.

It's all part of the charade I'm playing, I remind myself, tugging on the sleeve of my Armani jacket and adjusting my cufflinks before leaning back into the soft leather seats of my limousine. Nothing to prepare. My finance manager arranged the transfer of funds this afternoon, and my scriptwriter emailed me the same cut-and-paste version of the speech I've already given at least five times this year.

Only the name changes, with a modified reason why the cause is so important to Barrett Enterprises.

Except this one *is* important to me…personally.

The We Are Family Foundation is committed to the care of orphans in the US and around the world—a cause I deem important. No one should be alone because they don't have parents or a family.

There are eight fucking billion people on the planet. Few of them with the sort of money I have to contribute, to make a difference. Still, I'd rather have sent a check and sat at home, sipping on my Macallan Gold, watching porn, and jacking off.

Or rather, ordering in.

I don't mean Chinese food.

Truth is, I don't watch porn. I have no need for it. If I want a woman spread before me, I can have one at any time.

I'm Connor Barrett, one of the wealthiest and most powerful men in New York City.

Yet, I'm not who I say I am.

I'm both a ghost and, ironically, one of the most visible men in America. Why hide in the shadows when you can hide out in the open? The opposite of what they trained me to do in the marines.

Even more ironic—I have skilled security protecting me, which even they know is unnecessary. I'm six foot four, broad and muscular. And I've been trained to kill.

I *have* killed.

Still, I can't look over my shoulder while running a billion-dollar empire, doing deals with politicians and untrustworthy businessmen who would love nothing more than to see me fail.

That happens when people owe you favors. They know I'll come knocking, and when I do, they won't say no.

No one says no.

I'm the founder and CEO of Barrett Enterprises. Entrepreneur, philanthropist, investor, and prolific businessman.

Men want to destroy me.

Women want to fuck me.

I reach for the crystal cut glass filled with whisky in the console beside me and bring it to my lips, remembering the last woman who slid down my black silk sheets and wrapped her red-stained mouth around my cock.

God, I could do with round two.

It's been weeks since I've had a good release without using my fist. I should've booked someone for this evening, but I didn't think ahead.

Booked? Yes. They're not prostitutes—I'm paying for their discretion. I'm paying for control.

Something I never give away.

But I'm careful about the women I fuck. By the time they enter my penthouse, they've accepted payment and signed a confidentiality agreement—one no lawyer would ever let their client sign—which demands their silence and agreement to the terms of our time together.

One, should they break, that would destroy their lives.

So, not prostitutes, but they *are* escorts.

They're instructed to undress and blindfold themselves in my private elevator. I'm not fucking Batman—everyone in NYC knows my address—but it just sets the scene. One which makes it clear why they are here, and that intimacy is not welcome.

I'm not looking for a wife.

I need to stay a ghost.

If my enemies knew I was alive, I would be hunted.

The last words my father said to me…*Never tell anyone who you are, son. Run!*

The familiar grinding of my teeth, the pain slicing up the back of my neck from my fury, brings me back to the present, and I blink. I stretch one of my legs and check that the knife strapped just above my sock remains invisible. Just as all the other weapons on my body are.

I don't leave home without them.

"We're going to be a few minutes late, sir," Benson, my driver, says. I pulled him out of the military a few years ago. He knows how to scan for bombs, drive if we're attacked, and protect both of us if shit goes down. "The traffic was built up near Madison Square Gardens."

I'm silent, my body tensing, and my eyes slide over to Mack.

As if on cue, Mack Turner, my head of security, turns from the passenger seat and gives me a reassuring look. "It's an accident, Mr. Barrett. Turn up here, Benson. Then take 27th Street."

My body relaxes.

Mack is one of three men I trust with my life. He's by my side ninety percent of the time.

Not when I fuck.

That's not my kink.

While the We Are Family Foundation is important to me, I don't give a damn about being on time—I'm the VIP guest, and they'll wait for me. However, when you're hiding in broad daylight from the mafia—that's correct, *all* the mobsters and cartels—and are as powerful as I am, it would only take two minutes to go from being the *hunter* to the *hunted*.

Because I *am* hunting them.

They just don't fucking know it.

Glancing at my Rolex, I note I'm ten minutes late. I run my hand over my solid jaw, rubbing my dark scruff. I need to fuck. I've been agitated and impatient recently. As a dominant and controlling lover, the act helps me release built-up energy.

I nearly snort at the word *love.* There's no love in my life.

"Keep the car close when we arrive, Benson," I say darkly. "I'm only staying an hour."

"Yes, sir."

When the limo pulls up outside the Convention Center, I wait for Mack to open the door, then I climb out and stand, running my hands over my Armani tux and glancing around.

The red carpet is empty. Everyone inside is waiting for me.

In and out. That's the plan.

"Give Billy the night off tomorrow," I say to Mack without looking his way. When I take a few steps and he hasn't responded, I turn.

My dark eyes connect with his.

"You need a new location. It's not safe, Connor," Mack replies.

I nod.

He's not disagreeing with me. No one would. He'll have his reasons, and I trust him.

"Arrange it," I say, then step into the hotel lobby. The sign for the event points to the large conference rooms in the back.

To be honest, I'm surprised someone from the company organizing the event is not greeting me. I was told they would. But it's one less annoying person on this planet to deal with, so I couldn't care less.

I make my way through the space and find the room and the main door. As I reach for it, it flings open.

Ommph.

"Oh, shit!" the small body who just slammed into me whisper-yells, and the door closes behind her with a click.

Then I feel it…

Wet, cold, and seeping through the front of my tuxedo.

As I grip the petite brunette's arms and remove her from my chest, her eyes fly open wide, and I can't ignore the magnetic pull from the crystal blue globes.

Jesus, she's fucking gorgeous.

My cock wakes up and begins to swell. I imagine gripping all that long dark hair and wrapping it around my fist. Then, as panic fills her eyes, I'm tempted to smirk. But I never smile, and my hands, which have released her, want to touch her again, and that bothers me.

Who is this young woman?

"Connor Barrett," she gasps quietly, knowing who I am. Her eyes drift down over the dark liquid on my shirt, and she bites her lip, letting out a soft curse. Then those lids dip further down my body.

Don't look any lower, sweetheart, or…

Too late.

Her eyes shoot back to mine, and I say in a dark, thick voice, "You shouldn't have done that."

As she swallows, my lips curl up at the corners.

Tonight just got a whole lot more interesting.

GET THE DARKEST KING FREE NOW!
www.books2read.com/thedarkestking

ALSO BY JULIETTE N. BANKS

Get all my books at www.juliettebanks.com

THE MORETTI BLOOD BROTHERS
Steamy paranormal romance
The Vampire Prince – **FREE ebook**
The Vampire Protector
The Vampire Spy
The Vampire's Christmas
The Vampire Assassin
The Vampire Awoken
The Vampire Lover
The Vampire Wolf
The Vampire Warrior
The Vampire's Oath
The Vampire's Fate
The Vampire's Obsession

THE DARK KINGS OF NYC
Steamy dark mafia romance
The Darkest King - **FREE ebook**
The Ruthless King
The Savage King
The Avenged King

THE DUFORT DYNASTY
Steamy billionaire romance
Sinful Duty - **FREE ebook**
Forbidden TouchTotal Possession
Desire Unbound
Dark Surrender

Ruthless Surrender
Naughty Festivities
Wicked Praise
Beautiful Ruin

THE MORETTI BLOOD WOLVES
Steamy paranormal shifter romance
The Claimed Wolf - **FREE ebook**
The Alpha Wolf

REALM OF THE IMMORTALS
Steamy paranormal fantasy romance
The Archangel's Battle **- FREE ebook**
The Archangel's Heart
The Archangel's Star

LET'S STAY IN TOUCH

To receive information about my new or upcoming releases, new series and free giveaways join my **VIP BOOKCLUB.**

Sign up at

www.juliettebanks.com

Also, if you love my books, you are invited to join my VIP readers group on Facebook. It's a private R18 (and FUN!) space to talk about all my series and these sexy book boyfriends.

www.facebook.com/groups/authorjuliettebanksreaders